WELCOME TO NOWHERE

CAIMH MCDONNELL

Caimh McDonnell

Visit my website at www.WhiteHairedirishman.com

ISBN: 978-1-912897-11-7

❀ Created with Vellum

AUTHOR'S NOTE

Dear Americans,

This book, despite being set in your country and featuring mostly American characters, is still inexplicably written in Irish-English with all of the incorrect spellings associated with that. The author can only apologise for this. You see, the first person who'll read it is the author's mother and frankly, she is pretty hardcore on what she considers correct spelling. She doesn't give a monkey's for your opinion on this matter. The author therefore has no choice but to accede to her wishes as he has a freakishly large skull and the poor woman had to give birth to it, along with the rest of him.

Also, if any of this book feels a bit familiar, that's because you might have read the short story *Smithy's Revenge*. This book uses that as a jumping off point and the author wrote it as lots of people wanted to know what happened next in the story, not least the author himself. With this in mind, it'd be shocking form for you to complain about this as you got the short story for free and if you check, it warned that this might happen in the introduction.

Now that the apologies and threats are out of the way – enjoy the book!

PROLOGUE

Rock bottom.

Those two words had been bouncing around Smithy's head all day. This had to be rock bottom. It could take many forms for many people. He'd once known an alcoholic who had woken up naked in a kiddie's ball-pit. That had been the moment that had pushed him to finally get help, and the one that had cost him his job as a school vice-principal. The comedian Richard Pryor famously set himself on fire while free-basing cocaine and missed the once-in-a-lifetime chance to work with *The Muppets.*

So, rock bottom was different for everybody. Smithy wasn't naked, high or on fire. He was in full possession of his faculties, hiding in some bushes and dressed as a leprechaun.

He was also, he now realised with absolute clarity, a gambling addict. It wasn't as if he hadn't known that before, but there was knowing and there was *knowing.* Lying face down in the mud to avoid getting shot offered an excellent opportunity for a personal audit. The results were not pretty.

Three weeks ago, Jimmy Trike – who described himself as a "casting agent" but was really so much less – had approached him about a job. Five grand. For an acting gig, that was a lot. For one day's work, that was an awful lot. For an actor who'd not had a paid acting job for two years, four months and twelve days, that was one hell of an awful lot. On top of that, Jimmy mentioned it was five grand guaranteed, with a chance of it increasing to fifty.

Smithy had been around far too long not to smell a massive rat. It hadn't been an acting role at all. It turned out Jimmy Trike was who you went to if you were organising a leprechaun hunt and you needed prey. He hadn't phrased it quite like that, but Smithy had figured it out. Being a dwarf actor, he'd been offered a lot of leprechaun work in the past and had always turned it down, regardless of how much he needed the money, because it played into the bullshit narrative that the only parts people like him could play were inextricably linked to their height. As if the gamut of human emotion could be run only by somebody over six feet tall.

You want someone who can embody the human experience? How about someone who has to put up with a world designed for people two feet taller than them? And who has to suffer the indignity of people treating them like a novelty item?

Smithy had turned down the job, but only after getting into it with Jimmy. Shame on him for making people into some kind of humiliating sideshow for the gratification of Wall Street jerk-offs with the emotional maturity of pre-pubescent boys. He had been forthright, incisive and eloquent. He'd also managed to keep his temper in check. Smithy had a bit of an anger-management issue (at least that was what the judge had called it).

Smithy's girlfriend, Cheryl, had looked visibly relieved to hear that while he had given the scumbag a large piece of his mind, he hadn't garnished it with any physical violence. He had neglected to mention that he may have had a run-in with Jimmy's dumbass jeep in the parking lot afterwards. Who needs a jeep in Manhattan, for Christ's sake?

The whole thing had felt righteous.

Then, a couple of weeks later, Smithy had felt way too confident about a full house of kings over sevens, and he'd found himself in five grand to Benny Wong. Worse, he hadn't cleared a line of credit beforehand, assuring everyone he was good for it as he'd bet the pot. Benny didn't take kindly to such behaviour. You didn't run illegal card games in Chinatown for as long as he had without having some very strict rules, and without having people working for him who could see to it that those rules were respected, on pain of pain. Five grand bought a lot of pain, or possibly the end of all pain.

There had been rumours. Benny Wong knew a lot of people, and some of those people had occasionally ceased being people. Smithy had managed to negotiate a twenty-four hour grace period, and he'd been lucky to get that. Benny already considered him a pain in the ass – he'd banned Smithy from his games for three months after he had got into a fight with another patron who had refused to stop "rubbing his head for luck". The world was full of assholes.

Still, flat broke and down five grand to Benny Wong, Smithy couldn't exactly throw many stones. He'd got the extension only because the next day was St Patrick's Day. He'd explained about the hunt and how he'd be paid five grand for just turning up. The one part he'd neglected to mention had been the tiny detail that he wasn't in it.

He was banking on Jimmy Trike being a forgiving sort. After the last time, Cheryl had been clear – if Smithy got himself into another hole with gambling, they would be done. She had been right to say it. He was painfully aware she was out of his league, and frankly, if he couldn't keep his shit together, then she deserved a whole lot better. She was not a woman to hang around waiting for a deadbeat to wise up, and Smithy didn't blame her.

And so, he had swallowed his pride and gone to see Jimmy Trike again. It had gone as badly as he had feared it would. The human dumpster fire had lorded it over him, revelling in his discomfort and repeating back to him – word for word and in between gales of laughter – a lot of what Smithy had said at their previous meeting. Then, after he'd had his fun, Jimmy dropped the bomb that all ten positions for prey had been filled.

The following morning, Smithy had been sitting in a diner up by Grand Central, deciding what message he should leave on Cheryl's voicemail as he high-tailed it out of town, when the call had come. Jimmy, sounding a lot more friendly, informed him that a space had opened up. One of his contestants had got himself arrested overnight for public nudity. Happy St Patrick's Day! Smithy had flirted with the idea of telling him to shove it, but that would've been just another example of the dumb pride that had got him into this situation in the first place. Beggars could not be choosers.

He'd been picked up by a stretch limo out near the Brooklyn Bridge. There had been ten of them, and he'd been the last to hitch a ride. Some of the others he'd recognised from having seen them at auditions, some not. It wasn't as if the thing actually required actors; actors were just the easiest people to find and, statistically speaking, the most likely to be desperate for money. There had been no small talk. Whether that was because nobody wanted to bond with their fellow competitors, or because they were all simply too ashamed of being involved in this fiasco, it was impossible to say.

They'd been driven out to a country estate; Smithy didn't know where. His knowledge of New York stretched only as far as to the end of the subway line. At the venue, they had been met by people from the events company, suited and booted, all professional efficiency, as if this were a regular conference and not some *Wolf of Wall Street* fever dream.

Once they'd signed all the waivers and non-disclosure agreements – and there'd been a lot, because assholes don't like people knowing they're assholes – they had been issued with their uniform, complete with tall leprechaun hat. Every fibre of Smithy's being vibrated with righteous fury. He was all set to tell these people where they could shove it, including the hat, but then he thought of Cheryl and how much he enjoyed his working kneecaps, and kept his mouth shut.

He and the other actors got changed in a stable. A horse huffed as it watched Smithy stuff his clothes into a kit bag. A couple of shaven-headed heavies in sports coats stood by the doors, before a blonde woman in impractical heels asked them to assemble. The briefing was short and to the point. She referred to them as "participants",

4

clearly too embarrassed to refer to them as leprechauns. Poor woman – Smithy really wanted to stick her in one of these outfits and see how she'd feel then.

Each "participant" would be given a fifteen-minute head start before the hunters followed. The hunters would be wielding paintball guns. Once "shot", the participants were "out" and had to return to the house, where they would receive their pay – in cash, as agreed. There were four hunters, each with their own coloured paintballs, and the one who shot the most leprechauns would win. The blonde woman had mentioned this in the mistaken belief that the "prey" gave a damn about the other end of things. All they cared about was what she explained next: the last leprechaun standing got the fifty grand.

Smithy hated everything about this, but if he was going to feel caked in self-loathing for weeks, he might as well do it with money in the bank. Fifty grand would clear his debts with enough left over to live off while he got to work on his play. All he needed was a little time to get it done.

His group had been brought out to the start line – ten condemned men. Only at that point had it dawned on Smithy that they were all men – did these idiots really think that there was no such thing as a female leprechaun? He had no idea why this bothered him, but it did.

The four hunters had been there, waiting for them. Each one sat astride a quad bike, wearing what looked like the traditional get-up English people wore to hunt foxes. Smithy had only ever seen it on TV. They'd had their coloured flags on their bikes and large paintball guns resting on their shoulders. One of the hunters had been an immensely fat guy – Jabba the Hut-esque in stature – while the other three guys looked, if anything, bored by proceedings. As if this was their fifth leprechaun hunt of the season and they'd grown tired of them by the third.

The grounds were spectacular. The treeline was maybe one hundred yards away. It might've been the most obvious place to head for, but Smithy was still going for it. If one of those asshats was going to claim his scalp, they'd at least have to get off their damned bike to get it. It seemed the big guy was in charge, judging by how the blonde woman waited for his nod to get things started.

The participants had all made a run for it as soon as the horn had sounded. Seeing how bad the others were at hiding, Smithy could only assume that many of them had enjoyed considerably happier childhoods than he had.

During the briefing, the corporate blonde had mentioned some "little surprises". It turned out she had been referring to the fact that the woods were booby-trapped. He'd watched as a fellow contestant in front of him had plummeted, screaming, into a covered pit. Smithy looked down to see a mattress at the bottom, his competitor on it, unharmed, save for his bruised pride and possibly ass. At that point Smithy had heard the roar of engines behind him and ran. He watched from a distance as one of the hunters pulled up beside the pit and fired their paintball gun into it. Talk about fish in a barrel.

Judging by a couple of screams he'd heard from afar, these "little surprises" seemed to be dotted all over the place. Smithy had quickly decided that the best course of action would be to hunker down and wait it out. It was either that or risk getting hogtied in some trap while running for his life.

He chose his hiding place carefully. A hollow in the ground, shielded by bushes on three sides. It allowed him to keep out of view unless someone drove right by him. These idiots would be looking for moving targets. Patience would be the key.

Smithy wasn't wearing a watch, so he didn't know how long he'd been out there, but it had been a while. He'd heard whooping and hollering as the hunt progressed, and one by one the prey had fallen. The activity had settled down to quad bikes driving back and forth, up and down the paths. The dumbasses were that loud, they didn't exactly have the element of surprise. Smithy toyed with the idea of taking out one of the hunters, but while it hadn't been spelled out expressly, he guessed that the hunted becoming the hunter would be considered strictly against the rules. Nobody involved in this affair was interested in a fair fight.

Lying on the wet ground was starting to make his old knee injury ache. It had been sore for maybe twenty minutes now. He raised his head, checked nobody could see him, then risked standing up to try to stretch it out. Through the trees he could see the forlorn figure of one of the other leprechauns trudging back towards the stable. By Smithy's reckoning that must be nearly all of them. He wasn't an optimist by nature, but holy shit – fifty grand!

He dived for cover as rope twanged behind him. Someone let out a plaintive yelp.

Smithy turned to see another contestant – a red-haired guy he'd vaguely recognised in the limo, possibly from a couple of auditions. It was hard to tell if it was definitely him – he hadn't been dangling upside down from a tree the last time Smithy had seen him.

"Jesus, dude. Help me – please!"

He must have been sneaking around and not noticed the trap. His left leg was caught in a rope snare, hence the reason he was hanging six feet up in the air.

Smithy looked up at him. Technically, the man was his competition.

"Come on, guy, don't leave me hanging."

Fifty grand.

"Seriously? We're in this together. Us against them."

Smithy looked at the rope. The other end of it was attached to a stake in the ground. He could probably untie it.

"C'mon! You aren't going to leave a brother like this, are you?"

He couldn't. He just couldn't. It was bad enough that he'd lowered himself to participate in this debacle. He couldn't abandon all humanity and leave the guy hanging there, just to improve his chances at some cash?

He looked around. It didn't seem that any of the hunters had been close enough to hear.

He sighed. "Hang on."

The rope wasn't the easiest to untie, and the landing wasn't graceful, but he managed to get the guy down.

After the redhead picked himself up, he extended his hand and gave a broad smile. "Duncan."

Smithy shook it. "Smithy. Pleased to make your acquaintance."

"Hey, thanks, man."

Smithy waved him away. "Like you said, we're all in this together. Us against those juvenile idiots."

Duncan picked up his hat and dusted it off. "I know, right? This is insane."

Smithy nodded. "Yeah. Degrading bullshit. I wouldn't be here if I wasn't desperate for the money."

"Me either," said Duncan. "My Monica needs an operation bad."

"Oh jeez," said Smithy, feeling awkward. "Sorry to hear that."

"Yeah. I promised her she could get her boobs done. She's got the pair she wants picked out and everything. Got to keep the ladies happy, am I right?"

Smithy said nothing. He looked at the guy and waited for some indication he was joking. None came.

"OK," he said eventually. He was in no position to judge, but he did so anyway.

"So, what's your tactic?" asked Duncan. "Hiding? Yeah, cool. I've been relying on running. I'm pretty fast."

"Good for you," said Smithy. "Speaking of which, I should probably get back to, y'know …"

"Oh, yeah, yeah, yeah," said Duncan. "Totally. Thanks again. I'm going to—"

They both hunched reflexively as Duncan was interrupted by the blonde woman's voice. She was standing on the edge of the woods, shouting into a megaphone.

"Contestants – there are only two of you remaining."

Smithy and Duncan looked at each other.

"Holy shit," said Duncan.

Smithy extended his hand. "Whatever happens, best of luck."

"Yeah, you too," said Duncan, accepting the handshake. "Sixty grand is a lot of money."

Smithy nodded. "Sure is. It's fifty, though – not sixty."

"Sure," said Duncan, stepping back. "Sorry."

Something was suddenly off.

"You'd be amazed how much augmentation costs these days,' he continued. 'Got to get it done right. One of the guys promised me ten grand extra if he won."

"What?" said Smithy. "How can you—"

Before he could finish, Duncan pulled a small paintball gun from his pocket and shot Smithy in the chest.

Smithy had to admit Duncan hadn't been exaggerating. If the next fifteen minutes proved anything, it was that the guy really was good at running.

CHAPTER ONE

Fourteen months later

Diller took a long, thoughtful suck on the straw of his drink as Smithy watched him expectantly.

"Well?"

They were sitting in the back booth of the Porterhouse Lodge. Over the last few months it had become their unofficial clubhouse. They liked its casual ambiance. They liked Jackie and Phil, the regular barmen who were the primary source of the casual ambiance. Most of all, Smithy liked the fact that it was one of those rarest of establishments; one that would allow him to have a tab. A resting actor appreciates such things.

Along with all that, Smithy liked it for the privacy the back booth offered. He had spent the day looking after the dog that was sort of his, sort of his girlfriend Cheryl's, and sort of stolen. It was a Siberian Husky that Smithy had "acquired" from his ex-employer's dog-grooming shop to prevent its previous a-hole owner having it spray-painted to look like Gene Simmons from Kiss.

They had guessed, correctly, that someone would come looking for him at Smithy's place, so Cheryl had started taking care of him. They'd bonded and the dog had stayed with her, without it being discussed much. Smithy had moved in with Cheryl a few months later. Surprisingly, this had not been discussed that much either. His apartment had flooded and a temporary arrangement had become permanent. A lot of Smithy's and Cheryl's relationship worked on a "don't ask, don't tell" basis. The dog's original name was abandoned, and for a couple of weeks he'd been referred to as Not Gene Simmons. This led to NGS and then, eventually, Nogs.

Smithy had taken the day off from driving the cab to keep the goofy mutt out of trouble. Cheryl's landlord was dropping by and there was a strict "no pets" policy. Smithy didn't mind minding Nogs – he had kind of dumped the dog on Cheryl after all. The only downside was that a dwarf walking a large Siberian Husky around Manhattan attracted a lot of unwanted attention. He was used to people staring, but it didn't mean he liked it. A four-foot-five guy, walking a dog that wasn't far off his own height, Smithy suspected that people kept expecting him to hop astride it and try to ride off into the sunset. So, it'd been a long day, and he'd been glad of the comfort of the back booth at the Porterhouse Lodge, where Nogs was snoring away happily under the table.

Having finally finished taking his deliberately long drink, Diller placed his fist to his mouth and belched softly. "'Scuse me. That's a kick-ass lemonade. That's why this place is the bomb. Most bars have really crappy ones. I guess they figure they're just gonna mix it with—"

"Diller?"

Diller shifted nervously on the padded seat of the booth. "My mom always says, if you can't say anything nice, don't say anything at all."

"She's such a fount of wisdom."

Diller squinted. He was very sensitive about his mother.

Smithy raised an apologetic hand. "I meant no disrespect. What d'ya think is wrong with the plan?"

"First off, the fact you have a plan," said Diller. "Nothing good can come from this."

"Oh, for Christ's sake," said Smithy, picking up his whiskey and then putting it back down again. "Need I remind you what this bastard did to me?"

"No."

"He gets me, and nine other people ..."

"I don't need to be reminded."

"... And makes us dress up as leprechauns! Leprechauns."

"But you're going to remind me anyway."

"On St Patrick's Day! And the guy is on a quad bike. He's, like, four hundred pounds. Massive. As if the prick couldn't do with the exercise of chasing us on foot!"

"I know all this, but I'm gonna let you get it out."

"Then him and his rich asshole buddies hunt us, like ... like ..."

"Leprechauns?"

"Animals! Like we're less than human. And let me tell you, those paintballs hurt. They leave bruises – physical and emotional."

Smithy was absent-mindedly shredding a beer mat into strips as he spoke. Diller watched him with concern. Mostly, he was a calm and thoughtful guy, right up until the point he wasn't. His temper had landed him in trouble before – and that was only the trouble Diller knew about.

"I know," said Diller. "It was horrible. No question. You only did it because you needed the money."

"He took advantage of me needing the money."

"I said you never should have taken a loan from Benny Wong."

"Whose side are you on?"

"I'm just saying, you needed the five grand."

"I could've done with the fifty-grand first prize, but that other little ginger bastard cheated me out of it. Still though, if this fat ... I mean, I don't mean to be harsh, but the dude is a whale. Screw it, I'm gonna call him the whale."

Diller pulled a face. "Let's not make it a weight thing."

"I'm not ... You know me, I don't judge. Me and Big Dom are tight."

"Dom is looking good these days."

"I think that gastric band thing he got is really working for him."

Diller nodded enthusiastically. "I'm so pleased for the guy. He's been trying real hard. Did you know seventy percent of weight gain is genetic?"

"Really?"

"Yeah. I'm reading this book called *The Obesity Code*. Calorie counting doesn't work."

"Why are you reading that book? You're as skinny as a rake."

Diller shrugged. "The library had it and I've read most of the stuff there."

"Well, he ... Wait." Smithy looked up from his rant, distracted. "Did you say you've read most of the stuff in the library? Seriously?"

"They don't get a lot of new stock coming in, so ..."

"That's insane! Marello's – over by the Brooklyn Bridge – has a quiz night. We should hit that."

"Isn't that the place you got barred from?"

"People cannot use their phones to google stuff." Smithy prodded the table to emphasise his point. "There's no point having rules if nobody is enforcing them. What were we saying?"

"You were explaining how you don't overreact to stuff."

Smithy shot Diller a look that was notable for its lack of appreciation for the last remark. "My point is, this rich fucking ... Well, now I don't know how to describe him without referring to his weight."

"Just use his name."

"I can't. His name is Lou Reed."

"And?"

"That's the same name as, well, Lou Reed. I love Lou Reed."

"Who is Lou Reed?"

"What? You've never heard of Lou Reed? The Velvet Underground?"

Diller's expression was blank.

"C'mon. They're one of the definitive rock bands of the twentieth century."

"The twentieth century?" exclaimed Diller. "I'm twenty-two. I was barely here for any of it. You're really surprised that a 22-year-old black dude from Hunts Point doesn't know who this guy is?"

"The point is that Lou Reed, Bowie and Iggy Pop are my holy trinity."

"I've heard of Bowie."

"I'm going to do you a mixtape."

"A what?"

Smithy narrowed his eyes. "Are you trying to distract me from talking about the plan?"

"Hey, I'm not the one getting irate about dead guys."

"They're not all dead. Iggy is still alive," said Smithy, then paused. "I'm ninety percent certain he's still alive. I gave up reading the news for the last couple of months to focus on the play."

"Time you spent on this plan, apparently."

Smithy glowered. "Man, for such a sweet guy, you've got a real eye for the low blow."

"I'm just saying, maybe you're ..."

"What?"

"Is it possible ..." Diller ran his hands over the table top, as if he'd left the right choice of words on it and couldn't quite believe they'd disappeared.

"What?" repeated Smithy.

"Is it possible that your writer's block has maybe made you focus on this a teeny-tiny bit more than perhaps you should?"

"No."

"Just—"

"No," repeated Smithy emphatically. "In fact, now you mention it, I think it's this wrong – this big, massive, throbbing, monumental wrong – sitting there, festering away in my subconscious, that is draining the creative spirit out of me. I think if I resolve this situation then the play will just flow."

"Making it one of the many fine ones written in prison."

"Oh, for ... Now you're just being dramatic."

"At least one of us is."

15

"Alright," said Smithy. "Anyway, the point is, this rich ... Damn it! What do we call him? I refuse to refer to him as Lou Reed."

"OK," said Diller, pausing to push the ice cubes at the bottom of his glass with his straw. "How about we call him Fat Lou? No, that's not good. Big Lou?"

Smithy shook his head. "I knew a guy called Big Lou. One time, he helped me get back into my trailer when I was locked out."

Diller's eyebrows shot up. "You lived in a trailer? When did you live in a trailer? You've got a whole backstory we have never discussed."

Smithy shrugged. "It's not uncommon."

"I've never known anyone who has lived in a trailer."

"That's because you've never left New York. I mean, have you ever even seen a real-life cow?"

"Yeah," said Diller, before running his hand over his tightly cropped hair. "I saw one at a petting zoo the school took us to this one time. I remember it because it didn't seem that happy."

"How so?"

"Y'know, just its general vibe."

"Vibe?" repeated Smithy. "Have you ever met a happy cow?"

"I dunno. Like I said, I only ever met one."

"Precisely. You've got no frame of reference. Cows are not creatures predisposed to joy. The only one you've ever seen smiling is the cartoon one on those ads. Come to think of it, how messed up is that? This cow is supposed to be delighted because you're eating cheese made out of the milk it produces to feed its babies. That ain't natural."

"Doesn't the cow also talk?"

"Whatever. You're dragging us off the point here, Dill."

"Me? You're the one asking about cows. I wanted to know about you living in the trailer, but you never talk about your mysterious past."

"No big mystery. Just picture me in a trailer with a bunch of Lou Reed LPs. Speaking of which, back to the topic in hand ..."

"What's an LP?"

"Don't even ... Wait. How about Louis? The rich a-hole – we can call him Louis."

Diller nodded. "I don't know anybody called Louis."

"Perfect."

"Lousy Louis?" offered Diller.

"Done. Point is, this Lousy Louis fucking fucker" – Smithy was enjoying verbalising the name now it had been freed from unkind stereotypes and musical legends – "what he did, it cannot be allowed to stand."

"Can't it, though?" asked Diller. "I mean, it's been over a year already."

"That was only because I was forming my plan. Lulling him into a false sense of security."

"Clever," said Diller. "Here's another idea – you could just move on? Living is the best revenge."

"Only for people who don't have a plan. And besides," said Smithy, picking up his glass again and wafting it around to make his point rather than drink its contents, "if we let the rich assholes run riot – do what they like – what happens to the world? This is America, goddammit."

"Umm," ventured Diller, "the rich do pretty much—"

"Not on my watch!" interrupted Smithy. "If the system doesn't stop these monsters, then the individual must. I'm going to do it for me and the other persons of reduced height who were involved."

Diller's eyes widened with concern. "Oh Lord!"

"What?"

"Do you not say 'dwarf' any more?"

"What does that matter?"

"You promised me that if the right word ever changed, you'd tell me. I don't want to end up like the old guy in that diner. Remember? He looked horrified when the waitress told him you can't say 'coloured' now. You could see he didn't mean to be, y'know ... Poor guy looked so upset. I think most people don't mean to offend, but you've got to try to help the good ones because language can get confusing. I met a British guy at that audition last week – told me that

17

'Asian' means a whole different bunch of people over there than it does over here. Isn't that crazy?"

"Diller," said Smithy, "stop trying to distract me."

"I'm not."

"You were."

"Alright, I was, but only for your own good."

"You can't distract me," said Smithy. "I'm on a mission."

Diller's eyes opened even wider and his mouth gaped. "Oh my God, why didn't you say? Is this from ...?" Diller pointed at his head and then looked around, before directing his finger towards the ceiling nervously.

Smithy sighed. "No, it's not from the voice."

Diller slumped in his seat, clearly disappointed. "Oh."

"We've discussed this: it ain't God."

"I disagree."

"You disagree? It's in my head."

"Exactly. You're the worst person to judge. It's like why you should never cut your own hair."

"It's nothing like that. The damn thing is just an auditory hallucination caused by post-traumatic stress following a car accident."

"Or," said Diller, "the voice of God is speaking to you following a near-death experience."

"That's a matter of interpretation."

"Everything is."

"Well," said Smithy, glancing around and lowering his voice, "as it happens, it doesn't matter, seeing as I haven't heard 'it' in weeks. I think 'it' might be, y'know ..."

"Gone?"

"Shush. Don't say it. You'll jinx it."

"I hope I do. I liked the voice. I think it helped you to make very good life decisions."

"You're welcome to it in your head, then, my friend, because I was getting sick of it."

"Speaking of voices of reason, what does Cheryl think of this plan of yours?"

Smithy shifted awkwardly. "She doesn't need to know."

"Meaning that you're too chicken to tell her because you know exactly what she'll say."

"If we know what she'll say, why do we need to tell her?"

"That's ..." Diller scrunched up his eyes. "It feels like all the words in that sentence make sense on their own, but somehow they're collectively stupid."

Smithy sat back in his chair and tossed up his hands. "OK. Fine. Don't help."

"What?"

Smithy was taken aback by the edge of outrage in Diller's voice.

"If you don't want to—"

Diller cut him off. "I said it was a terrible plan. I never said I wouldn't help. I'm your friend. You ask me to help, I'm gonna help."

"Oh. OK. Well, thank you."

"Yeah, well," said Diller, still looking put out, "you're welcome."

Smithy held up his drink in a toast. "You're a good friend, Dill."

"Yeah, and it's still a terrible plan."

CHAPTER TWO

Smithy and Diller sat on the large wooden crate in silence, save for the quiet rocking motion of the van as it moved down the street. The only source of light inside the back of the truck was a sliver of sunlight at the bottom of the roll-top rear door. The heat was unpleasant – an unseasonably hot May in New York that felt more like July. There was an uncomfortable lack of air conditioning inside the vehicle – unsurprising, given that it was not designed for human transportation.

Diller pulled at his shirt, which was already starting to cling to him. "Do you think this feels like the D-Day landings?"

Smithy looked up in the direction of Diller's voice. "Nope."

"Y'know, the tension. Waiting to go over the top?"

"That's the wrong war you're thinking of. They didn't go over the top in the Second World War."

"Actually, they did. There were still trenches. I accept your point, though. On D-Day it was landing crafts. 'Waiting to storm the beaches' is what I should have said. Do you think this is a bit like storming the beaches on D-Day?"

Smithy shook his head. "No, Dill. I don't think we can compare our current endeavour – namely, you delivering me in a dishwasher crate to a penthouse apartment on West 57th Street – to the sacrifices made by so many members of our greatest generation on the beaches of Normandy. The comparison falls down on several levels, not least being that, as far as I'm aware, on that fateful day nobody on either side came dressed in a silly costume."

"I'm not in a silly costume," said Diller, sounding defensive. "I'm wearing the correct costume for my part."

"I know."

"A costume you provided, I might add. I haven't been to many costume parties, but I don't think many people turn up dressed as a UPS guy."

"True."

"You, on the other hand …"

"Me being dressed as a leprechaun is the whole point. You know I hate it."

Diller nodded. "I do. In fact, you hating it so much is what got us into this mess. Actually, come to think of it …"

"What?"

"Nothing."

"What's nothing?" insisted Smithy.

"You won't like it."

"Try me."

"OK, well, I mean – you know how you've brought your regular clothes in your gym bag? To change into before you make your escape?"

"Yes. So?"

"Could you not just have brought the leprechaun suit in the bag and changed into it later on?"

"No, because …" Smithy paused to consider this. "I …"

A moment of awkward silence followed, save for the van's creaking suspension as they took a right turn.

"Damn it!" conceded Smithy.

Diller sucked his teeth. "That's the thing with a plan. You think you've got it all laid out, but …"

"It's nothing," said Smithy. "It doesn't affect anything."

"Yeah, but if you missed that teeny-tiny detail, what else have you missed?"

The van took a left turn.

"Seriously?" said Smithy. "You're trying to mess with my head this close to go time?"

"I'm just pointing it out. It's not too late to—"

"I'm doing this."

"Sure. OK," said Diller. "I think maybe you should take one last long, hard look at the plan."

A little more of that awkward silence fell between them.

"Don't look at me like that," said Diller.

"It's dark in here. How the hell can you know I'm looking at you?"

"I just know."

"Hey," said Smithy, "hang on a minute. You hate the dark. How come you didn't ride up front with Big Dom?"

"It's, like, y'know – your last few minutes before the thing. I figured probably you could do with some company."

"Oh. Thanks."

"And besides, I don't think we can call him Big Dom any more."

"I know," said Smithy. "He told me he's lost 126 pounds. That's basically what I weigh."

"That's incredible," agreed Diller. "And I'll tell you what else. He looks great. I mean, it's not just the weight, it's how he's lost it. He's not got that flappy, jowly skin that some people get."

"He's a new man," pronounced Smithy. He raised his voice. "Hey, Dom, should we still call you Big Dom?"

"Yeah," came the shout back. "But more importantly, shut up. It's against company policy for people to ride in the back."

"Right. Sorry."

"S'alright. We're five minutes out. You sure about this?"

"Damn it, Dom – not you too?"

"I'm just saying ... Whatever, man. We're three blocks away. Time to batten down the hatches."

The two men hopped down and Smithy turned on the flashlight

on his phone. He pushed the wooden lid off the crate and looked inside.

"Helium – check. Balloons – check. Bag full of clothes – check. Paintball gun – check. Crowbar – check. Douchebag Bluetooth headset – check. Phone ..." Smithy waggled the device in his hand. "Check." He pulled on the pair of leather gloves he had also brought with him. "Gloves – check. Right, that's—"

Diller pointed into the crate. "Leprechaun hat. You didn't say 'leprechaun hat'."

Smithy sighed. "Yes, alright. Leprechaun hat – check. I was trying to preserve the small amount of dignity I still have."

"Oh, right," said Diller. "Sorry."

"OK, then."

Smithy swung the beam of his flashlight around the back of the truck.

"Something wrong?" asked Diller.

"Not as such, but ..." Smithy sighed again. "I can't see anything to stand on. Could you lift me into the crate, please?"

"Oh. Right. Yeah."

CHAPTER THREE

Sitting in the dark of the crate, Smithy listened to the *thunk-thunk, thunk-thunk* rhythm of the hand truck as it trundled across the sidewalk. It provided a slightly out-of-sync backbeat to the sound of Diller whistling "Born to Run".

Diller wasn't a fan of Springsteen any more than he was a fan of Lou Reed. Dale Grayson, however – the name of the character he'd come up with for the delivery guy he was playing – was. He had gone into far too much detail, but Smithy had let him run with it. Diller tried to turn every situation into some form of acting exercise, and today he was a 23-year-old UPS guy from Jersey, adopted by white parents at the age of six.

'Dale' had found acceptance in his new world through sport. He'd been offered a shot at playing baseball in the minors – but had declined, because his mother was sick. Instead of playing ball, Dale had stayed home and taken night classes in aquatic engineering at the local community college.

If that's what it took for Diller to help out with the plan, Smithy reasoned, then fine – he could be all that. As long as he also delivered the crate.

Big Dom actually worked for a rival courier firm to UPS. While he was happy to give them a lift with the crate, he would not take part in a fraudulent delivery, he said – it was against the code of the courier. Smithy was pretty sure the code of the courier didn't exist – not to anyone other than Dom, at least – but he hadn't queried it. Dom was an especially serious guy and Smithy could respect that.

They had met when Dom was the prop manager at a theatre company he'd worked with briefly before it had imploded, as so many of these things do. Big Dom was a great guy, and when he occasionally needed someone to listen to him while he talked, Smithy was happy to be that ear. It was just over a year since the big guy had been jilted while standing at the altar – literally – and it had left him with some understandable trust issues. The best man and Big Dom's intended had taken the honeymoon to Cancun. In spite of it all, Dom remained a kind soul with a good heart. Even now, he was sitting around the corner in his van, waiting to give Diller his bike back on his return.

Smithy had more confidence in the plan than Diller had, but that was because he hadn't wanted to tell his friend exactly how much time he had dedicated to its formulation. For the last two weeks, Smithy had taken a job in the florist across the street from Lousy Louis's apartment building, just so he could watch the comings and goings.

The two daytime doorpeople split shifts – four days one week, three the next. The woman was in her late forties and conscientious. She liked things to be just so. She paid a great deal of attention to deliveries, kept the reception area studiously neat, and was polite to the other staff. The man, on the other hand, was in his late twenties, and while he was gushingly effusive to the residents, laying the charm on thick, he was lazy and rude to the other staff, particularly the Guatemalan cleaner who had rebuffed his sexual advances.

He was, in short, a lazy douchebag – which was perfect. You could rely on a lazy person to be lazy, and him being a douchebag meant that if it cost him his job, well – instant karma. If the building's owners had any sense, they would give the job to the nice Guatemalan cleaning lady, who would be an awful lot better at it.

Smithy had learned all of this by carefully watching the building's toings and froings from his vantage point between the roses, tulips and peonies in the window of Petal to the Metal. It was amazing how much you could learn if you paid enough attention. He'd also discovered that he both enjoyed and had a flair for arranging flowers.

That's not to say he'd been sad to give up the gig two days ago. Being hit on by Phillip, the bitchy old queen who owned the place, hadn't bothered Smithy in the least, but Phillip's statement of "I find myself weirdly attracted to you" meant he could go take a long walk off a short pier. "Weirdly"? Seriously, did he think that was some kind of compliment? It always amazed Smithy how some people seemed to have no grasp of even basic manners. There were a lot of weirdos out there. Coming from a dude dressed as a leprechaun who was hiding in a crate so he could take vengeance on someone who'd paid him five grand for an afternoon's work, that was really saying something.

The crate took a right turn and Smithy steadied his breathing. He heard the *whoosh* of the automatic doors opening and the change in sound as the hand truck's wheels moved from the sidewalk to cold, smooth marble.

"Hey, how ya doing?" said Diller – or rather Dale, in his admittedly well-judged New Jersey accent.

"I am fine, thank you. How are you today, my friend?" said a bright and chipper voice that was not supposed to be there. Smithy had planned it so that the lazy douchebag doorman would be on duty. He'd never heard the man speak, but he was willing to bet that he didn't have a West African accent.

"Yeah, y'know, I'm getting by. Like the Boss sang, it's just the working life."

That seemed a little much.

"What boss?" said the unknown doorman. "Whose boss? I don't understand."

"The Boss. Bruce Springsteen."

"Ah, right, the singer. Is that crate a delivery from him?"

"No," said Diller. "I was just ... Hey, never mind. I got a delivery here for apartment 2601. The penthouse."

"I see," said the doorman. "Well, I have nothing on the list here. I will take it and put it into the back room."

"What? No. I was told it's gotta be delivered up into the apartment. Got to be left in there."

"Hmmm ... I have not been told anything about this."

"Yeah," said Diller. "The guy left really clear instructions. If you don't mind me asking – are you the regular doorman?"

"No, I have been sent here by an agency."

I should have come by and checked this morning, thought Smithy. *Why did I not come by and check?*

"Ah," said Diller. "Maybe he left instructions with the other guy?"

"Well, we cannot ask him. He has been fired."

"Oh."

"Yes. He was found attempting to have sex with a domestic appliance."

"Excuse me?"

"Yes. A vacuum cleaner. He has been removed from his position with immediate effect. I do not know what they have done with the vacuum cleaner."

"Right," said Diller.

"No, it is very wrong."

"Yeah, I mean, obviously."

"There are some very sick people in this world, let me tell you."

"You ain't kidding, buddy. All kinds of weirdos."

Smithy, while trying to focus on staying calm, couldn't help thinking that this new information put the doorman's interest in the Guatemalan cleaning lady into a new and even more disturbing light.

"Yes," said the doorman. "Follow me and we can leave this delivery in the storage area."

"I wish I could, fella, but my instructions were really clear. This has got to be delivered right into apartment 2601."

"Hmmm. What is it?"

"It's a dishwasher."

"I see. Perhaps the tenant was concerned that the doorman might attempt to have sex with it. Such a disgusting man."

"Too right," said Diller. "This is what happens when people do not let the light of Jesus into their lives."

"Praise the Lord."

"Praise the Lord."

This was precisely why Smithy had wanted Diller to be the one to deliver the crate. It should have been straightforward. The former doorman, being the lazy sort, used to accompany delivery men up to the apartments to drop off big deliveries directly. He didn't want to do what the doorwoman did and take them up personally when the tenant came home. You could rely on lazy – except when lazy got caught being a sicko with a vacuum cleaner and then, well, you couldn't rely on it at all. Smithy could rely on Diller, though. He was a people person. It was a remarkable ability. He knew how to get on with anybody. Praise the Lord.

"So," said Diller, "can we just drop this crate upstairs, please? I would hate to have to come back. My church has a social tonight and I promised my auntie I'd help with putting the chairs out."

The doorman paused to consider this. "I will tell you what I will do – I shall call the tenant and confirm the instructions. We have a sheet of working hours contact numbers for residents for this eventuality."

"Ummm. Oh, there's no need to trouble the guy."

"It is no trouble – apartment 2601, you say?"

"Yes," said Diller, because what else could he say?

"I have a number here that says it is for his office. Let us call and see."

Smithy sat in the dark, listening as a firm hand punched buttons on a phone.

"It is ringing," said the doorman.

"Honestly, you don't need to—"

"Hello, may I speak to Mr Lou Reed, please?" Pause. "Thank you." Another short pause. "They are putting me through. Isn't that the name of a famous singer? Maybe that is why Bruce Springsteen is sending him a— Yes, hello. My name is Jacob Anan and I am the temporary doorman at Mr Reed's building. I am contacting you regarding a delivery."

Pause.

"I see. Will he be in the meeting long?"

Pause.

"Oh, I see. I believe it is a delivery from Bruce Springsteen."

"No," said Diller, "it's …"

"Yes. I just wanted to know if he wants it delivered directly to his apartment?"

"Sorry," tried Diller again. "I think there's—"

"OK," said Jacob. "Thank you for your time."

The phone was put firmly back in its cradle.

"It's not a delivery from Bruce Springsteen." Diller sounded increasingly exasperated.

"Oh," said Jacob. "She said you could take it straight up if it was."

"It's less of a delivery. More of a gift."

"Ah, OK. Well, follow me. This Bruce Springsteen, he seems like a very generous man."

"Yes," said Diller. "Yes, he is."

CHAPTER FOUR

"Aw, hell no!"

Smithy had already put on his Bluetooth headset, so he took his phone out of his pocket and speed-dialled Diller.

His friend spoke in a whisper. "Is everything OK?"

"No."

"Oh God. Have you been arrested?"

"What? No. And why are you whispering?"

There was a moment's pause as Diller realised he didn't have a good reason for his low voice. He coughed. "I'm ... My throat is sore."

"Yeah. Hey, great improv with the doorman, by the way. I thought we were royally screwed there."

"I know," said Diller. "I'm just glad that Lousy Louis was in a meeting, otherwise we'd have been done for."

"Yeah."

"Did everything go OK getting out of the crate? Oh my God, are you stuck in the crate? You're stuck in the crate, aren't you? I knew it!"

"Dill, relax. I'm not stuck in the crate."

In fact, Smithy had discovered that crates were harder to open from the inside than the outside, but it hadn't been anything the crowbar couldn't sort out. Once he was out he'd blown up a dozen helium balloons and filled the crate with them. When Lousy Louis came home, he'd discover someone had inexplicably sent him a crate full of balloons, but hey, who didn't love balloons?

Last year, Smithy had scored a short-lived delivery gig for a gift company. In the two weeks he'd worked there, he'd delivered a colonic irrigation gift set; a basket of muffins, upon each of which was an iced picture of a supreme court justice; and a "congratulations on your divorce" basket that contained everything a person might require for some quality alone time – unless they were the ex-doorman of this building.

In short, a crate full of balloons wasn't that weird. More importantly, you wouldn't open it and think someone had used it as a means by which to sneak into your apartment. Smithy was particularly pleased with this part of the plan. It was essentially a modern-day take on the classic Trojan horse. If it ain't broke ...

"OK," said Diller. "If you're not stuck in the crate, what's the problem?"

"Guess what this a-hole has on his bedroom wall?"

"You know I love a guessing game, Smithy, but this feels like it could take a while."

"I'll give you a clue – it's a sort of trophy."

"Oh God. The guy who won the leprechaun thing – he had him stuffed and mounted?"

"What?" said Smithy. "No, of course not. Why on earth would you guess that?"

"Well, I dunno. You seem pretty angry."

Smithy looked up at the wall again. "He has – I shit you not – Han Solo encased in carbonite. I mean, like, the real one."

"Yeah, that would've taken a while to guess. Define 'real' here?"

"I mean the actual prop from the film. There's a framed certificate beside it and everything. Signed by George Lucas."

"Cool!"

"It is not cool, Diller. It is annoying. Something like this should be in a museum somewhere, not hanging in this douchebag's bedroom. I mean, of all the places! Who has that in a bedroom? I bet it really sets the mood with the ladies."

Having been understandably distracted by the sight of Harrison Ford trapped in carbonite, Smithy hadn't paid much attention to what else was on the wall.

"Holy crap."

"Now what?"

"He's got one of Han Solo's blasters, too."

"Sweet!"

"How are you not outraged by this?"

"Because I'm a dude from Hunts Point who has only ever seen one cow, and this guy's place sounds awesome."

"Your priorities are messed up, Dill."

"Says the guy dressed in costume in the middle of a burglary. Speaking of which, aren't you supposed to be hiding somewhere? What happens if he comes home?"

"Relax. It's Tuesday. He goes to see some lady every Tuesday. I'd like to think she's a therapist but best not to ask."

"How long have you been following this guy?" asked Diller, incredulous.

"Not that long." This was technically true. Ish.

Most of Smithy's time had been spent trying to find the guy – it turned out the filthy rich weren't in the phonebook.

"The point is, he's not going to be home for ages. What I'm doing right now is figuring out a hiding spot. I've got plenty of time – I haven't even been in the living area yet. I'm going to have to stay hidden for hours, so I want to be comfortable and— Holy shit!"

"Now what?"

"He's got a floating bed!"

Smithy hadn't noticed when he'd walked in because, well, Han Solo was on the wall, but now he saw that the large bed, up on a platform in the centre of the room, was actually floating in mid-air.

"Cool. Do you mean it's hanging from wires or something?"

"No, I mean it's actually floating in mid-air. Seriously, is this some kind of voodoo? How evil is this dude?"

"I bet it's magnets," said Diller.

"Magnets? How can it be magnets?"

"I've seen it in a magazine. In fact, I'm pretty sure it was *TIME* magazine's Best Invention a while ago. Damn, I wish I was with you. This place sounds tight!"

"It's not tight," said Smithy. "What it is is grossly, offensively decadent. And what stops the bed from floating off?"

"Science."

"Science," mumbled Smithy disapprovingly. "Science wasting its time on crap like this is why we don't have a cure for cancer."

"Take a picture of the bed."

"Really? I've broken into somebody's apartment and you want me to take pictures so I have incriminating evidence on me?"

"Take a picture, send it to me and then delete it."

"So, to be clear, Dill, you want me to send you incriminating pictures linking you to this crime?"

"Oh, never mind. You've taken all the fun out of it. What other cool stuff has he got?"

"What is this? Lifestyles of the rich and the shameless? It's a big, gaudy, expensive-looking penthouse with a floating bed, an actual original Han Solo in carbonite on the wall, and a bona fide laser pistol. I'm getting out of this room before I throw up."

"How big is his TV?"

Smithy looked around. "D'you know, I haven't actually seen one."

"Oh. I don't trust peeps who don't have a TV."

"You don't have a TV, Dill."

"Yeah, but I can't afford one. That's different. I'm guessing this dude can."

"True."

Smithy looked at the various doors in the room. In addition to the one he had come in through, there were two others. He walked towards the one closest to him and stopped.

"These doors don't have handles," he told Diller.

"What?"

"They don't have ... Wait a sec." He waved his hand in front of a dimly glowing panel on the wall and the door whooshed left, *Star Trek*-style, to reveal a large walk-in closet.

"What was that?" Diller asked.

"Nothing."

"I bet it was something cool and now you won't tell me."

"It was nothing exciting. I'm in the dude's walk-in closet."

"What's it like?"

Smithy looked around. Rows of expensive-looking suits hung beside about three dozen shop-fresh shirts, with sweaters neatly folded on shelves, followed by T-shirts, slacks, chinos, and several drawers that were no doubt full of freshly laundered underwear. There were about fifty pairs of shoes, most of which were buffed to such a high shine that you'd get a migraine if you looked at them long enough.

"Just lots of fancy clothes. He's probably got a suit made out of Dalmatians in here somewhere."

"So, is this where you're going to hide?"

Smithy spun around slowly, giving it an appraising eye. There wasn't anywhere he could actually hide himself – at least not where he wouldn't be spotted as soon as someone walked in.

"Nah."

"You need to find somewhere."

"No kidding. I'm guessing under the bed is out – I ain't lying in magnetic fields all night. That don't sound healthy. I'll find somewhere. This place is massive, and it's just me and the bag."

Smithy shifted the gym bag on his shoulder, which contained his street clothes, leprechaun hat, paintball gun and a small canister of helium.

"Is the plan still ...?"

"To wait until he's asleep? Yes."

For reasons Diller didn't fully understand and wasn't entirely comfortable with, a lot of Smithy's recent ideas seemed to have drawn inspiration from the films of Mel Gibson. Last year he'd used *Lethal Weapon 2* to help their friend Bunny with a situation. He'd watched *What Women Want* with Big Dom in an effort to prime him for his return to the rigours of the dating game. Then there was this idea, inspired by *Braveheart*.

After William Wallace, played by Mel Gibson, is betrayed by the Scottish lords, he escapes and hunts them down one by one. In one particular scene, a lord is asleep in his bed, having a nightmare in which Mel is coming after him on horseback – wild-eyed, in full face paint. The full Gibson. The lord wakes up, terrified, and is relieved to realise it was only a dream. Then, his bedroom door flies open and in rides Mel on horseback – a vision of terrible vengeance made real – and proceeds to slam a kind of cannon ball on a chain into the lord's head, smashing it like a pumpkin.

Admittedly, in Smithy's version, a lot of that had changed. For a start, he wasn't actually going to kill Lousy Louis, and despite what his acting CV said, Smithy couldn't ride a horse. Even if he could, he would have needed a much bigger crate.

No, in his plan, Lousy Louis is asleep in his douchy floating bed and wakes to find a leprechaun standing over him, holding a paintball gun. Smithy had a shortlist of four planned speeches, but was yet to settle on one. He thought he would wait and see what felt right at the time. Then, as Louis is lying there thinking he's about to die, he'd be hit with the mother of all paintball barrages.

Smithy had spent quite a lot of money he didn't have on a gun that the guy in the shop said had something called a motorised, gravity-fed hopper. Smithy hadn't understood most of the technical lingo, but he'd grasped the important bit – it could shoot twenty paintballs a second. The dude had waxed lyrical and called it a triumph of engineering elegance and excellence. Smithy considered the phrase more appropriate for a feat of design such as the Brooklyn Bridge, but he had let it slide. Besides, he was fully intending to return the gun in the morning and say it was a present that hadn't been appreciated. Failing that, he'd stick it on eBay and hope for the best. This project had gone way over budget, not least because it wasn't supposed to have one.

The other change in Smithy's version of events was that, unlike the deceitful lord, this would be only the beginning of Lousy Louis's nightmares. If Smithy's plan went as he hoped it would, Lousy was going to learn a valuable lesson – one that would stay with him for the rest of his life – about how to treat human beings.

Smithy moved back into the bedroom and walked up to the other *Star Trek* door. He waved his hand in front of the sensor.

"Aw, hell no times a hundred!"

"Now what?"

"He's got a whole wall of Lou Reed's album covers – like the actual, proper musical genius Lou Reed. Full vinyl LP covers – all thirty-five – that's twenty-two studio and thirteen live albums."

"Oh," said Diller. "OK."

"OK? OK? It is not OK!"

"What? This guy can't like the same music as you?"

"He can, but he doesn't. Because if you actually like Lou Reed, you would not have his album covers on the wall of your bathroom."

"Oh."

"Yes. One of the greatest artists ever to grace the planet deserves more respect than to have his life's work gazed upon by some fat dipshit while he takes a dump."

"We said we weren't going to mention his weight again."

"All bets are off! This is an affront that will not stand."

"Oh boy. And so it begins."

"What are you talking about?"

"Well," said Diller, "I can always tell when you're totally losing your temper because your speech gets more and more Shakespearean."

"That is ridiculous."

"Is it, though? That fight in the karaoke bar, the last thing you said was, 'If this brute dares to place his hands on me once more, I shall smite him.'"

"I never—"

"You did. You said you were actually going to smite that Australian dude, which turned out to mean putting his head through a framed picture of Gloria Estefan."

"How do you know who Gloria Estefan is, but you don't know Lou Reed?"

"Now who's changing the subject?"

"Alright, I'm just ... I once had every Lou Reed album on vinyl, y'know. They got lost in a fire."

"Oh."

"I know these aren't the exact same ones, but it's just ..." Smithy ran his gloved hand over the framed covers, as if trying to comfort a wounded animal. "This is just ... Aw, hell no! Hell no! Hell no!"

"Now what?" asked Diller. "Has he stuffed and mounted Lou Reed?"

Smithy looked up at the wall. "I think he ..." Smithy had to work to hold back the emotion in his voice. "I think these album sleeves still have all the original records inside them."

"So?"

"*So?*" Smithy could feel his blood starting to boil. "Dill, do you have any idea what a steamy bathroom will do to rare vinyl recordings?"

"No."

"Well, neither do I, but I bet it's not anything good. I'm going to rip down every single one and take them with me. This is an affront in the eyes of God!"

"Hello again, Mr Angry Shakespeare," said Diller. "If you're gonna steal stuff, can you get me the Han Solo laser pistol?"

"I am not stealing stuff. I'm here to make an important point."

"Couldn't that point be that bad people don't deserve nice things?"

"Dill, don't—"

Smithy froze. It was only 4:30pm – Lousy Louis wasn't supposed to be home for at least three hours. So why had he just heard the front door open?

CHAPTER FIVE

Lou Reed – the one who wasn't dead – came barrelling through the front door, his phone pressed to his ear.

"I don't give a fuck, Morris. Just get it done, or else go fill out a job application for Dunkin' Donuts, because that is where you'll be working next week."

He snapped his phone shut with a pleasing *thunk*. Flip phones were hard to come by these days, but he'd found a place in South Korea that did custom builds. He enjoyed being able to snap the device shut to terminate a call. It felt boss. Speaking of bosses ...

He looked at the big crate sitting in his kitchen of polished marble surfaces and glittering chrome. His fridge had more processing capacity than NASA had when they'd put a man on the moon. It currently housed some pickles and a jar of mayonnaise past its expiration date.

"Alright, alright, alright!"

He walked around the crate as if admiring a fine work of art. He'd hurried home right after his assistant had given him the message. Last year, Lou had spent a lot of time chasing Springsteen's people to try to book him for the company's Fourth of July party. He'd been told Bruce did not do private events, no matter what. He'd doubled the offer – hard no. Then he had doubled it again, and had gone to great lengths to find out where Springsteen lived. He had sent an intern over to deliver the offer in person with a bottle of champagne. The intern had been instructed not to take no for an answer. He had returned drenched in champagne and defeat. Last Lou had heard of him, the guy was working in Starbucks. That was too good for him – coffee is for closers.

Lou ran a hand over the crate affectionately. He'd known that Springsteen would have a price – all that "man of the people" stuff was just marketing.

"Samantha, call Pamela."

"Calling Pamela, sir."

Samantha was the state-of-the-art home management system that he'd had installed earlier this year. It controlled everything. He'd also paid a small fortune to get that hot chick from that show he liked that'd got cancelled to record the voice for it. It was totally customised. One of a kind. Lou was all about rarity.

"Hello, Mr Reed." Pamela's voice came from the speakers in the ceiling. Lou could make and receive calls anywhere in the penthouse.

"How the hell am I supposed to open this thing?"

"Ummm, what exactly?" asked Pamela.

"What? The crate! The crate from Springsteen! It says on the side that it is a dishwasher."

"Right. Of course. Sorry. Do you want me to send somebody over?"

"No. I want … Wait a second." Lou spotted something on the floor. "It looks like they left a crowbar. I guess I'll have to do it myself."

"Sorry, sir."

Lou took off his suit jacket and tossed it on the marble counter. Then he took a long, hard look at the crate.

"Do you have any idea why he would send you a dishwasher?" Pamela asked.

"Well, it's a gift. Obviously."

"It's kind of odd, though."

Lou looked around the crate again. "Musicians are odd. We

booked Bowling for Soup a few years ago and they sent us a crate of Fresca. Did Hiroshi's people call back?"

"Not yet, but—"

"Call them again."

"It's five thirty in the morning there now, boss."

Lou stopped and glared at the ceiling. "Did I ask you what time it was in Tokyo or did I ask you to make a call?"

"Yes, Lou. Sorry, Lou."

He placed the tip of the crowbar under the lid of the crate and rested his weight on it. Unexpectedly, it offered little resistance, as if it had been held in place only loosely. Lou stumbled messily as it flew off.

Then he looked up.

His scream, carried by the speakers, echoed around the apartment.

"What is it?" asked Pamela. "Are you OK, sir? Lou? I'm calling 911."

Lou fell to the ground and stared up at the kitchen ceiling in horror. "B ... B ... Balloons!"

Pamela's voice was a mixture of confusion and terror. "I'm ... Lou? Do you need ...?"

"He ..." Lou was breathing hard. "He sent me fucking balloons! What kind of monster sends somebody balloons?"

There was a pause at the other end of the line. "Right. That's ... weird. Are they ... ordinary balloons?"

Lou looked up at the ceiling as the balloons bobbed there ominously. "They're balloons, Pamela. Big, fucking creepy balloons. What can you possibly not understand about that?"

"Right. Maybe he thought they'd be" – her voice lowered, as if she was already regretting starting the sentence, but she couldn't avoid finishing it – "nice?"

"Nice?" said Lou, as he crawled out of the kitchen on his hands and knees. "*Nice?* Are you out of your fucking mind? Everyone knows I hate balloons. What a sick bastard. Jesus Christ, Pamela. Get over here now. I need you to get rid of them."

"Right. I'll send somebody."

Lou, having reached the hallway, placed his hand on the wall and dragged himself back to his feet. "No. You. I want you."

"I can't, Lou. Remember, we discussed this. I've got to take Michaela to the doctor's about her throat."

"Cancel it."

"I ... I can't do that. It took six months to get that appointment."

"Fine."

"I'm sorry. I could come after? Or ..."

"No, no – it's fine. If you're not dedicated to your job, then that's not a problem."

"Look, I'll send someone else."

"No," said Lou firmly. "Nobody else. I don't want strangers. Not now."

"The building's concierge, then?"

"No. He's new. He tried to talk to me on the way in. I don't want him. It's fine."

"If you're sure."

"Yes. I'll just have a room in my home I can't use because you can't fix a simple problem."

"I can come over after the—"

"No," said Lou as he walked through to his bedroom, pulling off his tie and tossing it on the floor. "I need a shit."

"OK, I'll leave you to—"

"Take me through my schedule for tomorrow."

"I ... Right."

Lou went into his bathroom and proceeded to drop the kids off at the pool while Pamela took him through his agenda of meetings for the following day. He was straining to push out a particularly big one when he heard a whooshing noise from the bedroom.

"Goddammit, Pamela. You said the guy had been round to fix that problem with the doors."

"He did. He came yesterday morning. He assured me it was fixed."

"Well, it isn't. Get him back first thing tomorrow. Christ. Can't anyone do their job around here? I've got a stressful week ahead. The last thing I need is doors opening at random in the middle of the night. It freaks me the fuck out! I'm a light sleeper."

"Right, sorry, I'll—"

"Samantha, end call."

"Sorry, Lou, can I just—"

"Call terminated," came the automated voice from the ceiling.

"Wah, wah, wah," Lou whined in a mocking tone. "Like it's my fault your kid is sick. Samantha, place a call to Steffon Birch."

As he wiped his ass, Lou informed his company's head of human resources that his PA wasn't working out, and that he'd need yet another new one.

Having unburdened himself of both lunch and his useless PA Lou walked back into the bedroom. "Samantha, how come nobody can do even simple things right?"

"Sorry," said the automated voice, "I do not have that function."

No, he said to himself, *you don't*. He walked into his closet and changed into slacks and a sweater, leaving his suit on the floor for the maid to deal with in the morning.

When he left the bedroom, he passed the glass enclosure of the kitchen. Since he'd bought the place, he'd had the kitchen redesigned three times, which corresponded to the number of times he'd used it to cook an actual meal.

"Samantha, darken kitchen glass to max."

He watched with satisfaction as the glass tinted until it was impossible to see into the room. It was a useful feature, allowing him to move around his apartment in privacy while the maid cooked his breakfast each morning. Lou liked to go clothes-free for the start of his day.

He needed to take his mind off the balloons. Fucking Bruce Springsteen, trying to play some kind of sick and twisted joke on him. People were weird.

"Samantha, TV."

Lou sat down on the couch and placed his feet on the coffee table as the floor-to-ceiling windows darkened and the twelve-foot screen descended from the ceiling.

CHAPTER SIX

Smithy felt his phone vibrate in his pocket. That must have been about the tenth or eleventh time now. He reached down slowly, careful not to disturb any of his cuddly friends, and took it out of his pocket, cupping the screen with his hand so that the glare wouldn't reflect off any of the windows. He looked at the array of unread text messages.

Diller: "What happened?"

Diller: "You OK?"

Diller: "Smithy?"

Diller: "Answer me!"

Diller: "Oh God, this is bad."

Diller: "Why aren't you answering?"

Diller: "Not that I know where you are."

Diller: "Or had anything to do with whatever you are doing."

Diller: "I've been busy all day."

Diller: "I'm going to call Cheryl."

Smithy cursed silently to himself and then thumbed a response quickly.

Smithy: "All fine. DO NOT CALL CHERYL!!!"

After twenty seconds, the phone vibrated again.

Diller: "What happened?"

Smithy: "He came back early. I think he was excited to see what Springsteen had sent him."

Diller: "Oh."

Diller: "Oops! "

Diller: "How did he not see you?"

Smithy: "I was always good at hide-and-seek."

Actually, it had been a combination of luck and quick thinking. Mostly luck. Thankfully, because it was a big apartment and Lousy Louis was loud, Smithy had been able to shut himself in the walk-in closet using the *Star Trek* door without drawing any attention.

Smithy had nearly screamed when the automated voice of Samantha had come blaring over the speaker in the otherwise silent space. Between Lousy Louis's booming voice and the phone call being carried right around the apartment, he had been able to ascertain where Lousy was. He had also heard more than enough to reaffirm his opinion that the man was indeed an unspeakable asshole – one who was, inexplicably, afraid of balloons. If Smithy had known that sooner ... Still, too late now. As it was, he'd barely managed to avoid being seen.

When Lousy had proclaimed loudly that he was going for a dump Smithy had been able to escape from the closet. He'd also been lucky that when Lousy had heard the door open, he'd assumed it was down to some fault in the fancy-pants system. What on earth was wrong with ordinary door handles? They had worked fine for centuries. Lousy Louis deserved all the problems he'd got – and a whole lot more.

As soon as he'd fled from the bedroom, Smithy had looked around, desperate to find somewhere else to hide. There had been that moment – the point of no return. He'd stood facing the glass-enclosed kitchen, considering whether to make left for the front door and freedom, or head right and stick with his faltering plan. Then he had heard Louis make that crack about the PA's kid – Smithy had turned right. Then he'd turned back. Not to leave – he'd realised that he'd messed up and left the crowbar behind. He padded into the kitchen, snatched it up and then made his way back into the apartment.

He'd only been in the kitchen, bedroom and bathroom so far. The open-plan living area was made up of a massive sunken lounge with a sofa stretching the length of it that could comfortably seat about ten people. The enormous wooden coffee table in front of it was about the size of Smithy's entire apartment. Even as he'd looked around in panic, he couldn't help but wonder how they'd managed to get it inside. Had they taken out some of the windows that opened on to the huge balcony?

The view of the sun crawling across the Manhattan sky was a billion-dollar one, literally. They didn't call this stretch of real estate Billionaires' Row for nothing. Smithy had considered the balcony as a possible hiding place but rejected it. There was some furniture out there, but not a great deal, and the shrubbery wasn't the kind that would offer much cover. Besides, all he'd need was for Lousy to lock it and he'd be stuck out there all night.

The sunken lounge offered no concealment either. There was a bar in the far-left corner of the room, but that hadn't seemed a good strategic choice either. It had struck Smithy that it was highly likely Lousy Louis was a solo drinker.

To Smithy's right was a wall hung with massive movie posters. As Smithy had scanned the room, he'd ignored them pointedly. He couldn't afford to get distracted. He'd walked further into the apartment, between the lounge and the wall of posters. There must be somewhere in this ...

Smithy had turned the corner and stopped dead. Leonard Nimoy was staring right at him.

Smithy's phone vibrated again.

Diller: "Where are you hiding?"

Smithy: "I'm in *The Muppets*."

Diller: "What?"

Around the corner from the lounge lay an area about twice the size of the massive bedroom, filled with ... everything. Lousy owned the most ridiculous collection of memorabilia known to man. He had a life-sized waxwork of Leonard Nimoy as Spock, his hand held aloft in the traditional Vulcan salute. He had the pinball machine from *Tron* – the original film, not the awful remake. He had a Batman suit, a Captain America suit, a suit of samurai armour – all displayed on full-sized mannequins. Alongside them was a velociraptor from *Jurassic Park* and life-sized models of both the Alien and the Predator. In the centre of the room, dominating proceedings, was what appeared to be the Batmobile from the original TV series. However they had got the immense coffee table inside now looked like it must have been a walk in the park. And there, against the far wall, was a massive collection of what appeared to be every single member of *The Muppets*.

Smithy had been considering going for the closed door at the back of the "museum area" when he heard, "Samantha, darken kitchen glass to max." He'd panicked and dived in amongst the Muppets, burying himself in their furry safety. It had been instinctive. He came from a generation that didn't trust politicians, the press or damn near anyone else on TV, but everyone trusted the Muppets. He'd rearranged them hastily, placing five-foot tall Fozzie Bear to the left of him, Gonzo and a few of the chickens to his right, and the bass player from Dr Teeth and the Electric Mayhem standing behind him. Elmo sat on Smithy's lap. It had left Smithy just enough room to look out, but invisible to all but the most interested of observers.

Diller: "You're hiding with *The Muppets*?"

Smithy: "Long story."

Diller: "Has he got loads of other cool stuff, then?"

Smithy: "I'll tell you later."

Diller: "Does he really not have a TV?"

Smithy: "Bit busy right now, Dill."

Diller: "Oh right, sorry. Good luck."

Diller: "And if you happen to get your hands on that pistol ..."

Smithy: "No."

Smithy was starting to worry he was a bad influence on Diller.

After all, the kid had enough on his plate – maybe he should stop involving him in his dumb ideas?

Over the next few hours, he had made good use of Lousy's – well, not TV. You couldn't call a twelve-foot HD screen that appeared out of the ceiling a mere TV. It was no doubt a "home entertainment system" or something. They watched a hockey game, which the Islanders had lost 4–3 to Arizona, bringing an unexpected trip to the play-offs to its expected end. There had been a point when Lousy had frozen the picture on one of the Islanders' scantily clad "ice girls". These women were like NFL cheerleaders, only they had to clean the ice between periods while waving at drunken fans. As Lousy had sat and stared at her frozen image, Smithy had feared the worst. He had looked away and covered Elmo's eyes. Then, thankfully, Lousy had gone back to live TV in time to see the Islanders massacre another breakaway.

Lousy had put on the *Watchmen* movie after that, which Smithy had always quite liked, followed by an episode of *The Walking Dead*. That was an annoying move, as it was the season finale, and Smithy and Cheryl had been saving up the episodes to watch together. He hated watching stuff out of order. There was nothing this guy couldn't ruin. Halfway through the episode, the two large pizzas Lousy had ordered from some place called Ragadoni's turned up. Lousy had offered the delivery girl a hundred bucks if she came in and burst some balloons for him – no questions asked. The kid had called him a pervert and hightailed it out of there.

Once the initial terror of being discovered had receded, Smithy had found himself becoming quite relaxed. His presence had clearly gone undetected, and Lousy, while not exactly a gracious host, seemed uninterested in admiring his ludicrous horde of collectibles. By about 11pm, Lousy had nodded off while a bunch of talking heads argued over who should play quarterback for the Patriots. Smithy could feel his own eyelids growing heavy. He needed to stay awake – aside from anything else, he had been informed by Cheryl that he talked in his sleep. That would be a really dumb way to get found out.

Before he knew it he was wide awake. Something had caught his attention. His instincts had twigged it and they were just waiting for the rest of him to catch up. What was it? Lousy hadn't moved; he was still snoring away happily. The TV continued to talk to itself. What was wrong? Was it simply a jolt of paranoia at falling asleep that had sent a shock of adrenalin through him?

Then, without a whisper of noise, one of the doors to the balcony opened and a figure clad in black stepped in from the night.

CHAPTER SEVEN

Not my problem.

These were the first words that popped into Smithy's head. Whatever the hell this was, it was not his problem. Lousy Louis was an appalling human being and it stood to reason that he had pissed off a great deal more people than Smithy alone. Or maybe he just had a lot of highly steal-able stuff.

Smithy sat amongst the plush Muppets and watched as the figure in black looked down at the slumbering form of Lousy Louis Reed – who seemed to be in a pizza-induced coma, drooling on himself contentedly. The figure was backlit by the light of the massive TV screen, so details were hard to make out – not that there was a great deal of detail to see. The intruder – well, technically the second intruder – was clad head to toe in the black apparel of a ... Well, Smithy felt embarrassed even to think it, but a ninja.

One person breaking into an apartment in costume was odd, but two doing it separately? Mind you, while the ninja outfit was a bit much, the person wearing it had magically appeared on the top-floor balcony of a twenty-six-storey building, so maybe it was unfair to lump them into the same category as a dude who'd run the New York Marathon dressed as a chicken.

The ninja stepped neatly onto and over the immense coffee table, and leaned in close to look at the snoozing Louis. Smithy couldn't say exactly what, but something about this person's gait made him feel sure it was a man. The ninja clicked his fingers – no response. It appeared Louis was an incredibly heavy sleeper. No sooner had that thought occurred to Smithy, another one bounced up from somewhere to contradict it. According to Lousy's own whiny complaint delivered to his soon-to-be ex-PA he was a light sleeper who got woken up by malfunctioning doors whooshing open in the night.

Smithy didn't have much time to think about it, as the ninja had just done something unexpected. Though could a ninja who'd just walked in from the sky ever be said to do anything truly unexpected? Still, pulling a sleek black rucksack from his back and taking out a camcorder was surprising. The figure looked around the room and seemed to make a decision – he placed the recording device at the end of the coffee table, on its small inbuilt tripod. Smithy still had no idea what was happening, but he had a very bad feeling about it.

Things were about to get worse as, with a sense of dread, he recognised the tingling sensation at the back of his mind. He'd thought it was gone. He'd thought wrong.

HELP HIM.

He felt suddenly queasy.

HELP HIM.

Smithy closed his eyes and tried to have a strong word with himself/the voice of God.

Look, this isn't my problem. I don't know what any of this is about.

HELP HIM.

It's really none of my business. How do I know that he doesn't deserve whatever this is?

HELP HIM.

Smithy opened his eyes and shook his head. He was done being dictated to by his own psychological illness.

HELP HIM.

The black-clad figure stood in front of the comatose Lousy Louis, looking back in the direction of the camcorder. Its small screen was turned forwards, so the person in front of it could see themselves being filmed and frame the shot. Seemingly satisfied, the ninja nodded at the camera and then reached over his shoulder and pulled out a sword. As the blade caught the light, Smithy was certain that it was very real and very deadly.

Oh crap.

HELP HIM.

HELP HIM.

HELP HIM.

Could he really watch an innocent man die? No, wait – that sentence didn't sound right. Could he really watch a man who was guilty of an awful lot of things die? No, that wasn't it either. Could he really watch an asshole who was guilty of being an asshole be executed in cold blood?

HELP HIM.

HELP HIM.

HELP HIM.

Crap.

If I die doing this bloody stupid thing, there'd better be a heaven, and this better score me some serious brownie points.

HELP HIM.

HELP HIM.

HELP HIM.

If you really are God, then no offence, but you're not much of a conversationalist.

As quietly as he could, Smithy stood up and – for no reason he could readily understand – put on his hat.

CHAPTER EIGHT

The assassin placed the edge of the blade across Lou Reed's throat and prepared to pull it back to deliver the death blow. After a moment's consideration he bent down and repositioned Reed's head carefully so that it was leaning on the other shoulder. The man mumbled in his sleep but otherwise did not stir.

He glanced at the camera once more to confirm that he had framed the shot correctly, and then pulled back the sword.

As the sword made its final descent, a flash of movement in his peripheral vision caused him to alter its course. A figure was hurtling towards him. The blade sang as it ripped through the air and tore through his attacker in one fluid motion.

The assassin watched in confusion as the severed head of Fozzie Bear spun off into the distance. He turned to see the only slightly less incongruous form of a leprechaun charging down the coffee table towards him. He swung the blade again, missing the Celtic mythical creature as it fell flat on its back and slid along the table's polished surface. As he drew back the sword to strike a downward blow, the last thing he saw clearly was the gun. Then, in a triumph of engineering elegance and excellence, twenty paintballs hit him square in the face.

As the ninja howled in pain, Smithy rolled right and dropped off the table. The man staggered back and brought his hands to his paint-soaked face, dropping the sword in the process. As he rubbed furiously at his eyes, the sword embedded itself into the table at the exact spot where Smithy's chances of reproduction had been only a moment before.

A paintball travels at approximately 280 feet per second, which isn't fast enough to break the skin in most circumstances. However, to deliver a barrage of them into a virtually unprotected face was considered an especially bad idea – even by people on YouTube. As ridiculous risks go, Smithy felt that the one he had taken had worked out remarkably well. His opponent's howls were enough to cause Lousy Louis to come around. Louis looked up to see a ninja with a face splattered in pink paint and screamed. Smithy, however, didn't have the luxury of time to scream, because his opponent was coming to terms with his surprising change in circumstances and was reaching his right hand around to the back of his outfit.

Smithy started to run.

He dived over the end of the couch as the TV exploded in a shower of sparks behind him. Not unlike a stopped clock's ability to be right twice a day, a temporarily blind man can still kill you by shooting in your general direction. A series of shots from the gun that Smithy had correctly anticipated rattled off in rapid succession.

Smithy felt the *whoosh* of air over his head as a bullet passed through the hat that, thankfully, started a foot above the top of his head. Amidst the exploding TV and the sound of bottles of – no doubt shamefully expensive – booze in the bar shattering, Smithy counted possibly twelve shots. That would have been a useful piece of information had he the first clue what gun his opponent was holding and how many bullets it held. He didn't. Smithy didn't like guns in general – and this one in particular.

He tossed the leprechaun hat in the air, hoping to draw a couple more shots. Nothing. When he risked a glance over the top of the sofa, he found himself looking down the barrel of a firearm, behind which was the half-concealed and entirely pink face of his opponent, who was all kinds of pissed off.

"Who are you?"

The man's accent was clipped, hard to place.

Smithy sighed and sat back on the floor. "I'll be honest, it's a really long story, and I'm guessing we don't have that kind of time."

Smithy closed his eyes.

WELL, YOU TRIED.

Smithy's last thought was about to be something very unkind about God, but then he heard the noise. He opened his eyes just in time to see the immense form of Lousy Louis Reed, who had managed to get to his feet and was hurtling towards his would-be assassin with all the energy he could muster. He caught the black-clad figure just as he tried to turn, wrapping his massive arms around him.

It was the nature of Smithy's existence that he was used to most of life towering over him. The everyday world was designed by men about six feet in height, who assumed that the rest of the planet shared their eyeline. Still, nothing had ever loomed over Smithy with such ominous presence as Lousy Louis Reed grappling inexpertly with a pink-faced ninja.

Smithy was trying to scamper away when, like an avalanche of assholes, the duo came crashing down on top of him, expelling all the air from his lungs and possibly shattering a few things. It was impossible to tell where the most damage lay – everything hurt too much to individualise the agonies. Hell was other people, or at least other people lying on top of you.

Louis was pinning both Smithy and his assailant to the ground. The good news was that Smithy knew where the gun was; the bad news was where the gun was. The ninja's weapon-holding hand was pinned beneath Lousy Louis's girth, leaving the firearm pointing directly at Smithy's face. Smithy needed to move his head quickly if he wanted to preserve its structural integrity in the long term.

Above them, Louis was panting and groaning almost rhythmically. Smithy guessed this meant that the assassin's other hand was free and throwing punches into Lousy's body in an effort to move him.

Straining, Louis raised his voice. "Samantha ... call ... nine ... one ... one."

Smithy tried to pull his head further away from the gun, but there was no give in that direction. He couldn't breathe either, which was becoming an issue. Smithy had learned not to expect a great deal from life, but dying while Lousy Louis grunted and groaned above him felt like a particularly ignominious way to go.

The automated voice of Samantha boomed over the speakers, "Calling ... Olivia Munn."

It wasn't as if the evening had gone to plan or, indeed, made a great deal of sense up until this point, but still – this was a bit much. As Smithy began to wiggle in the other direction while attempting to draw some air into his lungs, the thought occurred to him that surely this couldn't be *the* Olivia Munn.

The sound of a phone ringing out filled the apartment.

The only Olivia Munn that Smithy had ever heard of was the Hollywood actress. She'd been brilliant in Aaron Sorkin's *The Newsroom*, and criminally underused in the X-Men film she was in. He couldn't imagine that Lousy Louis knew her, but then he hadn't expected him to be the target of an honest-to-God ninja assassin either. The dipshit was defying expectations left, right and centre.

After two rings, the phone was picked up and a female voice boomed over the apartment's speakers.

"Hello."

It was hard to tell if it was her or not. Smithy was now inches from his goal. Louis continued to grunt and groan, his weight shifting slightly, putting yet more pressure on Smithy and shoving his nose into the carpet.

"Who is this?" asked the female voice. It did sound quite like her.

Louis shifted again, giving a pained gasp as his weight moved back the other way. Smithy drew in a desperate breath and sweet, sweet air re-entered his lungs.

"Is it you again, you fucking pervert?"

Smithy was beginning to think it really was Olivia Munn.

Lights were flashing before his eyes now. Smithy summoned every last desperate ounce of strength he had left in his body and prepared to do the world's hardest push-up.

"I don't know how you keep getting my number, but I'm going to hunt you down and kill you, you useless, pathetic ball-sack of depravity."

Damn. Munn Burn.

The call was terminated.

Smithy kept his eyes locked on the barrel of the gun and heaved with all his might. Above him, Louis moved a few inches …

Smithy pushed his head to the side and sank his teeth into the black-gloved hand holding the gun. Somewhere in the distance there was a scream – and the gun fired three times.

Smithy's ears rang, and as the sound of the explosions faded, he realised he was temporarily deaf. The pain in his ears was mitigated by the fact that Lousy Louis, keen to avoid getting shot, had rolled off him completely.

Smithy reared up, gasping greedily at the air, born again. After a few moments, he placed a hand on the side of the couch and pulled himself to his feet laboriously. Amoebas of light were floating across his field of vision. He reached up to feel wetness running out of his right ear.

Having detected the smoke from the exploded TV, the sprinklers in the ceiling started to shower the apartment in water. Smithy felt like Andy Dufresne after his escape from Shawshank. An alarm was sounding, but with his ears still ringing it felt as if it were happening miles away, in a whole other life.

As he regained his sense of his surroundings amidst the man-made rainstorm, Smithy looked around him. Lousy Louis was on the floor, propped between the couch and the coffee table. His assailant was now limping towards the door to the balcony. The black-clad figure opened it and stepped back into the night from whence he'd come. Smithy watched in incomprehension as he clambered up onto the stone balustrade and, in one fluid movement, rolled himself off the edge.

Smithy got to his feet and rushed outside as fast as the stabbing pain in his right knee would allow. The cool night air felt glorious. He'd developed a new-found appreciation for the joys of breathing. He staggered across the outdoor space and clambered onto the balustrade just enough to allow him a view of the street. Down below, he could see a small parachute collapsing on the ground. A vehicle sped up the road and scooped up the ninja, leaving behind the parachute as the only evidence the whole thing hadn't been a weird, if remarkably physical, dream.

"You have got to be kidding me!"

Smithy turned back to the penthouse. The ringing in his ears was starting to die away and he could hear the fire alarm more clearly – enough that he was relieved when it stopped. By the time he had limped back inside, the sprinklers had ceased too. The room was drenched. He glanced across at the soggy mass of muppetry and gave a sigh.

Lousy Louis was gawping at him, his eyelids flying at half mast, like a drunk trying to find sense in the world.

"Are you ... an angel?"

"No," said Smithy. "No, I'm not."

"But ... you saved me."

"Not my idea."

"What're you ... What're you doing here?"

Smithy ignored the question as he limped towards his hat and picked it up. He looked at the bullet hole in it, about two inches above where his head would have been. *Well, that's one deposit I'm not getting back.* This thought led to another. He turned and saw the paintball gun lying on the ground. The barrel was pointing at an angle and the hopper was cracked.

"Goddammit! Do you have any idea how much these things cost?" Smithy picked it up, pointed it at Louis and pulled the trigger. Nothing happened. "Great. That's just great."

"I'll pay."

Smithy glowered at the man who did not deserve the name Lou Reed.

"That's your answer to everything, isn't it? You narcissistic, megalomaniacal piece of shit."

Louis attempted to drag himself up onto the couch but found it too much. He slumped back to the floor. He waved a hand at Smithy. "You're one ... one of the leprechauns."

"I'm not a fucking ..."

Smithy looked at the sword sticking out of the centre of the coffee table and took a few deep breaths. The tempting idea of making Lousy Louis into a kebab had popped into his brain, and while he wasn't going to do it, he enjoyed the prospect for a few seconds.

"You saved me!" Reed was now wearing a weirdly blissful smile.

Smithy looked at the sodden carpet below his feet, took a long, slow and deep breath, and then let it all out.

"Shut up. You are a terrible person. Do you understand that? Awful. I don't know why that guy was trying to kill you, but I bet you deserve it. You treat people like objects. You think money gives you the right to do what you like. Well, it doesn't. Alright? It doesn't. And show the actual Lou Reed some respect. Take those records off your bathroom wall. You are the most pathetic human being I've ever come across – and believe me, that is really saying something. Re-hire your assistant and, and, and ... Don't ever call Olivia Munn again. Just ... Just try to be ... a person. Just a decent person."

Smithy raised his head and looked at Louis to see what effect his words had had.

The man was fast asleep again, snoring happily.

"Great. Just great." Smithy looked up at the ceiling. "Well, I hope you're happy?"

He limped to the far side of the room, picked up his rucksack from where he had discarded it, placed the sodden hat and broken paintball gun inside and headed for the apartment's front door.

As he reached it, a thought struck him. He turned and headed back into the living area. He marched over to something, picked it up and did a hasty about-turn.

As he walked by the unconscious form of Lousy Louis Reed, he held up his new possession. "I'm taking Elmo. You don't deserve Elmo."

CHAPTER NINE

A minute later, Smithy stood on the landing outside Louis Reed's penthouse. He opened the door to the stairwell and heard the sound of boots quickstepping. Two of the elevators were on their way up too. It made sense. Shots are fired somewhere on the darker edges of the city; they'll send a patrol car. Shots are heard on Billionaires' Row; they'll send a SWAT team. Someone might miss the person they're aiming for and accidentally hit some of the money.

With a heavy sigh, Smithy opened the nearby garbage disposal chute and climbed in, clutching a sodden Elmo to him.

As the hatch closed behind him, he placed his legs against the wall and started to shuffle his way down gradually, ignoring the pain coming from his damaged leg. For a plan that had been prepared so meticulously, none of it had gone as it should have. Such was Smithy's painstaking level of preparation that he had even managed to get hold of the blueprints to the building. He knew this chute led to a trash-collecting area three floors down that would, in turn, feed into the compactor in the basement. It wouldn't be on at this time of night – he just had to make it there in one piece. Then he could find a way to slip out of the building.

He felt that sickly tingle again.

YOU DID WELL.

"Shut up, God."

CHAPTER TEN

Diller took a long thoughtful suck on his straw as Smithy watched him expectantly. They were back in the Porterhouse Lodge. Jackie had opened up early and allowed Smithy to use the upstairs shower without asking why. This was an all-time great pub.

"OK," said Smithy, unable to take the silence any more. "I'll admit, there were some issues with the plan."

Diller finished his drink with a slurp and placed his hand in front of his mouth to cover a belch. "'Scuse me."

"C'mon, Dill, talk to me. I can tell you're annoyed."

"Annoyed? Why would I be annoyed?"

"I'm going to assume that's a rhetorical question."

"Would it be because I warned you it was a terrible plan, you ignored me and ended up nearly getting yourself killed?"

"Hey, be fair. I'd have gotten out of that dumpster before the garbage truck actually crushed me. Not that I don't appreciate the help."

"I'm not talking about that," said Diller.

"Although it does need pointing out there was a scandalous amount of recyclable cardboard and plastic in there. Those rich a-holes have no excuse not to be recycling. Makes my blood boil."

"Yeah," said Diller, "and we all know that you're not a man who gets angry easily."

Smithy nodded. "That sarcasm is both fair and warranted."

"Thanks. And no, I'm not talking about how I had to get up at five in the morning to sneak into a building and pick the lock on the dumpster to save you and your little friend here" – Diller nodded at the stuffed Muppet that was leaving a damp patch on the seat beside Smithy – "from getting compacted. Although that was fun. I'm talking about how you almost got killed by a – and I can't believe I'm saying this – a ninja wielding a sword."

"Don't fixate on the sword," said Smithy. "If anything, the gun was far more dangerous."

"There was a gun?"

Smithy shifted in his seat. "Oh. Did I not mention that?"

Diller sat there with his mouth wide, making a choking noise. It was as if there were so many words striving to come out at the same time that they'd formed a logjam in his throat. Eventually he simply shook his head. "Unbelievable. Unbelievable."

"OK, you're right, but come on, someone broke into the guy's apartment to try to kill him. Who could have seen that coming?"

"Well, he is the kind of guy who has someone wearing a leprechaun costume break into his apartment to try to teach him a lesson in morality, so it's not completely beyond the realm of possibility. I guess other people don't share your conviction in the power of the teachable moment."

"The guy has enemies," agreed Smithy. "It's not a surprise, given his limited social skills and deplorable attitude towards the rest of humanity."

"Yeah. Maybe it was another outraged Lou Reed fan?"

"I wouldn't rule it out."

"Speaking of which ..."

"No, Diller – I didn't take Han Solo's blaster for you."

He shook his head. "Course you didn't."

"I wasn't there to steal stuff."

"No. As it turns out, you were there to save Lousy Louis's life."

"What can I tell you? Not my idea."

Smithy picked up his drink. Technically, it was too early for Jackie to have sold him a whiskey but luckily Smithy didn't have any money to pay for it, so the terms of the liquor licence hadn't been compromised.

Diller leaned forward. "Wait a sec, do you mean ...?" He jabbed his finger at his temple excitedly.

Smithy sighed. He didn't want to say it but, after all he'd done, Diller deserved the truth. "Yeah, the voice came back. Made me save him."

"Ohhh," said Diller, sitting back. "This puts a different slant on things. Maybe God sent you there to save this man's life."

"God didn't put me there. This plan wasn't the voice – it was all me, for better or for worse."

Smithy threw back the rest of his whiskey. He'd spent a couple of hours stuck in a locked dumpster. He wasn't in a sipping mood. Who locks a dumpster? Rich people. That's who. He'd been delivered into it via the chute and trapped in there, encased in stinking garbage and a lot of material that should have been recycled.

"Yeah, the whole thing was your idea," said Diller. "But the voice didn't object, did it?"

"I've done a lot of stupid stuff. The voice doesn't chip in every time. It ain't like that. You know this."

"I'm just saying ..."

"It was just my conscience kicking in. I couldn't sit there and watch somebody – even that Lousy Louis piece of crap – get slaughtered by some lunatic with a sword. The assassin dude was filming it, too, by the way."

"Really?" said Diller. "What do you think that means?"

"Damned if I know. Maybe they were some kind of psycho who gets off on watching their work. Maybe their employer wanted proof. All I know is, Lousy Louis clearly has bigger problems than me on his plate."

There was a joke in there about plate size, but Smithy wisely let it be.

"So, how're you feeling?" asked Diller.

"I'm alright. Probably better than I deserve. My knee is bothering me, my ears hurt and I've possibly bruised a rib or two, but nothing too bad, considering."

"And how are you feeling?" asked Diller again, emphasising the "feeling" this time.

Smithy nodded. "Oh. Right. Like an idiot, OK? You tried to warn me, and I should have listened. Maybe I needed somewhere to put my energy after I gave up playing cards, and I chose the wrong option. I guess I have what you could call an addictive personality."

"Well," said Diller, "you live and you learn, and thankfully you lived."

"Yeah, and not to repeat myself but I really am sorry. No more stupid revenge plots. No more dumb ideas. I'm going to get my head down, drive the cab and work on the play."

"I'll drink to that," said Diller, looking down at the table where their empty glasses sat. "Not that we can."

"I could get another one?"

"Yeah, because drinking at eight in the morning is an excellent way to fill your time now you've given up being the Count of Monte Cristo."

Smithy raised his hands. "Point taken."

Diller leaned forward and lowered his voice. "So, seriously – this ninja dude parachuted off the freaking building?"

Smithy nodded. "Honestly, it was the coolest thing I've ever seen in real life."

"Sweet." Diller paused. "So ..."

"Yes, you can have Elmo."

"Sweet."

CHAPTER ELEVEN

Smithy was at the ass-end of a fourteen-hour shift and his back was starting to ache. The customisation of the front seat of the cab made it easy for him to drive, but nobody was meant to stay sitting down for that long. He kept meaning to get out and stretch his legs, but it had been raining steadily all day, which was manna from heaven for a New York taxi driver. Besides, after all the time and effort he'd put into the build-up to his revenge mission – not to mention the expense – he needed to be earning. The temporary job at the florist hadn't paid that well, although it had given him a further skill to add to his acting CV. You never knew.

Part of him really enjoyed the driving. It was simple, straightforward. It gave him time to think. He'd spent a lot of those spare moments taking a long hard look at himself. This week had been a wake-up call. He needed to grow the hell up and focus on what was important. He was in his forties now, well past the point at which repeatedly putting himself into stupid situations was anything less than idiotic. Sure, Lousy Louis Reed was a scumbag, but if Smithy hadn't got himself in the hole to Benny Wong they'd have never met. He needed to stop looking for villains and start accepting responsibility for his own life. He felt as if his head was clear for the first time in a long time.

He'd resisted it for a while, but Smithy had cracked eventually and started to work with one of the hailing apps. He was lucky – he had been gifted the use of his yellow taxi by his friend Marcel. This meant that, unlike so many other cabbies who'd bought theirs at inflated prices – only to see the value crumble due to the "Uber effect" – he wasn't buried in debt and desperate. Still, a lot of people preferred to use their phone to hail a cab, rather than sticking a hand in the air. Ignoring that fact didn't make it go away.

The app had been glitchy all day. It had kept trying to send him well out of his way to pick up fares, directing him to lower Manhattan when he'd been up in Harlem, and then over to Queens. It pinged him again, looking for a pick-up just off Water Street. It was still a little out of his way, but if he took it, maybe the thing would stop making angry beeping noises at him. He swiped to accept.

It was after 7pm so the Manhattan traffic was only bad, as opposed to its rush-hour, War-of-the-Worlds, evacuate-the-city levels of bumper-to-bumper honking insanity. If anyone ever found a way to turn rage into electricity, one set of broken lights in Manhattan could power the Eastern Seaboard.

The waving little green man on the screen indicated his fare was on the left-hand side of the street. The only person standing on the sidewalk amidst the stream of hurrying pedestrians was a woman in a red coat, holding a matching red umbrella over her head. As he pulled up, she stepped forward smartly, collapsing the umbrella as she slid into the back seat.

Smithy pressed the icon on the screen. "Ms Muroe?"

"That's right."

"And we're off to Lincoln Center?"

"Correct."

Smithy put on his turn signal and pulled back into traffic. "Anything good on tonight?"

"Not that I'm aware of."

"Oh. OK."

"I'm meeting someone."

"Gotcha."

"Actually, that person is you, Mr Smith."

Smithy was startled, then remembered that his ID was on the plexiglass screen between the seats. He laughed awkwardly. "Thanks, but I'm spoken for."

Not that he was interested, but the woman was certainly attractive. Late thirties at a guess, long auburn hair, with bangs over piercing brown eyes. She smiled brightly at him in the rear-view mirror, knowing he was looking.

"That's actually not what I meant, Mr Smith. Although I believe you prefer Smithy?"

Smithy hit the brakes so hard that the car behind him honked. He looked in the rear-view mirror again at the still-smiling Ms Muroe. "What is this?"

"Just a friendly chat, I assure you." She glanced behind them. "You might want to continue to drive, Smithy. Do you mind if I call you Smithy?"

"Maybe I want you to get out of my cab?"

"Ohhh," she said and tutted. "If you throw me out here, that'll be your third and final strike. The app will not tolerate a poor customer experience. I know that because it's owned by my employer."

The car behind them laid on the horn again. Smithy glanced in the side mirror and noticed the NYPD cruiser on the far side of the road, its driver giving him a questioning look. Smithy waved and moved off. He took a left and, in the absence of any other ideas, started driving toward Lincoln Center.

"Whatever this is, I'm not interested."

"Oh, come now, Smithy – I'm going to call you that unless you tell me to stop, by the way. How can you know you're not interested if you don't know what this is?"

"Wait a sec. Who owns this app?" he asked, pointing to the phone on his dash.

"Lou Reed," she said. "I believe you are acquainted."

"I don't know who that is."

"Really?" said Muroe, giving him a sardonic little smile that might've been cute in other circumstances. "I've got footage from a couple of CCTV cameras on my phone here that says otherwise." She pulled a smartphone out of her coat pocket. "Would you like to see it? There's a bit where you slide along a table, which is frankly pretty badass."

"I don't know what you're talking about."

"OK," she said, laughter in her voice. "We can play it that way if you like."

"How did you find me?"

She shrugged. "I could give you an answer like, 'It is my job to find people.' It'd make me sound all mysterious and sinister, but it has been a long day. When you competed in Mr Reed's little hunt you filled out legal paperwork. You didn't fill it out correctly, but you did so incorrectly in such a way that still gave us enough to go on. Look, relax – this isn't anything bad. Mr Reed wants to thank you for your assistance in dealing with certain matters."

"OK. Consider me thanked."

"He wishes to do so in person."

"No, thanks."

"Mr Reed is a very generous man."

"No, he isn't," said Smithy. "He's a guy who thinks his money can buy him anything. That is not the same thing."

Muroe gave a little nod. "OK, I shall rephrase. He's a very rich man who wants to meet you so badly that this time yesterday the app I used to bring you here was owned by somebody else. If he's willing to drop that kind of cash just to get your attention, imagine how much money he is prepared to give you."

"I'm not interested in him or his money."

"Everybody is interested in his money."

"Nope," said Smithy. "I'm not for sale. He's the physical embodiment of everything I despise and I've no interest in his gratitude or his cash. I wasn't in his apartment for either."

"Careful, Smithy, you just confessed there."

"Stop calling me that."

"OK. Mr Smith? Shall we go with that?"

No response.

"Mr Smith it is. You do have a temper, don't you? I can see why Judge Rodriguez said what he did."

"Those records are sealed."

Muroe laughed again. Smithy was beginning to hate the sound. "Actually, can I just ask? Help me settle a bet. Why were you in Mr Reed's apartment?"

There was a long pause during which Smithy said nothing.

"Right, sorry. You don't want to incriminate yourself. Although it is a little late for that. I think you were there to teach him some kind of lesson. My colleague reckons you wanted to kill him."

"With paintballs?" asked Smithy.

"Oops, incriminated yourself there again, Mr Smith. And yes, he thinks you were going to do something inventive with them." Her eyes flashed on the word "inventive". "Personally, I don't think that's your style. Not the inventiveness, so much as the murder."

"No comment."

She laughed again. "Oh, I do enjoy you, Mr Smith. Down to business. I'm empowered to offer you ten thousand dollars to meet with Mr Reed."

"No."

"Twenty?"

"No."

"Thirty is as far as I can go."

"Good."

"So, you'll take it?"

"No, but now you can stop asking." Smithy pulled the taxi over and turned around in his seat to look directly at Muroe. "It's been a real hoot, but you can tell Mr Reed I'm not interested. End of story."

"Look, just meet him. Hear what he has to say. Call him an ass and take the guy's money. What've you got to lose?"

"My self-respect."

She raised an eyebrow. "If the report I read this morning is accurate, the security consultant reckons earlier this week you exited

Mr Reed's building dressed as a leprechaun via a garbage chute. Exactly how high a price are you putting on your self-respect?"

"Look. Let's just forget the whole thing."

"Mr Reed is not prepared to do that."

"Well, he will have to get used to disappointment."

Muroe sighed. "I'm the easy way, right? You get that? I'm him asking nicely. He will ask in other ways."

"And I've turned down his request nicely," said Smithy. "He wants to come at me in other ways, that's up to him, but fair warning, I don't appreciate being pushed around."

"I know. I've read your psychological profile."

"Good for you. Now, if you don't mind, it has been a long day and I'd like to get home."

Muroe looked around. "You're throwing me out here? But we're not even at Lincoln Center."

"Sorry, lady. I'm no longer for hire."

"So be it." She slipped her hand into her pocket and took out a card. "Here are my details. My cell is on there. Think about it. I'm available 24/7. I really do think you're cutting off your nose to spite your face here." She held it out, but Smithy didn't take it. "OK." She tucked it into the seal on the plexiglass. "It's there if you change your mind."

She pushed open the door and shook off her umbrella. "Say hello to Cheryl for me."

"Wait. What ...?"

The door slammed and Muroe was gone, walking away in the opposite direction. Smithy watched her red umbrella bob out of view in the rear-view mirror.

After a moment he slammed his fist against the steering wheel. "Damn it!"

CHAPTER TWELVE

Sometimes you just know.

As soon as Smithy got into the hallway, he could feel something was wrong. The apartment he shared with Cheryl was at the far end of the hall and nothing looked off, but still he knew. He was panting heavily, having just run up four flights of stairs because the elevator was too damn slow. It was a good building overall, but the elevator sucked. There were ongoing arguments between the landlord and the tenants because, in the landlord's skinflint opinion, the thing still moving meant it was working, despite the fact it took two minutes to crawl up four floors.

Still, it was a nice place, down at the still-unfashionable end of Brooklyn. A lot of people seemed to share the perception that there wasn't an unfashionable end, but that's because they never got past the hipsters up in Williamsburg. Brooklyn was still Brooklyn. You could tell which ethnic groups were thriving just by checking out the shelves in the grocery stores and the new restaurants. Smithy loved that. The place itself was alive, ever evolving. New York might be the city that never sleeps, but Brooklyn is the one that never stands still.

His friend Pedro was a walking-tour guide and one of the true believers who maintained Brooklyn never should have given up its city status to become subservient to New York. He'd convinced Smithy to sign his petition to reverse it. It was pointless, and Pedro knew it too, but he possessed the zeal of the true believer and Smithy could respect that.

Smithy tried to exercise restraint and walk down the hallway slowly, getting his breath back as he went. All the way home, he'd been attempting to reassure himself. That Muroe woman mentioning Cheryl was probably her way of letting him know that they'd been taking a good look around at his life. That was all. Probably. Almost definitely. Still, once the thought had taken root in his head, there'd been no shifting it.

As he moved down the hall, he could hear an Ani DiFranco song he recognised coming from their apartment. Cheryl liked to listen to her when she cooked. The woman was as smart as hell, funny and compassionate, not to mention all the other stuff. She was a catch and a half. Also, her cooking wasn't worth a damn. It was amazing how bad she was at it, and how much it seemed to annoy her. It drove her crazy. It wasn't like either of them believed it to be the "woman's role", or any crap like that. It was something she couldn't do, and that pissed her off. In the weird equilibrium of their relationship, it meant Smithy couldn't cook either. He wasn't allowed to. She would master it if it killed her, or killed him first.

Cheryl had come to New York to study dance, only to have her dreams dashed by an ankle that couldn't take the strain. She'd bounced around a few dead-end jobs before ending up working as a pole dancer. She all but unionised the workforce, drove out a couple of sleazy club owners and ended up managing the Pink Slipper on behalf of its new female ownership. While she was at it, she became a certified Krav Maga instructor. There was a plan to open her own dojo, but she kept putting it off. Not that she was afraid of the challenge, but she worried she would miss the girls too much.

The door to the apartment was slightly ajar. Smithy examined the lock. Smashed in. He closed his eyes for a moment. Fearing the worst and being confronted with the reality were two very different things.

He couldn't hear much other than the music coming from inside, and could see nothing past the sliver of light.

Sneaking in seemed pointless – they knew he was coming. When somebody is expecting you to come through a door at any minute, the only advantage you can gain from doing so is by doing it a lot faster than they expect you to. He stepped back against the far wall. It wasn't much of a plan – hell, it could be more accurately described as a wish – but it was all he had.

He took a deep breath and pushed himself off the wall, slamming through the door and rolling across the carpet, before coming up to his feet in a fighting stance. The berserker scream died in his mouth.

Two men he'd never met before were on their couch, in front of which lay the shattered remains of their coffee table. Cheryl loved that table – it had featured a portrait of Lenny Bruce painted by a friend of hers. One of the men – big-framed, fifties, with a nose that had been broken too many times ever to sit right – sat there looking calm, despite having his wrists and ankles bound with duct tape. He was holding a bag of frozen peas to the side of his face.

The other man, who had dyed-blond hair gelled up into a mohawk was lying face down on the couch, hogtied, with tape across his mouth. He looked less content with his lot. At least the colour of the couch meant that his nosebleed wasn't going to stain it as badly as it could have.

Smithy looked around. A lamp was smashed, a chair was turned over, and there was a large indent in the plaster of a section of the wall. It looked a lot as if it had been caused by somebody's head. Amidst it all, Cheryl, red hair tied back and apron on, was standing by the stove, cooking.

"Oh, hi, honey." Her voice had an affected, cheery air to it.

"Are you OK?"

"Why wouldn't I be?"

Smithy walked towards her, glancing back at the two men as he went. He noticed Nogs the dog sitting over in the corner, happily chewing on the former leg of the coffee table. As he got closer, he saw there appeared to be bruising around Cheryl's eye.

"Seriously, are you—"

She picked up the lid of a pot and slammed it down again without looking in it. "I'm fine. I'm a little annoyed, though, seeing as you didn't tell me we were expecting company."

"I didn't know. I tried ringing you ..."

"Did you? I'm afraid my phone got busted when it collided with somebody's face." She held it up for Smithy to see the smashed screen.

Standing beside her now, he noticed the gun sitting on the counter.

"Jesus."

"So," said Cheryl, "when were you going to introduce me to the fellas?"

"I've never met them before in my life."

Cheryl opened the oven, noticed that there was nothing inside it, then glanced behind her at the leg of lamb sitting on a roasting tray. "Damn it!"

Smithy reached out to touch her hand. "Honey."

She pulled it away from him. "Don't you 'honey' me."

"I'm sorry, I—"

"Sorry?" she said, no longer holding back the anger from her voice. "Sorry about what? George over there and I have been having quite the chat." Smithy looked back at the two men. The larger one nodded. "So, which bits are you sorry for? That you got five grand in debt to Benny Wong and didn't tell me? That you took part in that fucked-up hunt thing, after telling me you'd turned it down flat? Or that you attacked the guy who organised it a few days ago?"

"I didn't—"

"I'm assuming that was the night you told me you were out doing an all-night shift in a cab as 'research' for your play? For Christ's sake, Smithy! Why can't you just screw around like an ordinary boyfriend?"

"You have every right to be angry."

"Stop being reasonable. It's too late for you to be reasonable," said Cheryl, slamming the leg of lamb into the oven so hard that she may have violated its rights under the Geneva Convention. "Your latest idiot scheme, which you didn't tell me about, has resulted in someone sending over hired muscle to try to use me as leverage. Leverage? I'm nobody's fucking leverage."

Smithy glanced at the couch again. "I think they get that now."

"And don't be charming. Don't be charming, don't be reasonable, don't be apologetic. This is fucked up. All of this shit has been going on, and you told me about precisely none of it. We're supposed to be a team."

"We are."

"We're not. It's like I'm your goddamned babysitter. I'm not the sit-at-home-worrying type, and you know that."

"I'm sorry."

"And don't be sorry. Above all else, don't have the nerve to say you're goddamned sorry." She turned to the man sitting up on the couch. "George, how is your head?"

The big man cleared his throat. "It's better, thank you."

"OK," said Cheryl, "then I guess you two will be leaving."

George nodded.

Cheryl picked up the gun and thrust it at Smithy. "My former boyfriend will show you out."

CHAPTER THIRTEEN

The trio of men stood awkwardly, waiting for the elevator. Smithy's hand was sweaty on the grip of the handgun, which he held in the pocket of his jacket. He'd thought of escorting them down the stairs but the elevator, while painfully slow, was easy to control. Plus, fewer neighbours would see them, which was probably a good thing. If they called the cops, Smithy would have to get into why these guys were here, and that was not something he wanted to discuss with the authorities. Breaking and entering was still a crime, and from what Ms Muroe had told him, she and Reed had plenty of evidence of him doing that.

The big guy, George, stood there calmly, holding on to his blond associate, who still had his hands bound behind his back and his mouth taped. Blood was flowing from his nose in a steady trickle. He looked a mess.

"You can take the tape off his mouth, if you like," said Smithy.

"Nah," said George. "I've heard more than enough from this *figlio di puttana*."

"My Italian isn't what it should be but I'm guessing you two are not the best of friends?"

"You could say that. I didn't want to work with him. For the record, he's the one who tried to get physical with your lady. I don't do that."

"Sure," said Smithy. "You're a saint."

George shrugged. "That, I definitely ain't, but I don't hit women. I agreed to do this on the understanding it was a simple leverage job. That's what the lady said."

"Ms Muroe?"

"I don't know who that is."

"Brunette, thirties, good looking. When I met her, she was wearing a red coat."

"Oh, yeah, that's her. Not the name she gave me, though."

"Maybe she doesn't give that info to thugs."

"Hey, man, if I was you, I'd be pissed too. Just because I was willing to do what I was told, doesn't mean I agreed with it."

"But you did it anyway."

"You never do something management told you to that you disagreed with?"

"Actually, no," said Smithy. "But then, I've never held down a job for very long."

George nodded. "Fair enough. I got kids, man. I'm an ex-boxer with two strikes. You know anybody that's hiring for honest work?"

"Leave your details and we'll be in touch."

Smithy wasn't in a sympathetic mood. These morons had attempted to threaten Cheryl. Admittedly, it hadn't gone well for them, but that didn't make him feel any better about having put her in harm's way. Then there was the fact that he'd never seen her that mad. There had been occasions when they'd argued before, but this felt different.

The blond guy started mumbling something under the tape.

"Shut up, Karl," said George.

Smithy looked up at him. "He's bleeding from the nose. Better take the tape off in case the dipshit suffocates."

George muttered something before reaching across and ripping off the tape. Karl yelped. "Fuck."

"Keep your voice down," said Smithy.

"Fuck you, midget."

Smithy slammed a fist into Karl's stomach, causing him to double over. George grabbed him by the hair and pulled him back upright.

"You deserved that, Karl. Don't antagonise the man further."

What Karl lacked in social graces, he more than made up for in stupidity. "Fuck you too."

Before Smithy could move, George had a meaty hand wrapped round Karl's throat. He slammed him into the wall.

George spoke in a calm voice. "Fuck me? Shut your mouth, you piss-poor amateur. We had clear instructions, but you decide to get physical with a woman. When she kicks your ass, you pull a gun? You dumb fuck. Nobody said anything about bringing a gun. I don't need hassle, you get me? Get your ignorant ass arrested on your own time. We clear?"

Just then, the elevator doors opened to reveal Mrs Spinola from down the hall standing there, her dog Ruffles sitting at her feet. Neither of them was fit enough to use the stairs any more. She took in the scene, and looked at Smithy nervously.

"Is everything OK?"

"Sure is, Mrs S. We're just running a scene for a play we're in."

Her eyes lit up. "Ohhh, very method! C'mon, Ruffles." They shuffled past George and Karl, and Mrs Spinola nodded at them as she did so. "I used to do some amateur dramatics back in the day. You boys are so committed. And may I say, Smithy here is a dab hand with a plunger. Such a helpful boy."

Smithy and George waved as she walked down the hall.

"It's nice that you help the neighbours," said George.

"Shut up."

"Hey, I got a mother too."

"I'm sure she's real proud."

George tossed Karl into the elevator casually, slamming him against the metal cage. "Low blow, fella. Low blow."

George walked in behind him and Smithy closed the gate on them. George placed the tape back over his associate's mouth.

"You not coming with us?"

"I'm going to take the stairs. It's quicker. I need to move fast as I've got to find somewhere to sleep tonight. Thanks for telling Cheryl about all my fuck-ups."

George shrugged. "She was holding a pan of boiling water when she asked. I wasn't gonna lie."

"How did you even know about Benny Wong?"

George moved over towards the gate and lowered his voice. "These people, they're looking into you. Believe me, they'll know it all. Look, from what I understand, this Reed guy, he just wants to talk. He has a proposition for you. Maybe hear him out?"

"Not interested," said Smithy.

"Man, you are stubborn."

"Yeah, well, coming around and threatening my woman was a great way to make sure of that."

"C'mon, guy. You know that ain't why she threw you out, right?"

Smithy shook his head. "You're giving me relationship advice now?"

"Hey, I'm a screw-up left doing dirty work like this while working with pieces of shit like this *jabroni*, but I've been happily married for twenty-five years."

"Congrats."

"I'm just saying. It's the lying that'll get you – every time. Whatever you've done, tell her the truth. That's my two cents."

With that, George pressed the button for the first floor and the elevator began its glacial journey to earth. Smithy started walking down the stairs, overtaking them as he did so. Karl mumbled and banged against the bars until George relented and took the tape off his mouth.

Smithy looked up as Karl shouted, "Hey, buddy, buddy."

"I am not your buddy."

Karl ignored his retort. "The gun. Could you leave it somewhere?"

"What?"

"C'mon, man. It's a loaner."

Smithy and George shared a moment as their eyes met. "Is he for real?"

George shrugged.

"C'mon," continued Karl. "Don't be a dick."

"Don't be a dick?" said Smithy, more to himself than anyone else. "The guy attacks my girlfriend, pulls a gun on her, but I'm the dick." Then he raised his voice. "Sure, Karl, no problem. Go to 639 West 46 street."

"Yeah."

"Be there at noon tomorrow. Stand on the steps for forty-five minutes, then turn around two-and-a-half times."

"Then I'll get the gun back?"

"No, then you need to cross the road. The body of water you'll see is the Hudson. Go throw yourself in it, because that's where your gun'll be."

"You fucking—"

Karl was silenced by George extending a hand and casually slamming Karl's head into the side of the elevator. "Hey, Smithy. Take care of yourself and think about what I said, man. She's something. You need to step up and make it right."

"Thanks for the advice, George. Good luck finding another line of work."

Smithy walked out the front doors of the building. The rain was coming down hard now. He'd been in a rush and so he'd parked the cab beside a fire hydrant. He pulled the ticket from the windshield without looking at it. That was just the kind of day he was having.

CHAPTER FOURTEEN

It was amazing, thought Diller, what people did and did not see. It must be something to do with the human mind – a peculiar quirk. Ronnie Stocks was a relatively smart guy, just not book smart. Ronnie had been a few years ahead of Diller in school, although he hadn't been there. He'd been kicked out before Diller had reached high school. Diller couldn't remember what incident finally saw him on his way – Ronnie had quite the rap-sheet. What Ronnie Stocks had was street smarts, which in their part of Hunts Point was the only thing that really counted. He could sense danger, he knew who to stand tall in front of and who to back away from. He might not know much trigonometry, but he could calculate the vig on a loan just fine.

Still, he – like everyone else in Diller's experience – had restricted ways of thinking. Ronnie would look at Diller's house, for example – not actually his house, but the derelict tenement building on a row of such that the Diller family had called home for the last six years – and he'd see it as having two entrances. The front and the back. In reality, there were four. There was a crawl space from the adjoining property that Diller could get through and, with some difficulty, gain access to his own home. It meant crawling through all manner of mud and mess – not to mention navigating some rat traps – but it could be done.

Unfortunately, from Diller's perspective if not from Ronnie's, that avenue was closed off. A couple of dudes had moved in next door recently, and they were less than hospitable. Between the neighbours, Ronnie, who was sitting outside Diller's front door, and Little Kris, who was standing guard at the back, Diller was left with option four as his only available means of entry. Logically, that avenue shouldn't have been open to him either, but thanks to people's restricted world views in general, and Ronnie's in particular, it was. Really, how many times in your day do you actually look up?

Diller was currently dangling twenty feet above Ronnie's head. There were some pretty thick electric cables running above his house, from one massive pylon to another. They probably didn't have these kinds of pylons and prominent electric substations in fancier neighbourhoods, but they did here. Once, Diller sat on the roof and watched as a repair guy had been lifted up on a crane, and had proceeded to attach himself to the wires with a harness.

Jackson Diller, as was his way, had paid very close attention, and it was how he had learned to climb the pylon without electrocuting himself. It was also how he had managed to construct himself a harness out of rope and tarpaulin that allowed him to move slowly along the wires over the rooftops to a point above his own house where he could drop down. The other reason this technique worked in Hunts Point was because there were virtually no working streetlights – a shape in the dark skies was difficult to notice by accident. Diller assumed that Gotham had similar issues and that was why Batman did so well. It also helped that Ronnie was wearing expensive-looking headphones that were playing music so loud that Diller could almost recognise the track. He didn't have to worry about making noise.

This was the first time he'd attempted this means of entry, but it was going surprisingly well. He hadn't been electrocuted or fallen to a messy death, which were big wins as far as Diller was concerned. He still had a good fifteen feet to go before he reached the point above his house, and then there would be the matter of getting down – he had a mechanism built into the harness for this, but he'd not yet tested it fully– but still, things were going undeniably well.

In the bigger picture, Ronnie's presence in front of his house was a problem. Diller didn't have his money, nor was he likely to for quite some time. What's more, he had zero intention of trying to get it. For the last six months, he had been saving every last cent for what he called "the Project". As of a couple of weeks ago, his big plan had finally clicked into place.

Diller didn't talk about his mom much, mainly because without context people didn't understand. Hell, even with context most people didn't understand. Unless you'd been there – been inside their story – you couldn't fully appreciate it. It wasn't that their situation was unique, but still, even without realising they were doing it, people made judgements, and Diller didn't want his mother being judged.

Monica Diller was a great mom. Growing up, Diller had been aware that they didn't have much, but it hadn't mattered. Every day he'd go to school with a juice box and a sandwich, and sometimes the juice box had been reused and refilled with water, and that was fine. Diller liked water. From the get-go it had been just the two of them, and like she'd always told him, that was all they needed.

Looking back now at a child's memories reinterpreted through an adult's eyes, his mother had not really had any boyfriends. On one hand it was surprising, as she was a good-looking woman who could light up a room with her effervescent personality. Diller guessed she'd been too focused on being a mom. Besides, where would she find the time? She'd worked two jobs – one as a cleaner and another at a food-distribution warehouse – and that, combined with looking after her son, had left her precious little time for anything else, including sleep. Not that she had complained.

Diller's favourite sound in the universe was her laugh. It was one of those big, joyous, full-body laughs, filled with warmth. The kind of laugh that was always with you and never at you. When he'd been young she'd read him stories, and he'd taken to acting them out, filling every part. She'd howled with laughter and applauded. In hindsight, that's where his obsession with acting had started. It hadn't been an easy life, but it had been a good one.

Then, when Diller was nine, his mother had fallen from a ladder as she was trying to hang a curtain. He thought back to that day all the time. He'd been in his room, reading a book. She should have called him to hold the ladder. Why hadn't she called him? On such simple moments, lives can turn. It hadn't looked like much at the time, but her back had been bad and had gotten worse. Eventually she took a shift off work and gone to the free clinic. Spinal stenosis was what they finally diagnosed. The recommendation of rest was dismissed. There was no more room for rest than there was money for an operation. Monica had put a little aside for a rainy day, but this was a monsoon, and so the doctor had prescribed pain meds to help her cope.

Diller had heard it described as the "opioid sinkhole". It was an apt description. At a certain point, the OxyContin became too expensive and his mom had swapped to other opioids that provided more bang for the few bucks she had. That was how a working mom became a heroin addict. Through it all, she had held it together. Diller knew, but he was kept away from it. She would do everything to be a good mom. She would find a balance and on it went, the three of them living through this – Diller, his mom and the wolf.

That was the name he had given it. Day after day, he had to watch as his mom fought to control it. Some days were good, some days bad, but the wolf was always there. That laugh he loved started to be heard less and less as Monica's life became less about joy and more about survival. Between the pain and the wolf, she had worked as much as she could. Getting herself out of bed on mornings when she could barely move. The wolf eased the pain, only for it to demand its pound of flesh later.

Diller watched on and could do little. He'd left high school early and gone looking for work. His mom would have been horrified, but he'd taken to stealing. It had always felt wrong, but he'd not seen any other choices. Their apartment had gone by this point and, as a temporary measure, they'd moved into one of a row of abandoned tenements set for demolition. That had been six years ago. Even then the money couldn't stretch to cover everything.

Diller took more and more responsibility for providing. He worked when he could find it, and when he couldn't, he did what needed to be done. Through it all, his dream of acting had been mostly put aside. Mostly.

He'd met Smithy when he had joined an acting group after seeing an ad. Diller had found one evening a week to dream a little and he'd loved it. Being someone else had been a beautiful release. The sheer pleasure of being surrounded by people dreaming the same mad dream, bonded together by a shared hope at which the rest of the world would sneer.

Smithy had pulled Diller aside and told him he was good, really good, and he could seriously do this. The thought had been nice, but trying to make it as an actor without any formal training and no money behind you? That was less like trying to win the lottery and more like trawling the gutters, looking for a winning lottery ticket that someone might have dropped. Still, in spite of it all – and while doing all he could to provide for himself and his mother – Diller had tried.

He had always been ashamed of the stealing. Hating himself for having to stoop so low. He'd never told Smithy this, but the reason he was so invested in his friend giving up gambling was that it had also been the day Diller had decided to give up stealing for good. If Smithy could stay on the straight and narrow, maybe he could too. Then, he and Smithy had helped their friend Bunny out with a situation, and Diller had come into some money. Not enough for him to make "the Project" a reality, but enough to make it at least seem possible. Not acting. That was his selfish thing. Maybe if he got past this, he could take a real run at that. First of all, his big dream, "the Project" – meant finally they would have to kill the wolf.

His mom had tried everything to kick her habit, but nothing had worked. What little support that had been available just hadn't done the trick. He remembered the cold-turkey days. Brutal minute after brutal minute, watching the wolf howling. There were some state-funded rehab places, but perversely, to get into a lot of the schemes you needed a criminal record. Monica Diller was, through it all, an upstanding citizen. The help had never been enough. Then, he'd met Shawna.

She was an old friend of his mom's. In fact, she had babysat for Diller when he was a toddler. They had fallen out of touch when they'd had to give up their old place and move into the tenement. Shawna was a nurse in a rehab facility. She had bumped into Diller's mom on the bus and, try as she might, Monica hadn't been able to hide the signs of her addiction from a trained professional. Shawna had asked around, and a friend of a friend had passed on the message to Diller that she wanted to see him. They'd gone for a walk in the park and Shawna, who had always been painfully direct, had got out of him the full, unvarnished truth of his mom's predicament. Once he had got over the sense of disloyalty, it had been good to talk, even if that was all it had been to start with. Cedarbrook, where Shawna worked, was a good facility with a high success rate in helping people kick the habit. But it wasn't cheap. Good help never is.

The problem was, Monica Diller had been living with the wolf for so long that getting clean was going to be a long process. Shawna's advice confirmed as much. Monica would need to do ninety days residential, and that would cost money – a lot of money. Diller had taken his windfall, then taken work doing whatever he could, and Shawna had talked to her employers, asking for a family and friends discount. Finally, they'd struck a deal. He had enough to get his mom into Cedarbrook and he'd find the rest.

When Diller and Shawna had come to his mom with their plan, she'd cried. Following advice, they'd not told her anything until it was time, and then, after Diller had pleaded with her, his mom had gone with Shawna. His mom, who had always seemed so tall and proud throughout his childhood, had looked small and frightened as she waved out the window of Shawna's Honda as they drove away.

It had been eighteen days now. Diller went out to see her whenever he could. It was hard, but she had always been a fighter. It was working. It was really working. Finally, after all this time, the wolf was being beaten back. Diller just had to keep up his end of the bargain. He had decided not to ask friends such as Smithy for money. He wanted to do this himself. Besides, Smithy was saving up for his own dreams. Doing the whole thing alone had taken on a near religious significance to Diller. This was his penance. So what little money he had was going towards making the fees to keep his mom in the clinic.

Unfortunately, the plan had left no money for unforeseen expenses. Like finding out that his mom owed more money to certain people than he had realised. Hence why Ronnie Stocks was standing outside his house. All Diller needed to do was keep ducking, diving and providing, while his mom fought her battle. Ronnie could wait. Luckily, Ronnie wasn't going to come into their house. The reason for that was Mrs James, a nice old lady from the neighbourhood who Diller and his mom had taken in years ago. She got a little confused at times, but she had a sweet disposition. His mom had just done it because, even with the wolf to deal with, she couldn't stand by and let someone else suffer. At least with them, Mrs James got a roof over her head and a hot meal most days.

Diller hadn't realised who Mrs James's grandson was, mainly because she wanted nothing to do with him. Marco James was a bad man. In and out of prison, even in Hunts Point, he was someone you gave a wide berth. Somebody had broken into Diller's place a couple of years ago, taking what little they had. More importantly, it had left Mrs James terrified and confused for several days.

Diller never found out what happened, but two days later their stuff reappeared, left on the front step in a cardboard box. After that, Diller had been told that their house was holy ground. Nobody was going to step foot in it again unless they had a strong desire to meet their maker. Marco had made that very clear. All of this meant that Diller's home was truly his sanctuary, providing he could get inside without becoming a brutal example of what happens when gravity goes wrong.

While people might not look up much, lights in the sky could certainly attract their attention. It was why the timing of Diller's phone ringing was especially bad. Diller flapped round, trying to grab it from the back pocket of his jeans, but his left hand got tangled in a strap. He freed it by twisting his body. At that sickening moment he felt the phone, dislodged by his movement, slip out of his pocket and fall free. Terribly, possibly fatally free. It was a cheap phone, but Ronnie would not take that into consideration when it landed on his head.

Diller's hand flew out reflexively. Somehow he grabbed the phone between the middle and ring fingers of his left hand. He caught his breath as he looked down at it, the screen painfully bright in the night sky. He had only the most tentative hold. Below, Ronnie Stocks rummaged around in his left nostril with an enthusiastic finger. The phone stopped vibrating as the call finally went to voicemail.

Slowly, painfully slowly, Diller turned himself enough to bring his other hand almost within reach of the device. It was no use – the straps prevented it from going all the way around. There was only one thing for it. As he felt the phone slip from between his fingers, Diller whipped up his left hand, dragging the phone a couple of feet in the air before he lost his grip on it entirely. His right hand came around just enough to grab it.

He held it to his chest. His heart was pounding now. That had been ridiculously close. Always the little things.

As Diller's breath returned to normal, the phone vibrated in his hand again. He was about to turn it off before it caused any more trouble when he saw the number and stopped. Shawna.

He looked down to check Ronnie was still oblivious, then answered the call. "Hi, Shawna, now isn't a good time."

"Sorry, Diller, but we got a problem – a really big problem."

CHAPTER FIFTEEN

Jackie stopped behind the bar to pick up the baseball bat he kept there for special occasions. Dressed as he was in his wife's fluffy dressing gown, in ordinary circumstances he might look comical. The presence of the bat would dissuade anyone from attempting to crack any jokes. Jackie was a nice guy but a big one, and one who'd run a bar down by the docks for a decade before he'd got the Porterhouse Lodge.

Whoever was outside pounded on the door again. "Alright, I'm coming. Jeez – it's almost two in the morning."

He looked across to the storeroom doorway where Smithy was standing in his underpants. Jackie pointed the baseball bat at him. "You told me you needed somewhere to stay for the night because your old lady kicked you out." He waved the bat towards the main door. "If this is the cops, you and me are through."

Smithy held up his hands. "I swear, Jackie, this ain't me. I told you the truth."

"Yeah, well ..."

A fist pounded on the door again.

"Alright," hollered Jackie, "I'm coming. So help me, someone better be dead, or someone is going to be." More to himself than anyone else, he added, "My wife will mention this. A lot."

Smithy took a few steps forward as his mind filled with horrible possibilities. It hadn't seemed at all likely, but maybe that blond asshole had gone back to Cheryl's apartment. Crap. He should have stayed outside in the cab and kept watch, comfort be damned.

Jackie finished throwing the bolts on the inner door, flung it open and stepped into the vestibule. "Who is it?"

"It's me, Jackie. It's Diller."

Jackie's body language changed and he looked back at Smithy, his brow furrowed with concern. Diller was not the type to bang down your door at 2am without a really good reason, and no good reason would be good news.

"Hang on, Dill," said Jackie. "Just a second."

Jackie moved back inside and deactivated the alarm, dropping the bat on the bar as he did so. He took a large ring of keys from the pocket of the dressing gown and picked out the ones he needed. As soon as the door opened, Diller all but fell through it. He was soaking wet, bedraggled, and his normally placid face was filled with a fearful desperation that Smithy had never seen before.

"Jeez," said Jackie, all anger long forgotten. "Are you OK, Dill? You're soaking."

"Is Smithy ..." Diller stopped as he caught sight of his friend. "Oh, thank God. I've been looking everywhere. Why didn't you answer your phone?"

"Sorry," said Smithy. "It ran out of juice. I didn't bring a charger. I was going to get one in the ... Look, what's wrong, Dill?"

As Diller moved inside, Smithy noticed he was limping.

"Diller," said Jackie. "How come you've only got one shoe on?"

"Lost it," said Diller, without turning around. He collapsed to his knees in front of Smithy and grabbed him by the shoulders. "You have to do it."

"Do what?"

"Whatever he wants. You have to do it. She ... It's her one chance. You have to. You have to!"

Smithy tried gently to prise Diller's fingers from where they were digging painfully into his skin. "OK, Dill. Relax. Whatever it is, we'll fix it. I promise. Just calm down."

He looked over Diller's shoulder at Jackie. "Could we get him a towel?"

"Sure," said Jackie. "I'll put the kettle on too."

They managed to get Diller somewhat dry and sat him down in their usual booth, his hands wrapped around a mug of hot tea. Jackie turned on the heating, as nobody at this meeting was fully dressed. He was wearing only his wife's dressing gown, Smithy was in his boxers and Diller was missing a shoe.

He and Smithy sat there in silence as Diller explained about his mom. Smithy had known bits and pieces of the story, but not the whole picture. Smithy more than anyone could appreciate somebody having parts of their life they didn't want to talk about, so he'd never pushed Diller to tell him more.

"So you see," said Diller, "this is her big chance. To get clean. To get right, finally."

He picked up his tea and took a drink for the first time. Smithy noticed he was still shaking a little under the towel.

"OK," said Smithy, glancing at Jackie. "We get it, but how can we help?"

"That's the thing," said Diller, setting down the mug. "Shawna – the lady at the rehab who helped get mom in – she rang me tonight. Said there'd been a change in management and that she couldn't stay."

"If it's money," said Jackie, "we'll chip in and—"

"No," said Diller. Lifting his head and looking Smithy directly in the eye. "The centre has a new owner. It's Reed Developments."

"Oh God, you mean ..."

Diller nodded. "Lou Reed. He left a message with Shawna ..."

"The singer?" said Jackie. "Ain't he—"

"Shush, Jackie," said Smithy, then remembered himself. "Sorry, I just ... No, not that guy. He's a rich property-developer asshole. What did he say to you, Dill?"

Diller looked down and shook his head. "It wasn't a message for me. It was for you. He said you had to meet him at eight in the morning, or else Mom would be out by nine."

"Oh," said Smithy, sitting back in his seat. He held his head in his hands. He'd been so damn sure. Arrogant. He was untouchable.

"So, will you?"

"Of course," said Smithy. "We'll sort this out. I promise. I'm really sorry, Dill."

He thought back to the business card Ms Muroe had left in his cab. He'd tossed it in the glove compartment.

Smithy stood up. "It's time for me to make a phone call."

CHAPTER SIXTEEN

Smithy and Diller sat at the table. The air held an aroma of polish, expensive carpet and something sweet, no doubt an attempt to mask the smell of polish. They were at a downtown hotel called the Dean, a location Ms Muroe had suggested as "common ground". Smithy had not been keen to return to Reed's apartment, just in case Reed decided to ignore the bit where Smithy had saved his life and focus instead on what he had been doing there in the first place.

Smithy had called Muroe as soon as Diller finished explaining the situation with his Mom. He'd been outmanoeuvred and they both knew it. At least the woman had had the class not to crow about it. Then again, threatening the recovery of someone suffering from a serious, long-term opioid addiction just to get a person to take a meeting wasn't the classiest of moves.

It had been a short call. Muroe had told them to come to the Dean at 8am, and they had. She'd actually only told Smithy to come, but Diller had insisted he tag along for the ride. It wasn't like Smithy could say no. He was feeling wretched. His dumbass plan to take vengeance on Louis Reed had now not only dragged Diller and his mother into the mess, but had quite possibly lost him the woman he loved. The week wasn't going great, and it was only Thursday.

The Dean was one of those "boutique" hotels. Its reception was decked in velvet, dark colours, and art that was trying way too hard. It looked like the ideal place for a pretentious vampire to enjoy a city break. They'd caught a cab and left Smithy's parked behind the Porterhouse Lodge. There was never any parking to be had in New York, and while Smithy knew some sneaky spots where you could get around it without getting a ticket, there was nowhere that wouldn't have involved a walk. It was raining and Diller was wearing sandals, seeing as it was the only footwear Jackie had that fit him. He had still somehow managed to avoid explaining how he'd lost a shoe.

They'd been shown into a meeting room, and a ludicrous array of pastries was brought in and placed in front of them. Diller reached to take one.

"Don't," said Smithy.

"What?"

"Don't eat the food."

"But I'm hungry."

"It's a sign of weakness."

"Do you reckon we're in a strong position as things stand?"

Smithy sighed. He had a point.

"I'm going to eat that blueberry thing. If you like, I can rearrange the rest of the stuff to make it look like there was never a blueberry thing? So we maintain our strong negotiating position."

"Just eat the thing."

Diller leaned forward and grabbed the pastry in question. There was that much left, the absence of one single piece made no noticeable difference. The fact that every member of staff they'd seen on their way in looked painfully thin now seemed even more incongruous.

Thankfully, Diller's mood had improved. He'd received a call from Shawna on the way over, assuring him that his mom was fine – at least for now. He had told her diplomatically – without going into specifics – that the problem was being taken care of. Even though he could hear only one side of the call, Smithy could tell the woman on the other end of the line was mystified. He couldn't blame her – he wondered what the hell was going on too.

The idea that Reed wanted to thank him seemed highly unlikely, given the strong-arm tactics that had been employed to ensure this meet happened. Similarly, if he just wanted revenge, there had been ample opportunity. Whatever this was, Smithy had a bad feeling about it.

Diller leaned forward, looked down at the table top and said something. Smithy, wrapped up in his thoughts, missed it.

"What?"

"I said, how do you think they get it this shiny?" asked Diller. "I can see my reflection – in wood! How is that even possible?"

"Money. Apply enough of it and you can make any shit shine."

Diller shook his head. "How did you get to be so cynical?"

"Experience."

Diller sat back in his chair as the door opened and the large frame of George – the guy who hadn't attempted to rough up Cheryl the night before – walked in. He was holding a black metal box in his hands, and took up position in the corner of the room. He nodded at Smithy, who nodded back.

He was followed into the room by Ms Muroe, who was wearing a smartly tailored burgundy suit and a delighted-to-make-your-acquaintance smile. Then came Louis Reed. His bulk was pronounced in a room this size. Diller made to stand but Smithy placed a hand on his arm.

Muroe's broad smile widened as she and Reed sat down. "Mr Smith, I'm so glad you could join us."

"Well, you didn't exactly give me much of a choice."

"Still, I'm sure you'll find that if we work together, this will be a beneficial arrangement for all of us."

"Yeah," said Smithy. "I see you didn't bring the other guy."

"Who?" asked Muroe.

"Y'know, the thug you employ who likes attacking defenceless women."

She leaned back and glanced in George's direction. "Oh, that. From what I gather, Ms Watts was a long way from defenceless."

"But he didn't know that, did he?"

She waved a hand dismissively. "Mistakes have been made on both sides. I think it is best if we move forward in good faith."

"So," said Reed, speaking for the first time. "You're the midget who broke into my apartment?"

Smithy pushed himself away from the table and stood up. "OK, we're done here."

"What?" said Reed, seemingly confused as to what offence could have possibly been taken.

"Sit down, Mr Smith."

"The fuck I will, lady. You and your boss can shove it up your ass."

Smithy marched towards the door and placed his hand on the handle. "C'mon, Dill." He turned to see Diller sitting at the table, pointedly not moving.

Muroe glanced at her phone as she spoke. "You can leave if you like, Mr Smith. We can negotiate the revised pricing structure with Mr Diller for his mother's care. It will be a competitive quote but reflective of the excellent standard of care provided by Cedarbrook."

Smithy closed his eyes, took a deep breath and moved back towards his seat. "You people really are something."

"I'll take that as the compliment I'm sure you intended it to be," said Muroe, before turning to Reed. "I'm confident we can all be careful with our choice of language from now on?"

"What?" said Reed again. "For God's sake, he is a midget. It's political correctness gone mad."

"Too right, fat ass," said Smithy.

The two men glared at each other across the table.

"Boys, boys, boys," said Muroe. "Can we dispense with the petty name-calling and move on?"

Nothing else was said, but Reed and Smithy continued to lock eyes. If you tossed a raw chicken between the pair, it would have cooked before it hit the floor.

"Excellent," said Muroe. "Peace has broken out at last." She turned to George. "Could you ...?"

George nodded and moved around the table, holding out the black metal box. "Phones."

"What?" said Diller.

"Your phones," said Muroe. "We need them to ensure this meeting is not being recorded. You understand." They didn't, but Smithy and Diller put their phones in the box, anyway. George then produced a device and ran it up and down them before nodding at Ms Muroe and resuming his position in the corner.

"Thanks, George," said Smithy. "Give my love to your wife."

"Tell Cheryl I said hey."

"Yeah, if I ever see her again. You people seem determined to mess up my life."

"All of this unpleasantness could have been avoided," said Muroe.

"You're right. I should have just let whoever it was kill Mr Reed. Make the world a better place."

"Nobody tried to kill me," said Reed.

Smithy looked at him. "Then your barber is a little hardcore, what with using that great big sword and all."

"It was a stunt to win a bet. They were never going to actually harm me."

"Really?" said Smithy. "And what was all that shooting about, then?"

Reed shrugged. "You attacked them first."

"Are you kidding me?" He looked back at Muroe. "Is this guy out of his damn mind? I'm being blamed for stopping the guy who was trying to assassinate him?"

Muroe raised her hands. "Gentlemen, how about we let me do the talking for a little while? See if we can't move this along."

Reed rolled his eyes and nodded.

"Good. What you are about to hear is strictly confidential information, Mr Smith. Any attempt by you, or Mr Diller here, to repeat it outside of these four walls will be met with punitive measures. You have already seen what we can do in that regard. If I were you, I'd think of it as having signed a non-disclosure agreement – one that has real teeth to it."

"No kidding," said Smithy.

"Mr Reed," continued Muroe, "is in an ongoing competition with some friends of his. They collect things. Hard-to-get, one-of-a-kind things. Points being awarded for each item obtained."

"What kind of items?" asked Diller. "You mean like Han Solo's blaster?"

"No, but think of it in those terms if you like."

"What is that supposed to mean?" asked Smithy.

Muroe ignored him. "What you saw was actually one of the items."

"Come again?"

"Proving you could have another contestant assassinated," interrupted Reed. "Fifty thousand points. Plus, there's points added for style. Hence the ninja. We're all about style."

"Yeah," said Smithy. "I really got that vibe." He leaned forward. "You do understand how batshit crazy that sounds? Like, seriously, a 'friend' of yours was trying to assassinate you."

"To prove he theoretically could," said Reed. "A very substantial difference. It was a last-gasp attempt to win the competition. One that did not succeed." Reed gave a little pout. "I have won."

"Congratulations. I'm really happy for you," said Smithy. "So, to celebrate, you thought you'd prevent my friend's mother from getting vital medical help?"

"Oh, please," said Reed. "She's just some junkie."

Over the last couple of days Smithy's life had already developed a surreal sepia tinge to it, as if he might well wake up at any moment and discover it had been a particularly long and detailed dream. Still, for all the pinch-me moments that he'd experienced, nothing caught him quite as off-guard as Jackson Diller totally losing it.

His friend was a blur as he launched himself directly across the table in one fluid motion. One of his borrowed sandals flew off and hit Smithy in the face. Muroe's yelp had barely left her mouth before Diller's hands were on Reed's suit-jacket lapels. The unstoppable force of Diller's rage meeting the movable object of Reed's bulk. They tumbled messily to the floor.

"Don't call her that. Don't call her that. Don't call her that!"

Reed's voice came out as a falsetto warble. "Get him off me."

Smithy was out of his chair as George grabbed at Diller's back and pulled him away, slamming him into the wall forcefully enough that a picture fell to the ground.

"Let him go," said Smithy. George had about 150 pounds on him, but he'd taken down a lot bigger. Even if he couldn't, he was still going to try.

"Enough!" Muroe's roar was loud enough that everybody in the room turned to look at her. "Everyone sit down and shut up."

Smithy saw the heartbreaking moment play out on Diller's face when the red mist cleared and the reality of his actions hit him. "Oh God, I'm sorry. I'm sorry, I'm sorry, I'm sorry. Please don't."

"I'm pressing charges," said Reed, still lying on the floor, his legs tangled in his chair.

"Really?" said Muroe, not even attempting to hide the contempt in her voice. "You'd like to explain the purpose and circumstances of this meeting to the NYPD, Louis?"

He jabbed a finger in Diller's direction. "Your whore of a mother is out. You hear me? Out!"

"No," said Muroe, "she is not. Not unless you have decided you no longer want what this meeting was set up to achieve?"

He looked up at her, all hurt feelings and indignation. "He assaulted me."

"How do people normally react when you insult their mothers?" She didn't wait for an answer. "I assume you have calmed down, Mr Diller?"

Diller nodded.

"Fine. George, put him down and pick up Mr Reed."

George released Diller and moved across to help Reed.

"You OK?" Smithy asked his friend.

"Yeah," said Diller. "I'm sorry." He looked across at Muroe. "I really am sorry."

She waved away his words. "Both of you, take a seat." She put Smithy in mind of an exasperated mother, who'd frankly had it up to her eyeballs with this nonsense.

With some difficulty, George helped Reed to his feet. Reed shrugged off his assistance ungraciously, flapping his arms about. George raised his palms and backed away as Reed smoothed down his suit, his face a red cocktail of exertion, rage and embarrassment.

After a brief knock, the door opened and a perfectly coiffed man, with the kind of tan leather would be proud of, poked his head into the room.

"Everything is fine, Antoine," said Muroe. "Just some high spirits."

The man glanced around the room, gave a tight smile and closed the door.

Reed pulled in a deep breath, but Muroe cut him off sharply. "Whatever you're about to say, save it."

"I think you're forgetting who pays the bills, Ms Muroe."

"No, I'm not. Believe me, it's the only reason I'm not out that door. I am also not forgetting what I have done to generate those bills. Now, do you want to win this petty squabble, or do you want to do what you hired me to help you with, which is win this damned competition?"

Reed opened his mouth and closed it again.

Muroe left it a moment and then nodded. "OK, then." She sat back down and turned to Smithy. "Let's cut to the chase here. This thing is all over bar a final event this weekend – in Hawaii, where they all meet up and Mr Reed receives his prize. To get it, he needs you there, Mr Smith. Everyone has to bring someone to this final dinner."

"Let me guess," said Smithy. "I've got to sit there in a fucking leprechaun outfit?"

"Yes," said Muroe, "you do. And for suffering that indignity you will get thirty grand. On top of that, Mr Diller's mother's treatment will be taken care of. It is crappy and degrading and all of that, but it is also one evening, and let's not pretend we don't have you. You're here." She tapped the table with a fingernail to emphasise her point.

"You fly over there on a private plane, stay in a nice hotel, spend a few hours in a room full of people I'm sure you'll hate, and in return, you get all that I've mentioned, plus your – whatever the hell that was, breaking into Mr Reed's apartment – is forgotten and you need never see any of us again."

"How do I know you won't turn around next week and try to screw with me or Cheryl, or mess with Mrs Diller's treatment again?"

"Because," said Muroe, leaning back in her chair, "hard as it might be for you to believe, the only way I can do what I do, is for my word to be gold-plated, one hundred percent unbreakable." She tapped the briefcase by her side. "I've got documents with me to lock it up but, more importantly, if I say you won't be bothered again, you won't be bothered again." She kept looking at Diller, but she wasn't speaking to him. "Mr Reed is well aware that the cornerstone of our arrangement is that he doesn't break any agreements I have made."

"What exactly is it that you do?" asked Smithy.

She gave him a tight smile. "Opinions vary. Do we have a deal?"

Smithy glanced at Reed, then back at Muroe, before looking down at the table for a long moment. When he spoke, his voice came out barely above a whisper. "OK. I'm in."

"Excellent," said Muroe.

"I'm going too," said Diller.

Reed went to speak but Muroe extended a hand to stop him before he got started.

"That isn't part of the deal."

"It is now," said Diller. "Smithy is doing this to help me. I'm going."

Smithy touched Diller's arm. "You really don't need to, Dill. This is my mess."

"I'm going," he repeated, before turning to Smithy. "Besides, I didn't want to mention it before, but I could probably do with getting out of town for a few days."

"Why?"

"Long story, but let's just say my shoe might have accidentally hit a drug dealer in the head from a great height, and he probably won't be at the point where he's willing to see the funny side of it just yet."

Smithy shook his head. "Fine, Diller comes too."

"OK," said Muroe.

"But—" started Reed.

"OK," repeated Muroe, more forcefully.

"And," said Smithy, pointing at Diller. "You fix that thing with the shoe."

"How am I supposed to do that?" Muroe asked.

Smithy folded his arms. "You're a fixer of some sort, right? It's what you do."

Muroe looked at the sky for a second before nodding. "Fine. Mr Diller, what is this gentleman's name?"

"Ronnie Stocks."

"And how much do you owe him?"

"Who said—" began Smithy, but Muroe cut him off with a look.

"Two and a half grand," said Diller.

"Done," said Muroe. "We'll fly out tonight. Until then, we'll put you both up in this hotel, which you will not leave."

"I need to—"

"No, Mr Smith, you don't," said Muroe. "You can fix your relationship, or do whatever else you need to do, when we get back Sunday evening. Until then, you are mine. Clear?"

Smithy left it a second and then nodded.

"Excellent. Now, we're done, and nobody is going to say anything else. And for God's sake, will somebody eat one of these pastries as I'm not going to be the only one."

Reed stood up and glowered down at the tray. "Why the hell is there no blueberry?"

CHAPTER SEVENTEEN

Smithy closed his eyes and took a deep breath.

"What's this one do?" asked Diller.

"I don't know."

"I'm going to press it."

"OK."

Diller pressed the button and the screen dividing them from the driver whirred down.

"Hey, Frank."

"Hey, Mr Diller. Everything OK back there?"

"Yes, Frank. Sorry, it's my first time in a limo. I'm just seeing what all the buttons do."

Frank laughed. He was a jolly guy from Queens. Diller had introduced himself before they'd even got in the car. Smithy had been trying to spend the day moping around, dreading the humiliation he'd no doubt have to endure over the next few days. Once he'd seen all the paperwork confirming his mother's all-expenses-paid stay in Cedarbrook, and spoken to the centre to verify it, Diller was busy making friends and enjoying the high life.

"No problem, Mr Diller. You tried that red one on the middle console yet?"

"No, I ... Ohhh!" The "ohhh" was because a drinks cabinet had appeared between the seats. "Cool."

"Finally," said Smithy, "something useful. Hey, Frank, are we OK to ..."

"Fire away, Mr Smith. It's all complimentary."

"Great, and call me Smithy, please, Frank."

"No can do, Mr Smith. Company policy."

"Fair enough."

Normally, Smithy would have raged against such a thing, but he wasn't in the mood. He picked up one of the decanters sitting in the display, removed the stopper and took a sniff. He didn't have the nose for these things, but it was definitely whiskey. He poured himself somewhere between a triple and a quadruple measure and raised it carefully to his lips. The first sip left a pleasing tingle in his throat. Smithy guessed whatever this stuff was, it wasn't cheap.

"What's up with you?" asked Diller.

"How do you mean?"

"You've been in a mood all day."

"You mean today? The day that started with me getting woken from the storeroom I was sleeping in because Cheryl had kicked me out, to find out my nemesis had started messing with your life and threatening your mother's treatment to get me to take part in some sick, twisted little game?"

"Yeah," said Diller. "But since then we got to stay in a fancy hotel, got given free stuff ..."

Muroe had provided them with a few changes of clothes, shoes and some toiletries. Annoyingly, the clothes she provided for Smithy fit better than the ones he already owned. He had gone with the garish green-and-blue Hawaiian shirt. He didn't know why – possibly as some form of self-flagellation.

"... we're in a limo and we're about to get on a private jet to fly to Hawaii! Even you've got to admit, some of this is pretty cool?"

"No, I don't," said Smithy. "All I'm seeing is excess and ostentation. Leading up to me being made into an exhibit in this rich a-hole's private zoo."

Diller sat back. "OK, you're wrecking my buzz now." He leaned forward abruptly and grabbed something from the bar. "Free peanuts – cool!" He tore open the packet with his teeth and offered it to Smithy, who shook his head. "So, what else?"

"I'm not hungry."

"No," said Diller. "I mean, what else is bothering you?"

"Isn't all of that enough?"

Diller shrugged and looked out the window.

Smithy raised his drink to his lips, but then took it away without partaking. "If you must know, I hate flying."

"Oh. Is that why you've been, y'know ..."

"What?"

"Well. You kept the barman in the hotel pretty busy too."

"That's part of it," conceded Smithy. "Plus, if I've got to go through this, I'll be damned if I'm not costing this fuck-knuckle a small fortune in booze."

"If you like, we could throw some out the window?" said Diller.

"Spoken like a true non-drinker. Don't you dare."

"Alright. I was just trying to help."

"Surely the bigger question here, Dill, is how come you're in such a good mood? I mean, I brought this to my front door through my own stupidity, but Lousy Louis Reed has nothing on you and he still threatened you and your family."

Diller shrugged. "I know, but Mom is OK now." He tapped his jacket pocket. "I've got the paperwork to prove it. I know this is shitty for you but come on, this time yesterday I was shinnying along a wire, trying to get into my own house without catching a beating. Now I'm in a limo about to go on a private jet. I've never been on any kind of aircraft before, outside of sitting in one on a trip to a museum. It's a day of firsts for me."

"And," said Smithy, "you got to launch yourself across a table and attempt to throttle a monster."

Diller blushed. "I feel bad about that."

"Why? He definitely had it coming."

"It's not my ... y'know. Mom brought me up to be better than that." Diller winced. "No offence."

Smithy laughed. "Hey, that's the least you could say. My stupidity got you into this in the first place. I've been trying to apologise to you all day."

Diller waved him away. "Forget about it. It's all worked out fine."

Smithy laughed again – a more bitter one this time – and took a large drink.

"Hey," said Diller, "did you mean what you said before?"

"What?"

"About Reed being your nemesis?" Diller's eyes lit up on the word "nemesis".

"I dunno," said Smithy. "I'm beginning to realise that maybe thinking like that is the reason I keep ending up in crap up to my neck, usually while standing on my head."

The car took a right turn and the noise from the wheels changed as it slowed down.

Diller looked out the window. "Looks like we're here."

"Great," said Smithy, draining the last of his drink.

CHAPTER EIGHTEEN

Ms Muroe met them on the stairs up to the aircraft as a crew member hurried past, carrying their bags. "Gentlemen, welcome aboard. I trust you had a pleasant day?"

"Wow," said Diller, "is this a Falcon 900?"

Ms Muroe looked around. "Er, I've no idea. Are you a plane enthusiast?"

"No, but when I knew we were going on one, I went down to the hotel reception and they let me use a computer to look at them."

"Right. Well, I guess you could go ask the pilot?"

"Sweet!" Diller noticed Smithy's expression. "I mean, yeah, whatever."

"When do we get our phones back?" asked Smithy.

"When we get back here. This group of people takes privacy very seriously."

"Really? Shame that didn't extend to mine."

"If it is any consolation, I don't have my phone either."

"No," said Smithy. "No, it isn't."

Ms Muroe gave one of those smiles that wasn't a smile. "This rather brings me to my main point. I appreciate, Mr Smith, that you have some resentments regarding the way things have panned out."

"You could say that."

"A word to the wise: get over them. Mr Reed is an argumentative soul and we don't need the two of you butting heads. Let's just get through this as smoothly as possible, shall we?"

"Or?" said Smithy.

Ms Muroe ran her fingers through her hair. "I think we're past the point where I have to make threats, don't you?"

Smithy was already regretting not bringing the bottle from the limo. "Fine. Let's get this over with."

"That's the spirit," said Muroe, clapping her hands and stepping aside to usher them on board. "Gentlemen."

Smithy tried hard not to be impressed. There were eight leather seats in the cabin they were shown into, four of which sat either side of a table. Smithy and Diller were directed to them by the smiling flight attendant who introduced herself as Sasha. Diller restrained himself to just three questions before she took their drinks order.

Smithy was feeling a little drunk, but not in a good way. He was hoping to knock himself out for the flight. Hell, he'd do it for the whole weekend if he could. After all, he simply needed to turn up and be a novelty – it didn't sound as if his brain would be required.

"Y'know," said Diller, "this might be the nicest room I've ever been in – and it is on a plane!" He looked across at Muroe, who was strapping herself into a seat opposite them. "What's through the curtain?"

"There's a galley and then another lounge-cum-bedroom. Mr Reed is back there."

"He doesn't want to be out here with the hoi polloi?" said Smithy.

"And what did we just talk about?"

Smithy restrained himself to muttering darkly.

"He's a nervous flyer," said Diller, which earned him a glare from Smithy. "What? You are!"

"Ah," said Muroe, "you should have said. Would you like something for that?"

"Like what?"

"I'm sure the flight attendant could rustle up a couple of

Klonopin, if you think it won't mess up your attempt to drink yourself into oblivion too much?"

"Since when do cabin crew give out prescription medication?"

"A perk of flying the friendliest of skies." She raised her voice. "Sasha." The flight attendant appeared immediately. "Can I get my usual, and the same for Mr Smith."

"I'm fine, thanks," said Smithy, before turning back. "Didn't your mother ever teach you about not taking sweets from strangers?"

Ms Muroe rolled her eyes. "She's not a stranger, she's staff. Even you can't equate getting on someone's private jet with getting into a stranger's van on the promise of seeing some puppies?"

"No," agreed Smithy. "It's a lot easier to get out of a van. I'm going to stick to good, old-fashioned booze, thanks."

Muroe smirked. "Have it your own way. Mr Diller?"

"It's just Diller, and thanks but no. I'm going to be wide awake and enjoying the view. Might not get the chance again."

"Well, let the hostess know if you change your mind." Muroe nodded and Sasha disappeared back into the galley.

"You really can sort anything," said Smithy.

"That's my job," said Muroe.

"About that," said Smithy. "What exactly is your job? I mean, your business card had just your name and a couple of numbers."

"If you need what I do explained to you, you can't afford it."

"How much exactly do you cost?"

She ignored the question. "Do you remember that drunk NFL player who hit three cars last year and then wrapped his Beemer around a tree?"

"No," said Smithy.

"The senator's kid who burned down her boyfriend's condo?"

"No."

"Or the Wall Street trader who sent a picture of his, what my mother used to call, private area, to thirty-six of his company's employees?"

"No."

"No," said Muroe, "and you're not going to. That's because I fix problems. How much I cost is way less than what not having me will cost you in money, reputation, divorce proceedings and jail time."

"And I'm a problem to be managed?" asked Smithy.

"Yes and no," she said with a smile. "This job is a little bit more ... unusual. Mr Reed needed some assistance in this competition and he paid me a large retainer to provide it."

"You help him collect *Star Wars* memorabilia?"

She gave him a subtly admonishing look. "No. Nobody needs someone like me for that. The items involved were much more *unusual* in nature."

"Like what?"

"Can you keep a secret, Mr Smith?"

"Sure, but let me guess, you're about to say, 'So can I.' Right?"

She grinned at him. "Oh, you're a big spoilsport. But yes. You might see some of the items at this event, but I'm not about to kiss and tell."

Smithy nodded at the curtain that sectioned off the back of the plane. "And it doesn't bother you to work for a guy like that?"

"The rich are almost always difficult. It comes from not being told no often enough. He's not the worst."

"Really? There are worse than him?"

Sasha reappeared through the curtain carrying a small silver tray.

"Oh," said Muroe, "I could tell you some stories."

"But you won't."

She laughed. "You are catching on."

Sasha lowered the tray first to Muroe, and then to Smithy and Diller. Muroe took two Klonopin and a glass of water as the plane began to taxi down the runway. Smithy took his large whiskey and Diller his orange juice.

Smithy took a sip from his tumbler as Diller watched him.

"Can you tell the difference between the expensive stuff and the ordinary, cheap stuff you drink?"

Smithy held the glass in front of him. "You make it sound as if I'm normally drinking hooch in a dumpster. But honestly, no. In fact, this tastes a bit ..." He smacked his lips. "I dunno – bitter? I've never understood all the fancy words for whiskey and wine. Peaty this and hint of elderflower that. I'm very much in the good or not-good school of thought."

"And," said Diller, "is that good or not good?"

Smithy shrugged. "It's free. Hard for any free drink to be bad."

Muroe took an eye mask and some earplugs out of her bag. "And on that note, gentlemen, have a nice flight. I'll see you when we reach the sunny shores of Hawaii. I hope you remembered to pack your sunscreen."

CHAPTER NINETEEN

Smithy woke up to somebody shaking his shoulder firmly.

"Mr Smith. Mr Smith!"

He looked up to see Sasha the flight attendant looking down at him and wearing a tight smile that didn't reach her eyes. "We've arrived."

Smithy opened his mouth to speak and felt the drool on his chin. He nodded and wiped it away, embarrassed. How much had he had to drink? His paranoia started to kick in. The little voice in the back of his head that worried about what he'd done while drinking himself into a state of unconsciousness. Some deep-seated instinct prompted him to check that he was still wearing trousers and that their zip was closed. Two for two.

He was having trouble processing. His head felt as if it were filled with chewing gum. It didn't hurt exactly – it was more that he felt numb. He'd heard that really good whiskey didn't give you a hangover, but he'd always thought that was a myth pushed by people trying to sell you thousand-dollar bottles of the stuff. His throat felt sore and scratchy, and his mouth was dry. He ran his tongue around it, searching for moisture.

As he tried to take mental stock, he watched Sasha shaking Diller by the shoulder to wake him up. That was wrong. That was ... What was wrong with that? Something. He was having trouble putting thoughts together.

WAKE UP. TROUBLE.

Oh Christ, not you. I don't need a speech about the dangers of drinking from my imaginary friend.

WE'RE NOT FRIENDS. YOU'RE NOT DRUNK.

And then they were moving. Smithy was on his feet and behind Diller as they were both shuffled off the airplane. Hands were pushing them, and then they were outside on some steps. Coming from the plane's air-conditioned interior, the hot air hit like a slap in the face. It was dry, arid. It irritated his already scratchy throat. He clenched his eyes shut to protect them from the dazzling sunlight.

"Wow," said Diller, in a slightly slurred voice. "Hawaii looks different to what I expected."

WAKE UP, IDIOT!

Smithy shook his head and pushed past Diller to get a better view. He looked around, soaking it all in. Allowing the wave of growing panic to clear his senses. "That's because this isn't Hawaii. Where the hell are we?"

Smithy felt something push against his back and found Muroe standing there, looking dishevelled. "Where the hell are we?" she asked.

"That's a really good question," said Smithy.

As far as the eye could see was sand. Not beach – desert. The only thing breaking it up was a hangar at the other end of the runway that looked all but abandoned.

"Look," said Diller, pointing at a cloud of dust rising from the direction of the sun.

A vehicle, or vehicles.

Smithy didn't need the voice to tell him this was all wrong. His head had been cleared by the sound of internal alarm bells. He turned around to go back into the airplane, and was only just able to catch Muroe before she fell over. Reed had been roughly shoved out of the airplane and into her by two men who Smithy assumed were the pilot and co-pilot.

"What in the—?"

Apparently they weren't taking questions. They slammed the door closed behind him.

"Where the hell are we?" said Reed, in a voice that proved it was possible to mumble and shout at the same time.

"That's a popular question," said Diller.

Smithy pushed past Reed and pounded on the aircraft's door. "Open up! What the fuck!"

In response, the aircraft started to reverse, causing the stairs to lurch alarmingly to the left.

"Oh, no you don't," hollered Smithy. He grabbed the handrail on the stairs and used it to pull himself up, before clambering across Reed's back. Using him as a springboard, he propelled himself onto the top of the plane. He overshot, and was in danger of skidding off the other side, until his scrabbling fingers found a handhold and he was able to steady himself.

Smithy was aware of Diller calling his name, but he was focused entirely on the task in hand. He managed to manoeuvre his body and slide it down the brow of the plane so that he could see into the cockpit, albeit while he was upside down. The two men inside wore satisfyingly shocked expressions as he appeared.

"What the hell are you doing?" roared Smithy. "Open that door, now! You can't leave us in the middle of nowhere." He thumped his fist on the glass.

The two men appeared to be arguing. The younger one pointed at Smithy, but his older, balder colleague didn't look up. Instead, he pressed a button on the control console and water squirted onto the windshield.

This enraged Smithy further. "You monumental asshole. What I'd give for a hammer! I'm going to find you and set every individual remaining hair on your head on fire. Then I'm moving on to the rest of the hair on your body and ..."

Smithy was interrupted by a wiper hitting him in the face.

"Agh, you ..." He could feel himself start to slip. "No, no, no!"

As he slid down the windshield, he saw the bald guy waving at him while the younger guy shook his head in disbelief.

Smithy's scrabble for a handhold proved fruitless on this occasion. All he could do was angle his body so he hit the ground in the safest way possible. Despite his best efforts, his skull took a sickening whack as he fell onto his back. There might have been sand as far as the eye could see but still he had managed to hit concrete. He was having that sort of a week.

The landing knocked the wind out of him. He lay there, trying to breathe, and looked up into the clear blue sky. A large bird flew overhead. It was especially large. Smithy had never seen one in the flesh but he would bet it was a vulture.

Diller's concerned face blocked his view. "Are you OK?"

"Yeah, I'm ..." He took Diller's proffered hand and was hauled to his feet. Smithy had been so consumed by his attempt to hijack a plane from the outside that he hadn't noticed the vehicles that had arrived.

Two Humvees and what could best be described as a dune buggy surrounded them. They'd all been modified and they were going for a particularly distinctive motif. Smithy shook his head, as if that might rearrange reality into a more normal configuration.

Reed and Muroe were looking back at him. Beyond them, standing against the lead Humvee was a face Smithy vaguely recognised. Last time he had seen it, it had been sitting on the back of a quad bike, looking bored as it waited for a leprechaun hunt to start. The man had sandy hair, in a standard side-parting cut that probably cost a fortune despite achieving essentially the same look Smithy got for ten bucks.

He was athletic in that "has done some rowing" way prep boys often have. He was somewhere in his thirties and handsome, if you were able to look past a weak chin and a strong sense of entitlement. He didn't look bored now. He was grinning from ear to ear.

Behind him, in stark contrast, stood a half-dozen large men who did not look as if they'd spent a lot of time at the polo club. They resembled the clientele of the worst bar you had ever been in, if they'd been dragged through a bondage shop and a weapons fair. Several of them were wearing face paint. There were quite a lot of shoulder pads, a good deal of leather, and one honest-to-god codpiece. It would have been funny had it not been for the amount of weaponry that accessorised it. Guns were much in evidence, but there was also at least one sword and a couple of spiked cudgels.

The rich boy extended his arms expansively. "Here he is, the mighty midget we've all heard so much about."

Smithy felt Diller tense beside him. "Don't."

"I'm not going to," replied Smithy. While twenty-four-hour news proved his state of mind to be a rarity, Smithy struggled to be confused and angry at the same time.

"Welcome. Welcome. Welcome to our little soiree. I'm Chaz." He clutched his hands to his chest. "And may I say – big fan of your work. And I see you've brought a friend with you. The more the merrier."

He turned his attention to Muroe and Reed. She looked as if she were trying to decide where she should position her emotions between scared, pissed off and her normal level of unflappable cool.

"Ms Muroe. You too are, of course, very impressive in your own right. Welcome."

"Yeah. Can I ask what the fuck is going on?" She waved a hand about. "Unless there's been some pretty big news we missed, this isn't Hawaii."

The man laughed. "No, no, it is not. Good to see that didn't slip past you. I, as host of this year's event, decided to call an audible."

Muroe looked between the man and Reed. "Call an audible?"

"It's a sports metaphor," said Reed.

"I know what it means," snapped Muroe. "I just don't get how the hell you think you have the right to drug and kidnap us?"

The man took a theatrical step back and feigned being wounded. "Kidnapped? Heavens, no. I'm afraid you are new to our little group, but we play pranks like this all the time, don't we, LouLou?"

Reed, up until this point, had remained remarkably quiet. He now shifted awkwardly. The bellowing behemoth had been replaced by a suddenly nervous schoolboy. Smithy guessed there was enough history between "LouLou" and "Chaz" to keep a therapist busy for a couple of years, and that was before you got started with the collection of large men in bondage gear that one of them had assembled as an entourage.

"Yes, of course, Chaz," said Reed. He turned to Muroe. "We do, sort of ... A couple of years ago, Rake had us go to San Fran. We all got shanghaied and ended up on a converted navy cruiser travelling up the coast."

"Exactly," said Chaz. "I just took shanghaiing to the ultimate." He gave LouLou an affectionate but hard slap on the back. "I'm afraid I had to buy off your whole flight crew. Wasn't cheap, let me tell you!"

"OK," said Muroe. "Well, you boys can play your little games" – she looked at the collection of goons standing behind Chaz – "with whatever the hell this is, but" – she turned to Reed – "our arrangement is officially at an end. You do not pull this kind of shit on me. Get me out of here right now."

Displaying impeccable timing, the airplane on which they'd arrived took off in the background as she finished her sentence. Muroe looked at the ground and swore under her breath.

"Stop embarrassing me," said Reed.

Muroe's head shot up. "Embarrassing you? *Embarrassing you?*"

"This is just like Hawaii, essentially."

"Really?" said Muroe, making no effort to keep the scorn from her voice.

"Oh, come on," said Chaz, sounding exasperated. "Where is your sense of adventure? Don't worry about the boys here. I've just gone for a post-apoc theme for this year's shindig. It's all just a bit of fun."

Diller spoke from the side of his mouth so only Smithy could hear. "You know what it looks like ..."

"Don't say it."

Chaz clapped his hands. "Boys, mount up."

The selection of extras from a film Smithy was not going to mention got back into their vehicles.

"LouLou, you ride with me in the lead vehicle. Ms Muroe and the boys can go in the second Humvee."

"I'm not going anywhere," said Muroe.

Chaz shrugged. "Fair enough. Looks like we'll have one less guest for dinner, boys. I do hope you brought some sunscreen."

Muroe looked hard at him. "I want to make a call."

"Of course," said Chaz. "No cell towers out here, I'm afraid, but come back to the camp and you can do it from there. Wait until you see it – it's an absolute blast."

Muroe paused for a moment, then walked towards the indicated Humvee. Smithy couldn't fail to notice that one of the road-warrior rejects took a long, unsubtle look at her ass as she did so.

Chaz turned to Smithy and Diller. "And will you gentlemen be joining us?"

Diller looked at Smithy.

THIS IS A TERRIBLE IDEA.

"Tell me something I don't know."

"I'm sorry, what?"

Smithy raised his voice. "Sure. We'd be delighted."

CHAPTER TWENTY

The Humvee thumped up and down as they drove along whatever desert road they were on, doing nothing for Smithy's mood. His malaise was further exacerbated by the blacked-out passenger windows – there was no way to see where they were going. He was developing a headache – possibly from the mild concussion he had received while trying to corral an aircraft, or maybe just from the stress of seeing his whole life go so totally off the rails.

"Don't worry," said Muroe, "I will sort this."

"Really?" said Smithy.

She glowered at him. "Really. Look – OK, these people are a tad eccentric."

"Eccentric?" said Smithy incredulously. "Eccentric was pushing it before we got on the airplane. It has long since ceased to be a word capable of covering the current situation. These people are fucking insane."

"Shush," said Muroe, "they'll hear you." She indicated the front compartment of the Humvee.

"Oh, what?" said Smithy. "Do you mean the dude with the AK-47 and the Charlie Manson vibe, or the guy with the mohawk, the 'mom' tattoo and the sword? Wouldn't want to offend those guys. They seem nice. I bet they volunteer at homeless shelters during the holidays."

"Being snippy isn't going to get us anywhere."

"She has a point," said Diller, which earned him a look from Smithy. "What? Look, we're in this situation. Let's just try to keep cool and we'll get out of it. We always do."

"I don't think we've ever been in a situation quite like this," said Smithy. "I'm not sure anyone has."

Muroe lowered her voice. "Does anyone have any idea where we are?"

"This time of year," said Diller, scratching at his chin, "with this kind of weather? New Mexico? Nevada? Texas? Maybe California?"

"OK," said Muroe. "Right. Well, the person who owns the second-biggest private helicopter supplier in the country owes me a big favour, so I reckon I can get us out of here pretty fast if I can get hold of a phone."

Smithy blew a raspberry.

"Helpful," snapped Muroe.

"No, I don't imagine it is. Thing is, a couple of points – one, Diller just mentioned four states in which you could successfully hide the moon, and, sorry Dill, but even that analysis is based on a false assumption."

"Is it?" said Diller.

Muroe sighed. "Yes. He's right. We don't even know for sure whether we are still in the United States."

"Oh," said Diller.

"That's not the biggest problem," added Smithy. "The biggest problem is that, seeing as they took our phones back in New York, nobody knows where we are or that we're even missing."

"How is that …?"

"Because if someone here has an evil little mind like mine," said Smithy, "they'd realise that if we disappear, our phones will be traced. What are the odds that right now they are in Hawaii, where I bet you told people you were going?"

Muroe said nothing.

"Course you did," said Smithy. "So, let's say someone takes out a boat, sinks it, and we are never seen again. Tragic accident."

Nobody said anything to this. Smithy was already regretting having said it out loud. A silence fell inside the Humvee, save for the grunts and groans as they got thrown around.

"Jeez," said Smithy, growing uncomfortable in the quiet he had created, "aren't these things supposed to have suspension?"

"It is spooky, though," said Diller.

"Oh, c'mon, Dill, now isn't the time."

"What?" asked Muroe.

"I'm just saying," said Diller. "This whole thing started with Smithy's plan—"

"Alleged."

"Alleged plan to teach Mr Reed a lesson, and it was inspired by a scene from a Mel Gibson movie. *Braveheart*."

"Allegedly."

"No," said Muroe, "I've seen that movie. Mel Gibson is definitely in it."

Diller smiled. "And now this whole thing has a real *Mad Max* vibe."

"Right," said Muroe. "What's your point?"

"It's just interesting, is all. Smithy's life seems to be a compendium of Mel Gibson movies."

Muroe shook her head. "Interesting? Christ, what is wrong with you?"

Smithy's voice came out louder than he intended. "Hey. Don't you dare take a shot at Dill. It's thanks to you he is in this mess. I'm an idiot, but he is just collateral damage, due to your Machiavellian bullshit."

Muroe looked at Diller, and then looked away.

Always the one looking to break any tension, Diller went to say something, but he never got the chance. The Humvee went into a handbrake turn that threw them all violently across the back seat, before it came to a stop.

Diller tried to remove himself as courteously as possible from his resting position on top of Muroe, or at least without making contact with any body part that would mean they were married in certain cultures.

"I guess we're here."

CHAPTER TWENTY-ONE

Smithy, Diller and Muroe were roughly assisted out of the back seat of the Humvee. They stood looking around them.

"Holy shit," said Smithy eventually.

"This is insane," said Diller, so at least Smithy knew he wasn't imagining it.

They had arrived at a compound in the middle of the desert. On one side, there were a few actual buildings – a couple of hangars, some sheds and what looked like a cabana. In the centre stood a sprawling one-storey house with big windows and angled walls. It would've been the height of modernity in about 1986, but now it was starting to look shabby, as time and the desert ate away at it. In front of it sat a swimming pool complete with a diving board. Outside of its location, all of that could be said to be fairly ordinary, certainly compared to what else surrounded it.

Around them loomed mountains of scrap metal, cars, trucks, and vehicles of all kinds piled up to form makeshift walls. There was half of what looked like a 747. Dotted about in the shade of those cliffs of metal were tents and makeshift crude structures formed from sheets of corrugated iron or whatever else was lying around.

Men sat in deckchairs and on loungers, drinking beer and

enjoying the sun. The smell of barbecue drifted from upwind of where Smithy and Diller were standing. The men were all dressed similarly to the guys who'd met them at the airplane, as if the end of the world had interrupted their bondage night.

To Smithy's left, a couple of drunk guys were trying to shoot a beer can off a guy's head with a crossbow. The beer-can proper-upper didn't look too pleased about this, but another man was holding a sword to his nuts to encourage his compliance. The whole thing was a health and safety nightmare. Other men were working on vehicles – buggies, cars – mongrels reclaimed from the scrap. Two other guys were fighting in an improvised boxing ring while a few more looked on without a great deal of interest. They seemed to be paying scant attention to the Marquess of Queensbury's rules. Women were noticeable by their absence.

Muroe's voice came out in a strained whisper. "Wow."

"Yeah," said Smithy. "This is one hell of a mid-life crisis."

"There's got to be a couple of hundred of them," said Diller.

From somewhere behind them they heard a wolf-whistle.

Smithy didn't look for the source. "Stay close to me."

"Thanks," said Muroe.

"I was talking to Diller."

Chaz, wearing a grin to which it was increasingly difficult not to attach the word "demented", appeared from around the jeep. "Welcome to Nowhere!" He threw out his hands again.

Smithy realised who the guy reminded him of – he was like Willy Wonka, if the man replaced his love of chocolate with post-apocalyptic homoerotic violence.

"I'm sorry – what?" said Muroe.

"Nowhere," repeated Chaz. "This is Camp Nowhere. Isn't it incredible? Some old lunatic had the house and the scrapyard out here already. Perfect for our needs."

"Yeah," said Smithy, "there's a lot of lunatics about." He winced as Muroe jabbed a heel into his foot. "What?"

"Rule one," said Muroe in a hissed whisper, "don't poke the crazy."

Smithy considered responding but didn't. She had a point. Luckily, Mad Max Willy Wonka hadn't noticed. He had turned away and was yammering a mile-a-minute at Reed, who was standing there awkwardly, gawping at everything while shuffling his feet. He looked like a man whose entire world was spinning out of control. Smithy could empathise.

Behind him, a man in a football helmet and nothing else did a cannonball off the diving board into the swimming pool. A guy in a tattered, pink bunny-rabbit outfit, with an assault rifle strapped to his back, applauded.

"Dill?"

"Yeah, Smithy."

"Remember when you asked me to describe what a bad trip was like?"

They stood there, drinking it all in. Smithy closed his eyes and opened them again. "Dill?"

"Yeah, Smithy."

"I was drinking, then I was drugged, then I hit my head a couple of times, so I feel I should check. You see that large wall of wrecked cars over on the right there?"

"I do."

"Good. I can't believe I'm asking this, but can you see an orangutan standing on the top of it?"

"Do you mean the orangutan that is holding what looks like the fender of a car over his head?"

"Yeah. I mean, it is by no means certain, but let's assume there are not multiple orangutans here."

"Then yes, Smithy. I can see him too, so you're not going crazy."

Smithy watched the orangutan as it moved up the wall, waving the fender above his head.

"Let's not rule out me going crazy just yet."

"Hey," yelled one of the guards, "it's Shitshow!"

Several of the nearby men looked up and cheered.

"That's not very nice," said Diller. "Why do you think they—"

"Duck," said Smithy, as the orangutan provided a dramatic

demonstration of the origins of his name. The speed at which he produced, aimed and fired was remarkable. He managed to hit a bald guy, who'd been engrossed in working on a motorbike, right in the back of the head, which drew an appreciative cheer from his audience.

Shitshow stretched himself to his full height and held his fender aloft triumphantly. With the sun directly behind him, it was a striking sight. More suited to a live re-enactment of *The Lion King* than a primate who had just successfully fired faeces with the speed and accuracy of a Major League pitcher, but impressive nonetheless.

The man in question did not see the funny side. He picked up a shotgun he had lying around and fired in Shitshow's direction. He pumped it to fire another, but before he had the chance, he was punched hard in the face by a man with enough facial piercings to make airport security a real drag.

"Leave Shitshow alone!"

The animal lover and the bald guy with a shitty head then proceeded to try to kill each other with their bare hands while others looked on, half interested. For his part, Shitshow grabbed his genitalia, waved them about while sticking out his tongue, then trotted back happily the way he had come.

Smithy's attention was drawn to an immense human being stomping across the compound towards them. He had never seen that much humanity crammed into one body. The guy stood six foot eleven at least, with limbs the thickness of tree trunks and a chest so wide you could probably park a car on it. You'd need off-road capabilities to get it up there, though, as the guy had muscles bulging out of places Smithy hadn't been aware the human body had.

When he walked, it looked like he were carrying invisible tractor tyres under each arm. His head was shaven and he had a squint that gave him a permanently confused look, or he might just have been perplexed as to why he was wearing a studded leather mankini in the middle of the desert. It was a fair question.

Most of the man came to a stop behind Chaz, but it was

noticeable that bits of him still flexed and spasmed, seemingly at random, as he stood there.

Chaz spun about and patted the man on the slab of beef masquerading as his arm.

"Ah, Zero, excellent. Everyone, this is Zero – my second-in-command." He addressed the large man. "Are the preparations proceeding to plan?"

Zero nodded.

"Good. Good. Good."

Chaz appeared to possess the annoying habit of repeating a lot of words three times. In other circumstances, Smithy might view that as a warning sign of an unstable emotional state. In this situation no warning was necessary.

"Come. Come. Come. We really must give you the tour!"

Chaz turned and began to walk away. Muroe, Smithy and Diller looked at one another.

"How are you feeling about that 'eccentric' diagnosis now, Dr Muroe?" asked Smithy.

Muroe didn't say a word. She simply followed Chaz and Reed. Smithy went to do the same, but Diller pulled him back by the arm.

"Hey, go easy on her, will you, Smithy?"

"Are you kidding?"

"None of this is her fault."

"Really?" said Smithy. "Dill – whose idea do you think it was to use your mom as leverage to get us here?"

Diller looked unsure.

"Reed is that nasty, but he isn't that smart."

"OK, but she didn't expect this."

The guy in the football helmet and the bunny rabbit were now rolling around on the ground. It was either a friendly fight or a violent embrace.

"Yeah, nobody expected this."

CHAPTER TWENTY-TWO

They were joined on their tour of the compound by someone called Finley. From the brief exchange between them it appeared that he, Lousy Louis Reed aka LouLou and Chaz had all been in school together. Smithy had seen Finley once before, riding the back of a quad bike, although he looked markedly different today. The 90s era Hugh Grant floppy hair was now dishevelled, hanging over several days of unkempt stubble, and his clothes reeked of stale sweat. The guy spoke very little but his eyes had an unnerving, pleading edge to them. He mentioned in the stilted conversation that he'd been there for three days. Smithy guessed that was enough time for this place to do that to a man.

Muroe tried to bring up with Chaz the promise of a phone call, but Finley's surreptitious, urgent shake of the head stopped her mid-sentence.

"Is Rake here?" asked Reed, trying to sound nonchalant.

"Oh," said Chaz, feigning disinterest. "Yes. Yes. Yes. The fourth musketeer is around."

This exchange was met with another pointed look from Finley, this time directed at Reed. Smithy couldn't read beyond it being anything but good.

After that, through unspoken agreement, the group took the tour in near silence, save for Chaz's almost constant stream-of-consciousness babbling. Smithy guessed the man would struggle to pass any kind of test that involved peeing into a cup. His pupils were dilated and he had a nasty head cold in the middle of the desert. Right now, he seemed to be on an upswing, excited to play host and show them his wonderful toys, but Smithy knew enough to know that mood wouldn't last.

The tour took in all the sights. There was the house where, as honoured guests, they would be staying. The junkyard appeared to stretch on for miles. Smithy had no idea how all of this stuff had got here. Chaz had mentioned that the "old lunatic" who used to own it had been a car fan. No kidding. If you went looking, you could probably find parts for every type of car produced since the Model T.

Most of the men they met were seemingly amusing themselves rather than doing any kind of training or preparations. At one point, Chaz turned to Zero and asked him if the men had been drilled today. The large man nodded. Smithy had limited experience of such things, but none of these guys struck him as capable of forming a well-drilled unit. Still, at least in Chaz's mind it appeared he thought he was building some kind of army. At some point, Smithy would need to get answers as to what the hell was going on here. That point would be sometime after they got the hell away from here.

Chaz had then taken them into the arena – an enclosure about the size of a baseball field. Walls of cars, six or seven high, encircled the perimeter in most places, and at one end there was a set of massive iron gates. It looked as if they'd been there first, and the arena had been built around them.

The tour then wound its way back across the compound. Chaz said hello to various men as they went. Smithy found the body language interesting. Chaz didn't know it yet, but these men viewed him as their meal ticket rather than their alpha.

"So," said Smithy, curiosity trumping his better judgement, "where did you recruit all these guys?"

"Oh," said Chaz without turning around, "you'd be amazed what you can find on the dark web. Men. Guns. Drugs."

"Right," said Smithy, whose experience of online world purchasing consisted of a failed attempt to buy a framed Iggy Pop picture on eBay in 2007 before giving up on the whole thing as a bad idea. He might not have understood how Chaz had assembled all this, or why, but he guessed he could see the trouble coming that Chaz couldn't.

"So," said Chaz, waving his hands at things as he spoke. "Over there – fuel store, armoury, food. We've got a twenty-four-hour taco van. I mean, he didn't think he was going to be twenty-four-hours but try getting some sleep when all these guys get hungry." Chaz laughed. It sounded exactly as unhinged as Smithy had expected. He recovered, oblivious to the fact nobody had joined in. The hand-waving continued. "And over there is the hangar. Big surprise in there to kick off festivities tomorrow, plus some other stuff. Y'know. Pharmacy. Commissary. Mrs Ramirez did a fine job setting the place up before ... Anyway."

"Mrs Ramirez?" asked Reed. "How is she?"

Chaz kept looking straight ahead. "No idea. She left my employ."

"Oh."

This was how the world ends, thought Smithy, *with an insane man who wants to watch it burn, and an organised woman who was willing to do the admin.*

Muroe, who'd been taking it all in silently, kept looking over at Smithy, as if having her worst fears confirmed. She tried to sound relaxed as she asked her question. "This is an awful lot of stuff for just a weekend?"

Chaz laughed and wiggled his eyebrows at her. "Yes. Yes, it would be."

He stopped outside a single-storey building. Next to the double doors in front of which they were standing was a large, metal, garage-style door.

"Now, the reason we are all here." Chaz moved across to Smithy and Diller, and placed one hand on a shoulder each. "But first, how rude of me, I must explain to my new midget friend and his boy what this is."

Smithy and Diller looked at each other. This a-hole had interesting ideas on what was and wasn't rude. Smithy saw the pleading look in Diller's eyes and gave him a subtle nod. Now was not the time to start setting this guy straight.

Chaz continued, "I, as a member of the Breddenback family, am part of a long and glorious tradition. It is our humble role to document and preserve the true history of this great land, and not the version peddled to the masses. And so, to do so, we have held a competition, always with carefully selected close friends, where we strive to find those unique objects that truly define our times. We are the collectors. The winner of this private competition becomes the keeper of this secret treasure trove of history through which mankind's achievements and foibles are so lovingly encapsulated."

Chaz's impassioned monologue was slightly undercut by the nosebleed that had begun halfway through it. He carried on, oblivious.

"I asked my friends – Finley here and Rake, who you'll meet later – to join me in this sacred competition. And, most importantly" – he lifted his hand off Diller's shoulder and slammed it against Reed's large chest – "I asked my friend LouLou here – Mr Louis Reed, to give him his full, so richly deserved title – to join too. He did so, and enlisted the services of Ms Muroe here." Chaz's face twitched slightly as he waggled a finger at her. "Which was a little bit naughty but not technically against the rules. And, with her help, he has become the first person from outside the Breddenback clan in the competition's one hundred and thirty-year history to win it. An incredible achievement!"

Chaz grabbed Reed's face between both hands and squeezed it. In the man's tight grip Reed's doughy flesh was comically squished. Reed looked terrified but did his best to smile.

"An achievement which, it has to be said, did not go down well with Grandfather, Father or Mother. Uncle Lawrence didn't mind, but then, he's lost it and spends his days licking the furniture." Chaz released Reed's face and his voice dropped from its ringmaster pitch to a normal conversational tone. "That's not to make light of mental illness, you understand. We have all, I'm sure, been touched by it."

YOU'RE BEING TOUCHED BY IT RIGHT NOW.

Shut up.

Chaz wagged a finger in the air. "But, as I'm sure you're aware, the Japanese word for 'crisis' is the same as 'opportunity'."

Smithy caught Diller's eye just in time for his subtle head-shake to stop him from pointing out that it was, in fact, the Chinese who had the same word for both of those things.

"And," continued Chaz, "I have taken this as an opportunity to break away from the ties that bind. Against my family's wishes, I have brought the collection here, so that my good friend LouLou may take possession of it."

"I don't really need to—" started Reed, but Chaz's raised hand silenced him.

"Rules are rules! Without rules, what would we have? Chaos!"

Somewhere in the background, something exploded and people cheered.

"LouLou gets the collection and I have decided to take my own money and use it to make myself a self-made man."

HIS OWN MONEY? HE MUST HAVE HAD ONE HELL OF A PAPER ROUTE.

"But enough about my humble plans. Let us bask in the magnificence of the collection!"

Chaz grasped the handles on the double doors and threw them open dramatically. He then dived out of the way to avoid the shotgun blast.

CHAPTER TWENTY-THREE

The second most noticeable thing about the man standing in the doorway was his immaculate attire: a long black tailcoat, a bow tie, a crisp white shirt, trousers with creases so well defined if they were any sharper they would be in danger of splitting atoms, and black shoes polished to such a shine that you'd be too dazzled to see your own reflection in them. He stood in front of a purple curtain and was sporting what appeared to be a fencing sword, sheathed at his waist.

The most noticeable thing about him was his shotgun, with which he had just blown a massive chunk out of the wooden door.

Chaz was on the ground in front of him, and everyone else in the party was crouched or cowering. Smithy remained standing, looking at the finely tailored man. The advantage of Smithy's height was that he was unlikely to get shot in the head by anyone blasting blindly at whoever was coming through a doorway. It wasn't a situation that came up often enough for it to be an enormous consideration, but it had happened frequently enough for him to be thankful for it.

Chaz squealed from his foetal position. "Jesus, Wilkins!"

The man looked down at him, and then settled the shotgun against his shoulder. "Forgive me, Master Breddenback. I did not realise it was you."

He spoke with a clipped British accent – the sort that probably didn't really exist but people affected as it floated the boats of the kind of folk who want a butler.

Chaz uncurled himself. "You could have killed me!"

"Respectfully, sir, if I had wanted to kill you, you would now be dead."

Wilkins had a point. From that range, it would have been easier to hit the target than to miss. The shot had been carefully chosen as a warning, albeit a forceful one. Having said that, had the behemoth Zero been standing at the front of the group rather than at the back, then they'd all be trying to remove bits of his permanently constipated facial expression from their clothing right about now.

Chaz picked himself up off the ground with the assistance of a hand from Wilkins. The man's demeanour was telling. Smithy guessed he had known Chaz for quite some time, as his air of subservience had a definite undercurrent of disapproval to it.

"What are you doing shooting at anyone?"

"I'm afraid a trio of your other" – Wilkins twirled a finger in the air that conveyed a remarkable amount – "guests, attempted to gain entry to the collection earlier. They had to be dissuaded."

"What?" said Chaz, before turning to Zero. "Zero, I want these men found and dealt with."

"How gallant of you, sir, but unnecessary."

"No," said Chaz. "I insist."

"Very well," said Wilkins. "The immense gentleman should look for one individual with a severe limp, another lacking a right ear, and a third who shall sadly be unable to reproduce – or indeed, urinate – unaided."

Chaz looked from Wilkins to Zero. "Right. Good. See to it."

Zero nodded, which seemed to be a real skill of his.

Chaz turned and resumed his tour-guide duties. "Ladies and gentlemen, this is Wilkins. The keeper of the collection. He has been with my family for generations."

"And may I say what an absolute delight it is to meet you all."

"Thank you, Wilkins."

"Yes, between this and getting to drag a priceless collection of one-of-a-kind artefacts to a cesspool in the desert, my cup doth runneth over with joy."

Chaz twitched. "Yes, well, that is your job."

"And one, may I say, that I enjoy more and more with each passing day."

The two men looked at each other, Wilkins a study in English stiff-upper-lippedness by which Smithy couldn't help but be impressed. If Chaz ever got to see the phalanx of therapists he needed, his relationship with Wilkins would probably provide a nice couple of weeks as a palate cleanser between the mummy and daddy issues.

Wilkins snapped a square of fabric from his breast pocket and held it out to Chaz. "Would you like a handkerchief, sir?"

"No, thank you."

"Are you sure? It would appear you have a nosebleed."

Chaz held up a hand to his face, then snatched the fabric from Wilkins's hand.

"Very good, sir."

Chaz, his paranoia kicking in swiftly, moved to one side, his shoulders hunched as he wiped at his nose. "Show them the collection."

"Nothing would give me greater pleasure."

Chaz said nothing more. Instead, he simply gestured for Wilkins to get on with it as he scurried out the door and around the corner.

Wilkins turned to face the rest of the group and gave them an appraising stare. Whatever silent test he was adjudicating they evidently failed, given the subtle disdain in the curl of his lips.

"Ladies and gentlemen, as previously stated you are about to view a collection of one-of-a-kind artefacts that are literally priceless. I say 'view' as you are not permitted to touch them. You will not breathe on them. If they are in a glass case, not only will you not open the case, but you will also not touch the glass of the case with your grubby little paws. Failure to respect these rules will result in no finger-pointing. By which I mean" – he tapped the hilt of his sword – "you will suffer the loss of a finger. One of the good ones, too. Are there any questions?"

There weren't.

Wilkins glanced up at Zero. "And if you are a hulking behemoth blessed with the natural grace and poise of an inebriated bull in a china shop, may I suggest that you stay here and enjoy the view of this curtain."

Wilkins stared up at Zero for several seconds. He eventually broke off and spoke to Muroe. "Does it speak?"

"I ... I believe he does."

"Really?" Wilkins raised his voice. "You. Stay here. No smashy-smashy."

Zero nodded.

"Excellent," said Wilkins, clapping his hands. "What a thrilling insight into the world of Jane Goodall that was. Now, I'm assuming the rest of you understood the rules as they have been explained?"

Smithy, Diller, Muroe, Finley and Reed all nodded immediately.

"Wonderful."

Wilkins pulled back the curtain with a flourish. Inside, various exhibits were housed under dim lighting. In one corner, a machine huffed out air at a no-doubt-precise temperature. He ushered them into the room and pulled the curtain closed behind them.

"Stay behind me at all times as we're walking," Wilkins instructed as he moved to the head of the group. "I shall give you the abbreviated highlights and then I will be delighted to answer any questions you have."

Smithy turned to Diller. "Don't even think about it."

"But he said—"

"He's British. They do that."

Wilkins stopped abruptly and turned on his heel. "Now, if you look to your left, you will see a case that contains the bullet that killed Archduke Franz Ferdinand in 1914 and started the Great War. A tragic series of events that led to the needless loss of millions of lives. To your right is the outfit Janet Jackson wore at the 2004 Super Bowl – or rather she didn't fully wear, which is why it became famous. At this juncture I would normally point out that while I maintain the collection, sadly I do not decide upon its contents. Moving on ...

"To your left, the infamous O. J. Simpson gloves. To your right, the impeccably preserved pretzel former president George Bush Junior choked on. Over by the wall there is the original ejector seat from the space shuttle *Enterprise*, lovingly removed and replaced by an identical one. In that one, while enjoying a private tour, a visiting dignitary had a brief dalliance with a former Miss Alabama that people in the know estimate had a greater impact on the socioeconomic development of the world than most wars do."

"Wow," said Diller.

"Quite. This collection gives you a perspective on the secret history of the world few are afforded." Wilkins stopped beside a case containing a large glass jar. "And here is the brain of JFK."

Smithy's lips moved before his brain did. "Bullshit!"

Wilkins looked down at him with a glare that could strip paint. His voice came out at a temperature below freezing. "I assure the diminutive gentleman that, while I may not select the content of the collection, I am in charge of verifying its authenticity. Nothing in here is fake."

"But ..."

"Actually," said Diller. "The brain of JFK did disappear from the National Archives."

"Yes,' said Reed, "it did. Everyone knows that. Don't be an idiot."

Smithy looked up at him. "'Don't be an idiot?' Thanks to you, we're here as the prisoners of your demented friend. And you think you should be throwing around insults?" Smithy looked around. "In fact, what the hell are we doing? Getting sucked into this madness. We're away from him and his henchman, Dill. Let's get out of here."

Diller turned to Muroe. "Are you coming?"

"Well, I ..." started Muroe.

"Why would we bring her?" asked Smithy.

"We can't leave her here."

"It's because of her we're here in the first place."

"I demand to go too," said Reed.

Finley grabbed Diller's arm. "Please, take me with you."

"Alright," said Smithy. "Let's all just—"

Smithy broke off. The tip of a fencing sword jabbing into your Adam's apple will have that effect. Without moving his head, he raised his eyes carefully to look at Wilkins. The man spoke in the same level tone he had employed throughout their acquaintance – that of someone admonishing staff.

"We do not have time for your squabbling. Master Breddenback has clearly lost his mind and he has assembled outside of these doors what might best be described as a pack of rabid dogs. Has anyone here had experience of how rabid dogs behave?" He glanced about the group quickly. "No, I thought not. They chase anything that runs. Run now, and you give them something to hunt. A gentleman by the name of Rake, who was a childhood friend of Messrs Finley and Reed, was here for the last couple of days. Yesterday, he tried to run. He got hold of a motorbike. Master Breddenback offered a ten-thousand-dollar bounty for his capture and the dogs hunted him down. They have a light aircraft which worked as a spotter; all the dogs had to do was follow. It was not pretty."

The group looked at Finley, who looked on the verge of tears. "He's right. Chaz was ... He's lost it."

Reed's voice came out quieter than it had ever been. "Is Rake ...?"

"No," said Finley. "I managed to talk Chaz down, just. Rake is alive but being kept as a prisoner, for now." Finley rubbed his face, as if trying to wake himself up from a nightmare. "Chaz hasn't slept in days, he's vacuuming up coke, pills and God knows what else."

"What happened?' asked Muroe. "I assume he wasn't always" – she pointed in the direction of the door – "that."

"No," said Finley. "He's ... he's unrecognisable. We'd no idea until Rake and I got on a plane to go to Hawaii early – supposedly to do some sailing – and we ended up here. He's been ranting and raving ever since. I still don't know where here is. And don't think about asking – he flies into a rage if anyone dares ask. He has totally lost it.

His family disowned him after, y'know ..." His eyes flicked briefly to Reed and away again.

"What?" asked Diller.

"After he lost the competition?" said Muroe.

Finley nodded. "And he's gone out and hired, well, you saw. He thinks he's building his own army out of those animals. It's all insane."

"Rather," agreed Wilkins. "As we don't know where we are, we don't know in which direction safety lies. Even if you were to acquire some form of transportation, trying to flee this place without a plan will most assuredly get you killed. I myself was brought here under extreme duress and wish to make good my escape, but I am awaiting means and opportunity. I waited for you to arrive because I was hoping your resourcefulness might be of assistance in this situation."

"Well," said Reed, "I think we should—"

"Silence," said Wilkins. "I wasn't talking to you. You have done more than enough. I was speaking to Ms Muroe."

Muroe looked taken aback. "Right, well, I guess. I mean ... Can't we call somebody?"

Wilkins shook his head. "Mr Finley and I have been subtly keeping an eye out for any form of communication device. Assuming there is one, Master Breddenback is keeping it locked away. And I don't—"

Wilkins whipped the fencing sword away from Smithy's throat so quickly that Smithy's hand flew up reflexively to check for blood.

"That is correct, Mr Finley," Wilkins began clearly. "The brain of John F. Kennedy did indeed disappear from the National Archives and ... Ah, Master Breddenback. Re-joining us, I see."

Smithy turned to see Chaz walking quickly across the room towards them. Zero loomed behind him. Chaz looked reinvigorated, in a chemical sort of way. "Yes. Why was Zero left outside?"

"He did not strike me as an individual with an appreciation of history."

Chaz gave Wilkins a suspicious look, which was met with one of true blankness that took decades of training to pull off. "Right. How's the tour going?"

"It is going."

"Super. Super. Super."

"Moving on," said Wilkins. "Over there you can see Princess Diana's wedding dress. Not the one from the TV wedding, but from the real ceremony. Over there is one of the images from the moon that wasn't released to the public. On closer inspection you shall see why. There is also a computer over there containing a record of the first disparaging remark made in the history of the internet. It occurred four minutes after the thing went live. Any questions?"

Diller raised his hand and was ignored. Instead, Wilkins waved the group forward.

"Over there are the missing sections of the Nixon tapes from the Oval Office. A surprising amount of discussion concerning certain attributes of the Brazilian prime minister's wife – as well as some light treason. And to your right, a lovingly preserved section of Evander Holyfield's earlobe as infamously removed by Mr Michael Tyson." Wilkins came to a halt. "I think that is everything."

"Show them," said Chaz, his voice coming out in a snarl.

"Well, if you ..."

"Do it."

"Right," said Wilkins with a tight smile. "Of course." He turned and moved towards a display case at the end of the room, which was concealed by a curtain.

"And now, ladies and gentlemen," Chaz's voice came out a high-pitched squall, with all manner of emotions washing through it, "the star of our show. The prize item that won this year's competition and ever so slightly destroyed my life ..."

Chaz threw an arm across Reed's back and guided him forward. "C'mon, LouLou. Your moment of crowning glory. Now is not the time to be shy."

"I just ..."

"Actually," hollered Chaz, "let's be fair. Credit where credit is due." He spun around and grabbed Muroe by the hair. "After all, she did the work." He all but spat the words.

"Ahhh," said Muroe, "you're hurting me."

"Come on!"

Smithy stepped towards them but before he could do anything, Muroe delivered a knee to Chaz's groin that bent him double. As he crumpled, Smithy watched her eyes widen, already realising what a mistake she had made.

Chaz, on his knees, scrabbled for the holster at his belt. He was stopped by the tip of Wilkins's sword that appeared at lightning speed to dance inches before his eyes.

"That won't be necessary, Master Breddenback. Let's not forget our manners."

Chaz looked from the tip of the blade to Wilkins, and then to Zero. The massive man took a step forward.

After a moment, Chaz shook his head. "Fine." He looked up at Wilkins. "Show them."

Wilkins pulled back his sword. "I'm not sure if—"

"Do your job and show them."

Wilkins hesitated and then sheathed his weapon again. "As you wish."

He stepped towards the case and pulled a cord to tug the curtain aside.

The case contained a blue dress, displayed on a headless mannequin. Smithy and Diller looked at it and then at each other.

"I don't get it," said Diller in a soft voice.

Smithy looked up at Muroe. "Is it?"

She gave him a tight nod.

"That's right, ladies and gentlemen," roared Chaz. "The one, the only Lewinsky dress."

"As in—" started Diller.

"Yes," said Muroe, who couldn't look at it.

"How did you?" asked Smithy quietly.

"It wasn't easy," answered Muroe, in a whisper tinged with regret.

"I'll bet."

Smithy turned around to notice Chaz was still slumped on the floor, with tears in his eyes.

"Look, look at me now, Daddy!"

In the distance, a horn blew. Chaz was up on his feet in a flash, rubbing at his face with his sleeve before clapping his hands and rushing back towards the exit.

"Come, come, come on, everyone. Dinner is served!"

CHAPTER TWENTY-FOUR

Night falls quickly in the desert. By the time the group was leaving the collection's museum, the light was already fading. As they reached the arena, a star-spangled sky hung above them. Long tables had been set out and were filling up with the camp's residents. To Smithy's eye, Diller's estimate of a couple of hundred men seemed about right.

Large floodlights had been placed on one side of the arena, causing massive shadows to dance along the far wall of wrecked cars when anyone moved in front of them. Between the lights, a couple of barrel fires, plus, bizarrely, candelabras on the top table, the full moon in the cloudless sky was well assisted in the illumination stakes.

In the corner of the arena stood a catering van with the words "Taco King" emblazoned on the side. Incredibly, men who looked as if they'd sell their own grandmothers into slavery for a six-pack formed an orderly line, waiting politely to order. An elderly Hispanic man in a cowboy hat took orders and delivered the food.

Smithy, Diller and the rest of their ragtag little party were at the top table with Chaz. They were on a raised dais, all seated on one side of the table, classic Last Supper-style. Chaz, of course, was in

Jesus's position. Muroe was to the left of him, with Reed on the right. Their host was talking non-stop, although it wasn't evident to whom his stream of consciousness was directed. Smithy doubted the Last Supper had been this awkward.

If anything, Lousy Louis Reed looked the most uncomfortable of all of them. All of his bluster had long since deserted him. Not even he could fail to notice that here, he was not the master of all he surveyed. Worse, his former friend was spiralling, and technically the blame lay with Louis for beating him in their ridiculous competition. If this was the Last Supper, then everyone knew who sat in the Judas seat.

Beside Reed, Finley still looked like a scared little boy trapped in a man's body. Both men looked ashen-faced as the behemoth Zero pushed out a large cage on wheels in which sat a dishevelled and pathetic-looking man. Judging by Louis and Finley's reactions, he was clearly the fourth and final member of the musketeers. Rake – that was his name. Smithy must have seen him before, sitting atop a quad bike, but his appearance rang no bells. To be fair, Rake's world had changed so emphatically over the last few days, he might not have recognised himself. He sat, huddled in the corner of his rusted metal cage, looking vacantly up at the sky.

Reed went to say something to Chaz, but Finley hushed him. Reed looked as if he were still considering it, but before he could find words their group was interrupted by the arrival of the food.

"Oh, chili," said Diller, sounding genuinely enthusiastic as a bowl was slammed down in front of him. "Cool."

Smithy looked down at his meal. "Yeah. Did you check how many fingers the guy who slopped it down had?"

Diller shook his head. "Ah man, why'd you have to go and say that? At least he was bald, so that excuses the lack of a hairnet."

"Yeah. Have you seen the other two guys bringing out the food?"

Diller looked. "Wow. ZZ Top have fallen a long way."

"Really?" said Smithy. "You know ZZ Top, but Lou Reed is a mystery to you?"

Diller didn't look up as he poked at the surface of his chili. "I saw a couple of late-night comics referring to them in gags, and you know I hate to miss a reference."

"That you do."

"So," said Diller, "are we going to eat this?"

"Well, look at it this way, it's not even in the top ten of things around here likely to kill you."

"You really are a terrible loss to the greeting-card industry."

Smithy picked up his spoon. "Dig in. Need to keep your strength up." He brought some chili to his lips, then stopped. He lowered his voice. "Oh, and about the other thing ..."

"What other thing?"

Smithy gave Diller a pointed look.

"Oh, right. Yeah."

Smithy glanced around subtly to make sure their conversation wasn't being observed. "You were right. Muroe stays with us. Sorry. I was being a dick."

Diller shrugged. "Don't worry about it. I get it. You're right to be mad at her and all. I just ..."

They both looked up as two men came careening off one of the long benches that stretched down the side of the tables, one of them jackhammering punches into the face of the other. There was no indication as to what might have caused the altercation. Other diners watched on as the one-sided affair unfolded. Finally, one of them stood up and, with a laugh, pulled the "victor" off the victim, who staggered away, bleeding heavily. The spectacle was met with cheers and the banging of tables.

"Jeez," said Diller, into his chili. "What a place."

They ate in silence.

Smithy looked longingly in the direction of the Taco King van. How good must his tacos be for the man to work unmolested in this crowd? Shitshow the orangutan sat up on one of the walls, fender by his side, watching proceedings quietly.

At the other end of the table, Smithy spied Wilkins, the keeper of the collection. He sat there, regarding the bowl of chili in front of him as if he were expecting it to break into song at any moment – and he wasn't looking forward to the experience. The Englishman caught Smithy's eye and gave a nod. Smithy nodded back. Wilkins had been right about a lot of things; they couldn't just run. They needed a plan. Most of all, they needed a way of getting the hell out of there that meant they didn't end up in that cage beside Rake, or somewhere even worse. The cage was where Chaz put one of his best friends, and Smithy got the impression he was not on that list. One of life's great disappointments.

Chaz stood, raised his hands and spoke loudly. "Gentlemen."

He was almost entirely ignored. He looked over at Zero, who stepped forward and hollered, "SILENCE!"

This, at least, got the attention of most of the audience.

"Gentlemen," Chaz began again, "for tonight's entertainment, I bring you something special."

On cue, the same two guys who'd driven the Humvee that had brought Smithy and Diller to the camp, led out a man in cuffs. The prisoner looked of Southeast Asian extraction and had an athletic build. His face showed signs of bruising that was fading, nearly healed. His guards pushed him into the vacant area in front of the dais. He stood there, hands cuffed behind his back, looking around, as if calmly assessing the situation. He glanced up in Smithy's direction.

WE KNOW WHO HE IS, DON'T WE?

Oh God, please shut up.

DO NOT TAKE MY NAME IN VAIN.

"This is Makasito, supposedly one of Japan's finest assassins."

This was met with roars and wolf-whistles from the crowd. Someone threw a spoon, which Makasito calmly side-stepped.

Diller looked at Smithy. "Is that …?"

Smithy shrugged, but deep down he knew the answer. It was the man he'd fought in Lousy Louis Reed's apartment.

Chaz pulled a wad of cash from the inside pocket of his jacket and held it above his head. "This is twenty thousand dollars. The prize for anyone who can best him in combat. Hands up who wants to—"

Chaz was interrupted by a fat guy with a fiery-red Grizzly

Adams beard-and-hair combo, wearing a leather jacket over his bare torso. He stood up from the nearest table and charged at Makasito.

"Wait," said Chaz. "I didn't ..."

The Japanese man remained absolutely still. At the very last moment he flopped backwards onto the ground and used his feet and the ginger lunatic's momentum to flip his adversary over. The hairy idiot flew for a moment before crashing headlong into the base of the dais, causing the table to shake. Makasito was back on his feet in an instant and sent a kick into the side of his attacker's head, connecting with his temple. The bearded man slumped to the ground, unconscious.

Makasito turned to the crowd, awaiting his next attacker as if he were waiting in line for a taco.

Chaz looked down at him, then back at his audience, considerably less sure of himself.

"Well, that's the opening act out of the way." Chaz's joke was greeted with a smattering of laughter. He waved the money again. "Twenty thousand dollars. C'mon now. We'll even leave the handcuffs on him."

Several men stepped forward, cheered on by their friends. A kerfuffle broke out at the back of the crowd, which then began to part. A man stepped out. He was squat and powerfully built, with tattoos covering almost every inch of visible skin, including his face. Smithy looked at his eyes. Once you'd been around enough fights, you knew what to look for. This man's eyes chilled the soul.

Those who had been jockeying for position moved away and a hush fell. The guy's hype man emerged from the crowd behind him, waving his hands in the air. He was taller, leaner and wearing a bandana. He danced around and jabbed a mocking finger at Makasito.

"Oh, ese, you so fucked now, man. The Cobra is in the house. You feel it? He gonna take you down."

The Cobra stuck out his tongue. Smithy assumed he'd got it done to fit the name, but it was possible the name had come second. Either way, it was split so it appeared forked. Its owner extended it as far as it would go, while hissing at the same time.

"Damn," said Diller. "That's method."

With one hand the Cobra drew a hammer from the back pocket of his jeans, and with a practised motion, pulled free a thick chain he'd been wearing around his waist with the other. He twirled both without once taking his eyes off Makasito.

"Ohhh, baby, you about to get bit! You feel me? This shit is gonna get real for you."

The Cobra showed he was smarter than the first guy by going for the slow, circling approach. When you've got an advantage, you don't need to lessen it by showing your opponent your hand straight away. Instead, he swirled the chain over his head, quickly whipping it up to a speed where any contact made with it would be damaging. Makasito moved around the circle, mirroring his opponent as best he could, trying to leave space between them. Despite his hands still being cuffed behind his back, his smooth footwork spoke of excellent balance.

The crowd began to chant. "Cobra. Cobra. Cobra."

It grew into a roiling mass as people from the back shoved forward to see more, and those at the front pushed back to avoid getting a dangerously close view.

Chaz stood, clapping his hands excitedly, while Muroe remained seated beside him, stony-faced. Having completed a half-circle, Makasito now stood with his back to the majority of the crowd. Smithy shifted nervously. Like the odds weren't bad enough already. The assassin obviously wasn't much of a street fighter, having made such a fatal error by leaving his back wide open. It was only a matter of time before ...

The hype man saw his opportunity and lunged forward, intending to push Makasito towards the Cobra. He was met by his target's right foot, which rocketed backwards and caught him full in the belly, doubling him over. As the Cobra charged, the assassin rolled himself over the hype man's back with the grace of an acrobat, putting him between them.

Clearly, this had been the plan all along. Makasito kicked the hype man in the ass, sending him tumbling into the path of the onrushing Cobra. The two men collided, causing the Cobra to lose control of the rapidly rotating chain. It whooshed into the crowd and the chanting stopped as people ducked to avoid it. One man, who had been enjoying the chanting a little too much, ended up having his chances at being crowned prom king ruined.

Meanwhile, the hype man, all flailing limbs, had taken down the Cobra in a messy heap. The tattooed man threw off his associate unceremoniously and scrambled to his feet, quickly enough that Makasito had to stall his advance. Smithy had been in enough fights to know that being the one on the ground meant nothing but bad news.

As the hype man scrambled out of the way, jeered for his troubles, the Cobra and Makasito stood facing each other again. The Cobra had lost his grip on the hammer, which now lay on the dusty ground between them. Both men eyed it. Makasito had no use for it, his hands being cuffed, but denying it to the Cobra was its own reward. The tattooed man feinted towards it and Makasito responded. The Cobra's tattooed face split into an evil grin as his tongue flicked out again. He reached into his boot and produced a combat knife. It always paid to be prepared – the Cobra might have been a Boy Scout back before his time as a walking piece of urban-decay art.

Makasito paused for a moment before surging forward suddenly, causing his opponent to step back. He slid onto the ground, his legs a whirling dervish as he attempted to floor the Cobra with a leg sweep. His foot made contact with his retreating opponent but not enough to take him down. In one fluid motion, Makasito hopped back up and bounced backwards, but not before the Cobra's slashing blade caught his right arm.

Makasito looked down at his bicep, where a steady flow of blood was darkening his black T-shirt and spreading down his arm. The Cobra flashed his tongue again, and the crowd cheered.

"He's got the hammer," bellowed the hype man over the noise of the crowd.

The Cobra looked at the ground. To confirm his fears, Makasito turned around partially and showed him the hammer clasped behind his back.

The Cobra raised his hands above his head, laughing. "What the fuck you going to do with that?" he roared.

In response, Makasito tossed the hammer in the air and swung into a roundhouse kick, making contact with the tool in mid-air. It flew across the clearing, striking the Cobra right in the centre of the forehead and sending his head snapping backwards. The rest of him followed, and he collapsed to the ground, out cold. It had happened so fast that a smile still played across his face.

Makasito turned and faced the crowd again, calmly awaiting whatever might come next.

After a few moments of confused murmuring, applause broke out – the mob loves a winner.

Smithy watched as those who had been putting themselves forward before the Cobra's coronation as the mob's champion faded back into the crowd.

Chaz raised his hands. "Brothers, brothers," he said, laughing. "I told you he was good. And tonight, he did not disappoint!"

The crowd cheered.

"Unfortunately, he has previously been bested by a midget!"

Smithy felt himself redden as the mob's attention turned to him. This was what he had been dreading. Even as Makasito had fought, the possibility had swirled in his mind. *Chaz might demand a rematch. I'm not going to do it.* Then came the image of Diller with a gun being held to his head.

Chaz rested his hand on the grip of the Glock he wore in the holster on his belt. "And if there's one thing we cannot stand for in this organisation, it ..."

Smithy tensed as Chaz drew the pistol.

"Is ..."

It dawned on him too late what was happening. He got to his feet. No thought in his head as to what to do beyond that point.

"Failure."

Makasito didn't see it coming, which was some form of blessing. The shot passed through the back of his head. He was dead before he hit the ground.

The crowd fell silent, those closest to Makasito's body looking at it, slumped beside the unconscious form of the Cobra.

Chaz clapped his hands gleefully. "Yes. Yes. Yes. Are you not entertained?"

Muroe turned away and retched under the table.

CHAPTER TWENTY-FIVE

Dessert had been Twinkies.

Having watched Chaz slaughter a man in cold blood, Smithy's appetite hadn't been at its highest, but on the other hand, Twinkies came in self-contained plastic packaging and had a best-before date that meant they would outlive the planet – so it was the safest food imaginable in their current predicament. Diller had lost his appetite completely, so Smithy had told him to shove it in his pocket for later. Nowhere seemed to be growing evermore chaotic, even in the short time they had been there. He wasn't taking the existence of breakfast in the morning for granted.

They were "escorted" to their quarters in the main house by Zero and a quartet of his goons. While it denied Smithy the chance to take an unsupervised look around, it at least spared Muroe from dealing with the advances of the less chivalrous elements of the camp's populace. As it was, plenty of comments still came their way, mostly but by no means all directed at her – Diller and Smithy had their admirers too.

At one point, Reed got hit in the head by a well-thrown beer bottle. The man said nothing. Smithy gave it a day before he was as squirrely and monosyllabic as Finley. Those boys didn't know how to deal with a world where the rules that had always favoured them no longer existed. Diller had grown up in Hunts Point, scrabbling to survive. It wasn't this or anything close, but at least the odds being stacked against him didn't come as a shock.

Muroe hadn't said much, but as far as Smithy could tell she was holding it together reasonably well. Whatever could be said about the woman, and Smithy could say plenty, she had to be tough to do what she did. As for Smithy himself, this all held a dreamlike quality, that his idiotic determination to seek retribution against Reed could lead them here. He'd allowed himself to be put in the position where he could be humiliated by Reed the first time, and then he'd run back and done the same thing, only worse. When this was all over, Smithy was going to sit down and try to get his shit together once and for all. But first, he had to make sure that he could get them out of this freakshow without incurring any losses that would haunt him for the rest of his days.

"I'm no expert," said Diller as they passed two men trying to have a fight but unable to do so given how stinking drunk they were, "but was it the best idea to give a group of men like this access to booze and whatever else?"

"That's not what worries me," said Muroe, who was walking between him and Smithy.

"No?" said Diller.

"No. What worries me is what happens when it starts to run out. This place has one hell of a hangover coming."

Smithy had to concede she had a point.

They reached the main house, which was notable for the security system it had in place. Zero punched in an eight-digit code to open the door. They were led down a hallway and Zero came to a stop in front of two doors. Immediately, Finley opened and walked through one of them. Zero indicated for Reed and Muroe to follow him.

"Actually, I'm going to room with these two gentlemen," said Muroe, nodding at Smithy and Diller. "They're my guests and I want to make sure they're well taken care of."

One of the guards sniggered, but Zero just looked at her blankly.

He blinked a ponderous blink, which Smithy regretted he'd not used as an opportunity to escape, then pointed at Muroe and the other door.

She gave him a quick smile and went inside, closely followed by Smithy and Diller.

The room was surprisingly, well, pleasant. It was much like you'd find at a mid-range hotel which, given that everything outside of it was like a post-apocalyptic Disneyland, was a refreshing slice of blandness. There was a double bed, a futon, a wardrobe and a door leading off to a bathroom.

Diller looked at the door as it clicked shut behind them. "There's no handle on the inside."

"Yeah," said Smithy. "And those windows don't open. They can keep referring to us as guests all they like – we aren't."

"So, what are we going to do?" asked Muroe.

"Well," said Smithy, "I don't know about anyone else, but I'm going to see if there's any water for a shower."

"But …" Muroe noticed Smithy's eyes as they motioned up to the camera in the corner of the room.

She gave a subtle nod.

"There's only one bed," said Diller.

"You two can have it," said Muroe. "I'll take the futon."

"But …"

She nodded at Smithy. "Before he can say it, it is my fault we're in this mess."

"I wasn't going to say that."

Muroe opened the wardrobe. "I am, however, going to take one of the dressing gowns."

"Go ahead," said Smithy. "I'm guessing they're not my size."

"Oh, right."

"You can have the first shower too, if you'd like?" said Diller.

Muroe sighed. "Thanks."

Forty minutes later they'd all freshened up. It was awkward, three adults in such a confined space, but they made do. Part of the politeness pact was ignoring the fact that everybody had had to wash their undies and hang them on the shower rail. The flight crew hadn't taken the time to toss their bags off the plane before deserting them. They were due one hell of a sniffy online review.

The trio moved around each other – Diller and Muroe in the dressing gowns, Smithy with a towel wrapped around his waist – as Diller dug out the extra bedding from the top of the wardrobe and gave it to Muroe.

"We should all get some sleep, I guess," said Diller.

"Oh no," said Smithy. "You've got that audition coming up."

"I do?"

"You do," said Smithy. "The secret to being an actor is always to assume there's an audition coming up. Lack of preparation equals death. Soliloquy – *Henry VI*, Part 3, Act 3, Scene 2. In your own time."

Smithy sat on the floor, leaning back against the base of the double bed. He patted the carpet beside him. "Ms Muroe?"

Muroe sat down beside him, carefully adjusting her dressing gown as she did so.

Diller looked down at them. "Really?"

"I like the theatre," said Muroe.

"OK. Fine," said Diller, who closed his eyes for a moment to clear his mind. Then he looked off into the middle distance. "Ay, Edward will use women honourably. Would he were wasted, marrow, bones, and all, That from his loins no hopeful branch may spring, To cross me from the golden time I look for!"

"Shakespeare?" said Muroe in a low whisper as Diller soliloquised. She kept her eyes fixed on the performance in front of her, as did Smithy.

"Really? You think a kid from Hunts Point can't tackle the Bard?"

"No," said Muroe. "Y'know, you don't always have to assume the worst of me."

"Sure. This is also the longest soliloquy in Big Willy's oeuvre."

"So the camera can't see us here," said Muroe. "Do we know if they can hear us?"

"Even if they can," said Smithy, "we don't know for sure that they're watching. Still – let's not find out."

"To take their rooms, ere I can place myself: A cold premeditation for my purpose!"

"What's the plan?" asked Muroe.

"Well, so far there isn't one. Tell me all you know about Chaz."

"OK, but it isn't much. He, Reed, Finley and that Rake guy all went to the same boarding school. They're friends in that 'do anything to beat them' way that guys have."

Smithy thought about saying something in response to that, but let it pass.

"The Breddenbacks are old money, like 'stole it from the Native Americans' old money. Reed hired me to win this damn competition for him. I got the feeling Chaz was more his bully than his buddy. The man wanted it bad."

"And he got it."

"Yes," said Muroe ruefully. "And don't think I'm not fully aware that doing so messed up life for all of us."

"Can I ... I have to know, is that really the Lewinsky dress?"

Muroe gave the slightest of nods. "Yep. I'm unfortunately very good at what I do." She shifted and looked down. "For what it's worth – I really did think we were going to Hawaii."

"OK. Were there any indicators this was going to happen?"

"No. I mean, I'm pretty sure Reed is more shocked than we are. Chaz is losing it, and he's taking everybody down with him – he explained his plan over dinner. Brace yourself – Suriname."

Smithy paused. "Isn't that the evil wizard from *The Lord of the Rings*?"

"No. Country. Smallest one in South America. He plans to take it over."

"Well, say there is no kingdom then for Richard; What other pleasure can the world afford?"

"You are kidding?"

"I wish I was. He says he knows a guy whose father used to be ... blah, blah. Look, it doesn't matter, it is insane. He thinks he's out here training an army. Closest contact I've had with anything military is a brief, regrettable infatuation with wearing epaulettes, but even I know what he has here isn't an army."

"Nope. What he's got is the worst of the worst, who'll toe the line until they don't, and then ..."

"Yes," agreed Muroe. "And we don't want to be here when that happens."

"We need to find out where that airplane is, or figure out some way to communicate with the outside world. That's our best ticket out of here."

"How on earth are we going to do that?"

Smithy didn't give an answer, largely because he didn't have one.

"Oh, sorry," said Muroe, shifting awkwardly. "I forgot to say ..."

"What?"

"Chaz mentioned over dinner, mid-stream-of-consciousness rant, that he'd something planned for you tomorrow."

"Oh. Great."

They sat there in silence for a moment, watching Diller.

"She did corrupt frail nature with some bribe, To shrink mine arm up like a wither'd shrub; To make an envious mountain on my back, Where sits deformity to mock my body—"

"Hang on, Dill," interrupted Smithy. "Great work, but a quick note there. Richard of Gloucester is angry. He hates his own body; he blames it for all that is bad in his life. This is as much about his self-loathing as his ambition. He's trying to find validation here."

"Right," said Diller. "OK. I'll take it from ..."

"Wherever feels good."

Diller nodded, took a moment and started again from a few lines back.

Muroe cleared her throat quietly. "This might be the Stockholm syndrome talking, but he is really good."

"He really is."

She nodded.

"You and I screwed up in different ways and got ourselves here, but all he did was be a good friend. If it comes down to it ..."

Muroe nodded.

"He's also our secret weapon. I don't have much of a plan, but if we've got a hope he is going to be it."

Smithy glanced over to see Muroe staring at the carpet. He paused. "You OK?"

"Look, I know I don't deserve your help ..."

"Forget it."

"No. Listen. Please." She licked her lips nervously. "This place, this ... We're getting out of here, but if it doesn't happen ... If we don't get out of here, I don't want to be around for what comes next—"

"It won't come to that."

"But if it does."

"And from that torment I will free myself, Or hew my way out with a bloody axe."

Smithy looked down at the back of his hands.

"You know what I'm asking."

"Yes."

"And ..."

"It won't come to that, but yes."

"OK. Thank you."

They sat in silence for a while and continued to watch Diller.

"Damn," said Muroe. "He really is good."

CHAPTER TWENTY-SIX

They got to have a lie-in in the morning. What that meant was nobody came to get them.

Smithy had slept fitfully. He'd spent the first hour in bed whispering sweet nothings to Diller. Actually, it was mostly nothing nothings, seeing as they had no plan beyond not wanting to be there. In other circumstances, two grown men whispering beneath the bedsheets would've felt weird, but it didn't even make the top five of awkward things that had happened that day.

He hadn't meant to, but Diller had managed only to add to the complexity of the issue. He wanted to see if they could bust out Rake, Finley and Lousy Louis Reed too. The guy was literally generous to a fault. Smithy might have changed his mind when it came to Muroe, but as far as he was concerned, the others could make their own way. He'd left it at 'we'll see what we can do', but he wasn't losing much sleep over rescuing the three musketeers from their boyhood-friend-turned-megalomaniacal-fruitcake.

Eventually, Diller had dozed off mid-sentence, joining the softly snoring Ms Muroe, who was over on the futon, in the land of blissful unconsciousness. That had left Smithy all alone. At least he really wished it had.

THIS IS GOING REALLY BADLY.
Tell me something I don't know?
HOW TO GET OUT OF HERE.
Shut up.

They couldn't see the sun out of their window, so Smithy had no idea of the time. The whole place was so disorientating. He hadn't seen a clock since they had been there. In that regard, Nowhere was like Vegas. In many regards, really. Judging by the noises coming from outside throughout the night, it was a twenty-four-hour kind of place, and the management seemed more concerned about everybody having a good time than about following the rules. All this place was missing was an Elvis impersonator and Cirque du Soleil.

At some point in the morning, the door opened and three brown packages were tossed into the room. Diller picked one up and looked at it.

"These are MREs!" he said excitedly, before noting the blank expressions on the faces of his room-mates. "Meals, Ready to Eat. Army rations."

"Really?" said Muroe. "I don't suppose there's a vegetarian option?"

"Let's see … One of them is vegetable crumbles with pasta in taco-style sauce. Any good?"

"Sounds delicious," said Muroe, who caught the package as it was tossed to her, and began to examine it.

"Wait," said Smithy., "You ate the chili last night, didn't you?"

"Did I?" said Muroe. "Or did I look like I ate the chili so as not to offend a coked-up megalomaniac? I've been to a lot of dinners over the years – you've no idea how many purses I've ruined by using them to stash meat."

"Right," said Diller. "Well, when I'm done processing all the other crazy stuff I've seen in the last couple of days, I really want to come back around and think about that some more."

"You're welcome," said Muroe. "And if either of you ever tells anyone in New York I said that, I will end you." She issued the threat with a smile.

Smithy chuckled. "Here's hoping we get the chance to find out if you mean that."

They sat on the bed to eat their meals, which were surprisingly decent. There was even a water-activated exothermic chemical heater that warmed the food, much to Diller's geekish delight. Smithy had the hash browns with bacon, peppers and onions, and Diller had the shredded beef in BBQ sauce. Smithy had been finishing his remarkably edible granola when the door flew open. The immense figure of Zero loomed in the hallway. Smithy started shoving the remaining food sachets into the pockets of his trousers.

"Well," said Smithy, "looks like our presence has been requested."

They were afforded the same guard of honour as the night before to lead them back to the arena. The sun was blazing hot. Smithy could feel his skin cooking under the Hawaiian shirt that he deeply regretted wearing. It wasn't the highest thing on his wish list, but some sunscreen would be nice.

Zero brought them into the arena through a small set of side doors. Their arrival was greeted with jeers and catcalls from the mob. The tables and benches from the night before were gone, and the space was back to looking exactly like an arena, complete with baying crowd. There were no bleachers, so the spectators were positioned on top of the piles of scrapped cars that made up the arena's walls.

Zero led Smithy, Diller and Muroe towards the far side of the arena where something lay under a sheet.

"Whatever this is," said Smithy, "it isn't going to be good."

"I haven't seen *Mad Max Beyond Thunderdome*, but was it a bit like this?" asked Diller.

"I haven't seen it either."

"Me neither," added Muroe.

"Feels like we might be missing a reference."

"And I know you hate that," said Smithy.

"No offence," said Muroe, "but you two are a little odd."

Smithy looked up at the walls of cars. Atop one of them stood a naked man. It appeared he had painted his various limbs in different colours. His unmentionables were a vibrant bright green. For his sake, Smithy really hoped that the paint also had a sun-blocking quality.

"Normally," Smithy replied, "I'd agree, but we might just be the most normal people in this place."

Everyone winced as a pained squeal of feedback from a PA system came from behind them.

"Oh," said Diller. "This might be Tina Turner's bit."

"Seriously?" said Smithy. "And you've never heard of Lou Reed?"

Muroe raised her voice. "Hey! Tina is an American icon!"

Smithy and Diller exchanged a look. *That's you told.*

The trio turned around. To the right of the main gates, scaffolding had been erected to form a viewing platform. At its base stood a three-piece band of guitar, drums and bass. At its top was a stage. Reed and Finley sat there looking awkward, Wilkins sat there looking bored, as only an Englishman can.

In front of them was Elvis – or at least what Elvis would look like if he'd been born in the back of a pick-up truck, run over by that truck, and then dragged behind it for a couple of hundred yards. While the man bore some kind of similarity to the King in the hair department, and he was wearing the sparkly jumpsuit, Elvis had looked considerably better than him on his worst day. Indeed, on his last day. At a push, this guy looked like what Elvis might have left in the toilet bowl in those fateful final moments.

He did the voice. "Thank you very much, Nowhere! How y'all doing today?"

He was met with a mix of jeers, cheers and a couple of gunshots. Junkyard Elvis, slightly unnerved by the reception, leaned over the edge of the stage and looked down at the band. "Hit it, boys."

They launched into what could best and very kindly be described as a death-metal cover of an Elvis song. Smithy wasn't sure which song it was, and it didn't sound like the band were either.

"Wow, just when you thought this place couldn't get any worse."

As they reached the end of the arena, Zero stood to one side and pulled a sheet away from what they had been heading towards. The three of them stood there in silence, looking at what sat in front of them.

"Are those ...?" started Muroe.

"Yep," said Smithy.

"What?" said Diller. "What are they?"

"Seriously?" said Smithy. "Have you never seen a ride-on lawnmower before?"

"Exactly how many large lawns do you think there are where I'm from? I refer you to the fact that I've only ever seen one cow."

Zero and the rest of their 'guard of honour' moved off, after indicating that they should stay where they are.

"I have a very bad feeling about this," said Muroe.

"Relax," said Smithy. "Maybe they just want us to mow the desert for them? Nah, you're right. This is bad." He pointed at Junkyard Elvis and his band. "Whatever that is, we may look back on listening to it as the highlight of our day. That's how bad this is."

They turned to the massive gates at the other end of the arena as they opened. The crowd looked at them expectantly. There was a murmur of disappointment, mostly covered by the disappointing music as, after a few seconds, a cow was pulled through by a man wearing a football helmet and pads.

Smithy raised his voice to be heard. "Hey, look at that, Dill – now you've seen two cows."

"Oh God," said Muroe.

The football player tethered the cow to a stake in the ground and ran off, dodging hurled beer bottles and other improvised projectiles as he did so.

"Look on the bright side," said Smithy to Muroe. "There's a good chance that after whatever happens happens, you won't be the only vegetarian here."

The three of them stood there in silence as the band played on. They might have done a couple more songs or they might just have played the same song worse. They weren't leaving room for applause between numbers, which Smithy felt was a very wise choice. Despite the total lack of any discernible talent, the band were sort of impressive, given how they had to keep on playing while the music lovers on the walls of twisted metal around them hurled in their direction whatever bits of vehicular debris they could find. The bass player took an exhaust pipe to the head and kept going. Something unidentifiable hit the drummer, which did affect him – Smithy noticed that for a few bars he inadvertently fell in time with the rest of the band.

Their set came to an abrupt end when the guitarist got poleaxed by a well-judged steering wheel. He and the drummer then got into a fistfight, which briefly improved their sound. While this was going on, the bass player calmly put his instrument in its case, and the vocalist took several more bows than the reaction to them finishing warranted.

Someone gave Junkyard Elvis a nod and he slipped into his role as MC for whatever the hell this was. It was a role that suited him better, seeing as it involved no singing. "Ladies and germs, guys and gals, Billy-Bobs and Bobby-Sues, listen up!"

"God, I really hate this guy," groaned Muroe, which was met with murmured assent from the others.

"Before we commence today's festivities, a reminder that tomorrow will see the event y'all been waiting for – the Nowhere Demolition Derby!"

His announcement was met with a genuine roar of excitement.

"Oh, cool," said Diller, in a display of his trademark misplaced optimism. Smithy didn't have the heart to point out that they might not be around to see it.

"Before that, though, please welcome your friend and mine, our host with the most, the mastermind behind Nowhere, our fearless leader ... All hail, Emperor Chaz!"

Chaz, wearing a tasteful gold crown and lamé cape, stepped forward onto the stage. His arrival was met with a level of enthusiasm normally reserved for support acts, and kids in nativity plays who aren't yours. Luckily, the guitarist struck up a riff, so Chaz's ego didn't appear to notice the lukewarm response.

"And today he is going to take on these challengers in a battle of wits, strength and guile!"

"Did either of you challenge Chaz?" asked Smithy. "I don't remember doing that."

Diller shook his head. "It's like the dude watched *Gladiator* and got confused over who the hero was."

Junkyard Elvis was really getting into it now. "These knights shall ride their noble steeds and wield their fearsome lances!"

Diller turned around and looked at the lawnmowers again. "Do you think he means those metal bars on the ground there?"

"I guess," said Smithy.

"And Chaz— I mean, the Emperor, brings you – the mighty dragon!"

Junkyard Elvis waved a hand towards the massive gates. On cue, the guitarist started playing what might have been a Black Sabbath riff, but Smithy decided to be respectful enough to their musical legacy and refrained from trying to identify which one he was strangling to death.

"What is ..." Smithy tailed off as the entirety of the large gateway was filled with something being pulled in by a couple of pick-up trucks. Whatever the thing was, it was covered in a massive tarpaulin and it ran on large tracks.

"Does anyone want to say it?" asked Smithy.

"I said it last time," said Muroe.

"Alright," said Diller. "I got a really bad feeling about this."

Whatever it was scraped through the gates. Someone must have had the foresight to measure it, but they'd not included enough leeway. The tarpaulin caught on an edge and was dragged off.

Smithy's mouth dropped open. There in front of them stood a dragon.

CHAPTER TWENTY-SEVEN

The thing was massive, painted in dark red and gold, its steel body gleaming in the dazzling desert sun. Its head was shaped to resemble a dragon, with brightly glowing red eyes to complete the effect.

"It's Dragonzilla 5000, from *RoboBattles*," said Diller excitedly.

Muroe turned to Smithy. "Did you understand anything in that sentence?"

"*RoboBattles*," repeated Diller. "It's this Japanese thing – you can watch it on YouTube. Teams of engineers build battle bots to take each other on."

"Wait," said Muroe. "I've seen *Robot Wars*, or whatever it's called, on TV, but those machines were, like, a couple of feet tall." She pointed at the metal behemoth being manoeuvred into the arena. "That thing is as big as a house."

"Yeah," said Diller. "They started a league for these massive robots to fight each other. Dragonzilla was the best one. It only had one-and-a-half fights, though. There was an accident. A spectator lost an arm."

"How did a spectator—" started Smithy, but he was interrupted by the sound of the robot's massive buzz-saw arm whirring into life. "I had to ask, didn't I?"

Smithy looked up at the platform where Chaz was sporting an elaborate-looking remote-control console around his neck, like cigarette girls used to wear back in the days when scantily clad women purveying convenient cancer was considered the height of sophistication.

"The league went bankrupt," explained Diller. "After all the, y'know, lawsuits and whatever. I heard that Dragonzilla got bought by a private collector."

"Well, it did," said Muroe. "That psycho."

Smithy watched as the thing's other arm began to move. A massive, mallet-like appendage at the end of it pummelled the ground repeatedly, which was met with a rapturous response from the crowd.

"I know this isn't the time," said Smithy, "but am I the only one who thinks Dragonzilla is the dumbest name you've ever heard?"

"You should point that out," said Muroe. "See if you can hurt its feelings."

They watched as the robot twirled through two 360-degree turns, its upper body rotating independently to the massive caterpillar tracks that moved it around.

"The thing has a top speed of thirty-four miles an hour," said Diller.

"Who remembers stuff like that?" asked Muroe.

"He does." Smithy watched as the thing lurched towards the tethered cow, which was looking at a beer can, as if trying to figure out if it could eat it. "Oh boy. This isn't going to be ..." A thought struck him. "Dill, seeing as it's called Dragonzilla, does that mean it can ...?"

The flame that shot out of the robot's head engulfed the cow. Diller turned to one side and threw up.

Smithy placed a consoling hand on his friend's back. "I'm going to stop asking questions."

They all looked away as the robot moved forward and put the animal out of its misery through the liberal application of the massive mallet-arm. All this served only to whip the crowd into more of a frenzy.

Even with the PA system at his disposal, Junkyard Elvis struggled to be heard over the clamour. "Knights, mount your steeds."

"I guess that's us," said Diller. The three of them turned to pick up a metal pole each and clambered on to the ride-on lawnmowers. "Is it just me, or is this not the fairest of fights?"

"I've been in worse," said Smithy.

"Really?" asked Muroe.

Smithy didn't answer – it would be bad for morale. "Hey, look, someone left us a note." He snatched it off the steering wheel of the mower where it had been taped. "One, sit on seat to engage battery. Two, press key into ignition. Three, depress clutch before four, turning key clockwise."

They followed the steps as described and the machines sprang into life.

Muroe turned to Smithy. "Would now be a bad time to ask if we've got any kind of plan here?"

"You're not going to like it."

When he'd finished, Muroe and Diller nodded. "You're right," she said, "I really hate it."

"Told you."

CHAPTER TWENTY-EIGHT

"Plan" was far too strong a word for what he had in mind. It was, at best, the merest glint of an idea, but it was all he had. Smithy felt incredibly uncomfortable with what he'd asked Diller and Muroe to do, but he didn't see how he had any choice.

They all strapped on their helmets in silence. As protection against a machine with an industrial buzz saw and a massive pummelling mallet for hands, plus the ability to breathe fire, the helmets felt about as useful as a winning smile in the face of a tsunami.

Junkyard Elvis hollered into the mic at the top of his lungs. "Dragon ready?"

The massive robot raised its arms and spun around on the spot. A display that was greeted with rapturous hollering. If you were going to be David taking on Goliath, it really felt as if the crowd should at least be on your side. Hey ho.

"Knights ready?"

Muroe started laughing.

"What?" asked Smithy.

She shouted over the engines to be heard. "Do you think we could say no?"

"Stick to the plan," he shouted back, trying to look more confident than he felt.

They both nodded. Diller gave a thumbs-up.

"Let battle commence."

Muroe went right, Diller went left, and Smithy turned his mower around and headed towards the wall behind them. The thing had a reasonably tight turning circle, which was good as it wasn't built for speed or battle. He heard the dragon breathing fire behind him, and the crowd roared. He just hoped the other two were keeping their distance and buying him the time he needed. He resisted the urge to look back. That wouldn't do anybody any favours.

As he reached the rear wall, he put the mower in neutral and leaped off. He looked up and, after a couple of moments, saw what he was looking for. Right near the top, of course. Quickly, he started to climb.

"Get back in there, coward!"

A few men were sat on top of the wall. As it happened, being at the far end of the arena from the main gates and viewing platform, it was the least densely populated – presumably only by those music lovers who wanted to be as far away from the band as possible. Still, they didn't take kindly to Smithy's attempts to flee.

He felt objects hitting him as he climbed. Something metallic and heavy slammed into his right hand, causing him to lose his grip and almost stumble backwards. A cheer rose as he struggled.

Smithy shook it off and tried to block out the pain. No time. When he reached the third level of crushed cars, a figure appeared before him. It was the naked man he'd seen earlier, who, for reasons probably known only to him, had colour-coded his various body parts. The man started to spit on him, demonstrating an even lower standard of etiquette than his appearance suggested.

Smithy kept climbing. Handholds were hard to come by, but he managed to reach the fourth level of cars, blocking out the sounds from behind him. In his hurry to get up there he'd ended up a car's length away from where he needed to be. The only way across was to go a bit higher and then make his way over.

His route brought him within range of the swinging legs of the painted man. His foot glanced off Smithy's helmet. Smithy kept moving, his arms aching from the effort.

The foot slammed into Smithy's helmet this time, jarring his neck and almost sending him backwards.

Once.

Twice.

On the third occasion, Smithy managed to move his head out of the way and the foot slipped past him. He slammed his head into it. The naked man screamed. His cry went up a notch when Smithy bit him.

With another yowl, the naked man fell past Smithy and onto the arena floor, a development which was also greeted with a cheer. Even the worst scum of the earth found the company of a man with painted genitalia a little much.

Smithy hung on by his fingertips. With a final effort he got to where he needed to be. He found what he wanted and tugged at it. The effort of pulling it free sent him tumbling down the side of the wall. Luckily, there was a naked man beneath him to break his fall.

An increase in surrounding noise caused Smithy to look up. The dragon was heading straight for him. He leaped up, ignoring the pain assaulting several parts of his body and hopped on to the mower, careful to retain his "lance". The machine kicked into life just as the dragon spewed forth fire. Smithy turned away his shoulder and felt the flames wash over him, his every nerve screaming in pain and primal instinct.

Being at the far end of the arena, Chaz's view was at its worst, which was why the dragon crashed into the wall behind Smithy as he accelerated away. "Accelerated" seemed the wrong word for a top speed of ten miles per hour, but thankfully it was just enough.

Smithy heard screams from the men on the wall. They dived for cover to escape the dragon that had collided with it, buzz saw first. The commotion gave Smithy enough time to at least clear the area. He slapped at his Hawaiian shirt, smothering the flames. He'd feel those burns later. That was assuming there would be a later in which to feel anything.

He looked for the others. In horror, he noticed the mower that Diller had been riding was now a flaming wreck of hammered metal at one side of the arena. Relief flooded through Smithy as he noticed that his friend was on the back of Muroe's mower and seemed OK.

He looked up at the sky and moved himself into position on the other side of the arena, ignoring the barbecued cow parts strewn about him. Only when he was where he needed to be did he allow himself to look back at the dragon. Chaz had extricated it from the wall, leaving a mess in its wake. It turned out to be no bad thing that the naked man had colour-coded himself – if he had friends that were so inclined, they'd at least be able to identify which bits of him were which as they collected him off the floor.

Smithy needed Chaz to come at him right now. He leaped up to stand on the seat of his mower and raised his lance above his head as if in triumph. This received an ovation from the crowd, because even the worst people enjoy an unexpectedly good fight. More importantly, it had the desired effect. The dragon started to accelerate towards him.

Smithy nodded at Muroe, who zoomed off in the opposite direction. He hopped back into the mower's seat and slammed it into gear, heading straight for the oncoming dragon. It was like a game of chicken, only one of them was several tons of speeding metal, and the other might as well have been an actual chicken.

Fifty feet.

Forty feet.

Thirty feet.

Being careful to keep his lance pinned under his left arm as he kept that hand on the steering wheel, with his right hand Smithy grabbed the thing clenched in his armpit that he'd nearly died retrieving.

In the background, Smithy heard a crash. Presumably that was Muroe kamikazeing her mower into the base of the scaffolding supporting the viewing platform. He had no time to look. Assuming their luck hadn't improved, her move wouldn't be enough to bring the structure down, but hopefully it would at least distract those on top of it, which was the whole point.

Twenty feet.

Smithy held out the mirror and moved it around to catch the sun. He twisted it in his hands, hoping against hope that it was hitting the light right. Chaz should be staring right at him and be temporarily blinded right about ...

Ten feet.

Smithy dropped the mirror, leaped up in the saddle and rammed the end of his lance into the ground in front of him.

The mower wasn't going that fast but it gave him the forward momentum he needed. He flew through the air, pole-vaulting towards the oncoming robot.

He felt the flush of flames over his head as he hurtled under the dragon's jet of fire. The whirring buzz saw passed within inches of his face, but he kept his eyes forward.

Smithy crashed messily into the body of the robot, landing on the protective plates above its tracks as it collided with his mower and annihilated it, sending pieces of shattered mower flying. Smithy scrabbled for a handhold. His momentum was in danger of carrying him off the dragon's smooth body. He found one – an actual handle. There to allow engineers easy access as they climbed the massive body.

Above him, the torso spun round and round and round. The flames whooshed and whooshed from the beast's head, as if it were incensed. Smithy was too close for the dragon to scorch him now. He'd been banking on this, but he still needed to keep himself pressed to the floor to avoid being thrown off. More than in any other fight he'd ever been in, if Smithy hit the ground in this one, he was all kinds of dead.

He looked around him. Desperate to find ...

There!

He pulled himself to a control box attached to the Dragon's central shaft. Damn it, the thing was locked.

The dragon stopped suddenly, like a bronco trying to unseat its rider. Smithy's shoulder thumped into the main shaft, jarring it, but he held on, screaming from the excruciating pain.

He wrenched the helmet off his head. Sweat was pouring down his face, mingling with the dust that the tracks threw up as they tore up the ground, reversing direction.

He slammed his helmet into the padlock on the control box.

Once.

Twice.

On the third attempt the padlock didn't break, but the metal on the control box buckled just enough. Smithy dropped his helmet and pushed his hand into the gap, the jagged metal slicing it. He felt around and found something hot and metallic. He pulled at it. Then he found some cabling and wrenched it with all his might.

For a second, nothing happened.

And then, the engine spluttered and died. The whirling torso coming to a stop. The dragon made an odd whining noise and juddered to a halt.

CHAPTER TWENTY-NINE

Reginald Wilkins did not want to be here. In this desert, at this camp, on this viewing platform. He didn't want any of it. Now into his sixties, he wasn't ashamed to say he enjoyed sitting by the fire in a climate that suited such an extravagance, drinking a fine port and reading a good book while enjoying the earlier works of Metallica, before they went all soft and commercial.

Master Charlie Breddenback was at least consistent; from an early age he'd been an ungrateful yet grating little shit, and he'd duly grown into a big one. That the man was undoubtedly losing his mind was irrefutable. This is what happens when terrible children are told they are wonderful. Charlie's mother had a great deal to answer for. Mind you, his father was such a monumental arse that Wilkins couldn't entirely blame her for doting on the boy. She wasn't to know she was enabling a continuing and rapid decline in the standard of Breddenback men.

Wilkins had been their butler, a role he had slipped into by accident after a rather "colourful" early life. His cousin Bernie had been working for a friend of the Breddenback family when they'd caught their original butler with his hand in the cookie jar. Wilkins had no idea how to do the job. He'd been a squaddie from Oldham, outside Manchester, and thanks to getting involved in some extracurricular activities beyond the traditional remit of the British army, he was technically AWOL and a person with whom Her Majesty's forces were very keen to have a chat.

Bernie had laid it out for him – just fake the accent, learn the made-up backstory, and mind your Ps and Qs. The Yanks aren't able to tell who is proper posh and who is some grunt from Oldham looking to hide out for a bit. That had been all the job was supposed to be – a temporary place to lie low – but he'd discovered that the more he did it, the more he liked it.

He had soon relaxed, realising that all his masters wanted was someone who could say, 'Very good, sir' and 'Will that be all, sir?' in the right accent. He was protected by something better than a watertight backstory. He was staff, an underling, and they didn't ask because they simply didn't care. They weren't interested in getting to know you, because it is weird to ask someone to clean up after you when you see them as a fully rounded human being.

Beyond his all-important looking-like-a-butler duties, his other main role was managing staff and, in all honesty, the housekeeper Mrs Jacobs did that without his interference. Some women are just born to be in charge of things, and once you get out of their way, life becomes easier for everybody. Early on, he'd realised that she was from New Jersey but putting on an Irish accent – again, for the look of the thing. He kept her secret and she, if she had any inkling, kept his. He also consistently miscounted the house's supply of whiskey in her favour.

He had played the part for over forty years now, and at some point the act had become who he was – the grunt from Oldham disappeared into the background. That wasn't to say that he hadn't retained some skills. When a former associate of Breddenback Senior had sent a team of four men to steal the collection to use as leverage, the butler had dealt with it in an unexpectedly brutal manner. Senior had asked no awkward questions, recognising an asset when he saw one.

From that moment on, Wilkins had become the keeper of the

collection. *His* collection. Nobody else called it that, and he had never dreamed of speaking those words aloud, but that is how he thought of it. He liked the role a lot more, not least because dealing with mewling irritations such as little Charlie Breddenback had become someone else's problem. At least, until now.

And so, life had gone on until Charlie had messed things up so completely. The "competition"' was supposed to be in name only. The idea was that you found the winning pieces before you invited the others to play. It was meant to be a way for the family to show off their collection to the right, carefully selected people while proving their worth in that most traditional of ways enjoyed by old-money types: winning a competition heavily stacked in their favour.

Instead, Charlie had truly tried to prove his worth and, although not in the way intended, he had. He'd screwed it up and lost. Even then, the family wasn't willing to give up the collection as stipulated in the rules – they took the far easier route of disowning Charlie, which had led to the boy losing his marbles. Charlie had sent six men to capture both Wilkins and the collection.

In hindsight, Wilkins was regretting not going down fighting. Somewhere along the line it seemed he'd lost his edge. In his defence, if he had known that they would transport him and his precious collection to some moronic hellhole in the desert, then he would have taken down as many as he could on his way out.

Breddenback Junior might be insane and crammed full of enough pharmaceuticals that even Keith Richards would need a lie-in, but Wilkins had to be careful when and how to push him. He had been able to ensure proper lodgings for the collection here, but he could not ignore Charlie's "invitation" to attend this debacle.

Reluctantly, he had made certain security arrangements to protect his precious things while he was away. The museum was locked up tight, but he doubted that would dissuade all but the most lackadaisical of cutpurses. On the other hand, the anti-personnel mines that he'd strategically placed ... he was keeping an ear out. The first explosion would be the sound of any interloper being discouraged – quite possibly, permanently. If he heard a second one, he'd make his apologies and return to man the battlements.

In the meantime, he sat there and tried to remain detached from the madness. The music, assuming that was what it was, had been like an aural root canal. Then, Charlie had turned up in his gold lamé cape and crown, reminding Wilkins of a child at play. The boy avoided looking at him, Wilkins noted, as if he were an unwelcome reminder of his family. That had proved helpful to a certain degree, but now he was "spiralling", as people called it nowadays.

It felt as if it were only a matter of time before Charlie decided that it would be easier to kill Wilkins than to have him about the place. That was assuming this monstrous folly didn't come crashing down around his ears before then. Either way, Wilkins knew enough that he and the collection needed a way out, and fast. He had rather pinned his hopes on Ms Muroe and her associates in that regard. It was therefore a great disappointment to him when they'd been led out to the slaughter.

The subsequent battle involving Charlie and his mechanical monstrosity had come as a delightful surprise. Embarrassingly, Master Breddenback had demanded his opponents to stand still, as if they'd gone against the spirit of the game by not dying. This Smithy character, whoever he was, lacked neither ingenuity nor bravery.

Messrs Reed and Finley had all but jumped off the platform when the industrious Ms Muroe had crashed her mower into it. Wilkins had remained seated and given them his best withering stare. What kind of man got on a platform without first giving its foundations a scan to see how soundly it was constructed? A little wobble wasn't going to take it down. Did they not recognise a diversionary tactic when they felt it? Master Breddenback had always had such disappointing friends.

As the robot had ground to a halt, Wilkins found he had to restrain himself from punching the air. In stark contrast, Charlie took defeat with all the grace of Elton John before he finally cleaned up his act. He screamed and hurled the remote control from the platform. He then snatched an AR-15 semi-automatic rifle from one of the nearby guards and emptied an entire clip in the direction of the now-defunct robot. This led several people to seek cover as bullets ricocheted off its metal hide.

"He cheated!" screamed Charlie as he tossed away the empty machine gun.

"No," said Wilkins, "he did not."

Charlie whirled around and glowered at him. "Excuse me?"

Wilkins cursed himself. He had not intended to speak. It had rather popped out. Still, in for a penny, in for a pound. If he died now, odds were good it would be quick, and that would be something. He didn't wish to go like a cow staked to the ground.

He stood up and spoke in a calm voice. "Respectfully, Master Breddenback, the diminutive gentleman and his colleagues did not cheat. I appreciate they used unconventional tactics, but traditionally speaking, small indigenous forces have always engaged in using such methods when faced with superior odds."

He watched as Charlie's right hand twitched and considered the gun holstered at his belt. The behemoth Zero was standing behind Wilkins. Wilkins's sword had been confiscated by one of the guards at the bottom of the stairs on their way up. He still reckoned that if he surged forward now, he had a good chance at taking Charlie over the side of the platform with him. If he had to die, he'd like to know it would be in the noble cause of ending this madness once and for all. The only thought that stayed his hand was of the collection that had become his life's work, and what would happen to it without him.

Wilkins shifted his feet, preparing himself.

"Right of challenge."

Both he and Charlie paused. The voice had come from down below.

A hand popped up at the edge of the platform, holding out a white tissue and waving it around. "Right of challenge," repeated the voice.

"What?" said Charlie.

The head of the young African-American gentleman – Diller,

wasn't it? – appeared and disappeared quickly, having scanned the platform. It then reappeared, looking understandably nervous.

"Right of challenge," he said again. "We claim right of challenge."

"What are you talking about?" snapped Charlie.

"This is, like, a Roman gladiator battle, right?"

"Yes."

"Well, as is traditional – as victors in the arena – we have the right to challenge someone. We wish to be allowed into that demolition derby thing."

Charlie placed his fingers on the grip of his holstered sidearm. "That's bullshit."

"No," said Wilkins, stepping forward. "The gentleman has it correct. In Roman times, if gladiators fought at the behest of the emperor and won, he gave them the right of challenge."

Wilkins locked eyes with Diller.

"Yeah," said Diller. "We claim that ... please."

Charlie gave a barking laugh. "Let me get this straight," he said. "You three would like to enter a car in the demolition derby tomorrow?"

"Yes, please," confirmed Diller.

Wilkins noticed the strained expression on his face. He guessed Diller didn't have the firmest of grips on the scaffolding below, but wisely thought that climbing up fully wasn't the best of ideas.

"Do you have a car? That's rather important for a demolition derby!" Charlie slapped Zero on one of his enormous pectoral muscles, enjoying his own joke even if nobody else did. Zero kept staring off into the distance.

"We don't have a car, yet," admitted Diller. "But there's all this scrap. We could build one, please ... Your Majesty." He winced, afraid that last bit might be a bit too far.

"And who is on your team, exactly?"

"Well."

Diller looked over at Finley and Reed, who ignored him steadfastly. "Me, Ms Muroe, Smithy – assuming he's still alive after you …" Diller thought better of the implied criticism in that statement.

"And me," said Wilkins.

Charlie turned to look at him. "What?"

"Yes, I've always enjoyed tinkering with vehicles and what not."

Wilkins stood there for the longest of moments as Charlie regarded him. He tried not to notice how Charlie's left eye twitched as he did so.

Eventually, Charlie reached his hand down to the regrettable Elvis impersonator, who was cowering at the side of the stage. "Give me the mic."

Elvis handed it over and Charlie turned to the arena. "As your beneficent Emperor I have decided to let these knights, who CHEATED to win this battle, have another chance to prove themselves honourable. Therefore, they shall take part in the demolition derby tomorrow. The Emperor has spoken!"

Charlie turned away, so thankfully didn't notice a couple of members of the crowd making gestures at him.

"Zero, make sure that our guests have everything they need, and that they don't attempt to use this as an opportunity to depart before they have a chance to redeem themselves."

Zero nodded.

Wilkins looked down at Diller and gave him the briefest of nods. He hoped that Master Breddenback was too far gone to go to the trouble of accessing Google – all the "right to challenge" stuff he and Diller had just trotted out was utter nonsense.

Wilkins had decided that this was his one chance of getting out of here. One way or another, he doubted he'd live to regret it.

CHAPTER THIRTY

A wave of relief hit Diller as he saw Smithy walking across the arena floor towards them. He had to resist the urge to rush across and hug him. Smithy wasn't big on displays of affection at the best of times, and Diller imagined that went double for them happening in front of a baying mob. To be fair, the baying mob had mostly wandered off – at least those who weren't going over to look at the remains of Dragonzilla. Diller was a little pleased on that front too. The remote control had almost hit him in the head when Chaz had thrown it away in his petulant tantrum. It was no Han Solo's blaster, but it was still pretty cool – a bona fide collector's item.

Behind Diller came Muroe and that odd Wilkins guy, plus Zero and their ever-present retinue of guards. When they got closer, Diller noticed that Smithy was limping and holding his shoulder.

"Are you alright?"

"Nothing a couple of months' bed rest and a lake of whiskey couldn't fix. I'm not sure I heard that right because my ears were still ringing from getting shot at a lot, but are we in a demolition derby now?"

Diller shrugged. "I thought ..." He looked around at Zero and the others. "It was that or, well, we saw what happened to the ninja dude."

Smithy nodded. "No, it was a smart idea, Dill."

"How are we going to build a car in twenty-four hours?" asked Muroe.

"Badly, I imagine," said Smithy. "I know a bit about cars. Does anyone else have any great expertise in that area?"

Wilkins cleared his throat. "I know a little. Speaking of which." He turned to Zero and pointed at the remains of Dragonzilla that several scavengers had already set to work on. "Seeing as these three bested that monstrosity, clearly they have salvage rights to it."

Zero looked down at him blankly.

Wilkins sighed. "So, you need to send some of your men over there immediately and stop those jackals stripping everything of use from it. Or should I take this up with Master Breddenback?"

Zero remained motionless for a couple of seconds, then pointed at the wreckage. Two of his men duly made their way across the arena floor and shooed away the interested parties. Diller noticed several of them still left with souvenirs, including the buzz saw.

"We shall also need somewhere to work," said Wilkins. "I am willing to offer my museum."

Zero nodded.

"OK," said Muroe. "Let's go."

"Splendid," said Wilkins. "I'll lead the way. Do stay behind me. Otherwise you might find yourself dispersed over a wide area."

As they left the arena, Diller noticed that it appeared a game of baseball was starting up. There was something heart-warming about the sight. Amidst all the insanity, and among the violent lunatics that surrounded them, it was heartening to see these men playing a simple game.

Then he noticed they were using the head of the painted naked guy as the ball.

CHAPTER THIRTY-ONE

Smithy, Diller and Muroe waited patiently while Wilkins disarmed his museum.

"I only have the two mines and a few improvised little distractions, but one does what one can." The way the man was talking, it was as if he were apologising for having only one kind of dip at a party.

Wilkins's next move was to set about packing away the contents of the museum. Diller's offer to help was very firmly rejected. The man really did not like people touching his stuff. The heavy ordnance should have been a clue.

"Right," said Smithy, clapping his hands. "We need a team meeting."

Muroe looked pointedly at Zero and his cohort, who were standing around wearing a collection of expressions that were an attempt to look tough and bored at the same time. "Team meetings have to be private."

"Says who?" asked the one with the eye patch.

"Oh no." Muroe shook her head. "We're not coming up with genius design ideas so that you can sell them to the other teams. Not on my watch."

"We gotta guard you."

"You can do that from the other end of the room."

Begrudgingly, the four men moved away.

Muroe watched them go, then turned to her team. "First off, has anyone got a genius design idea?"

"No," said Smithy. "I'm hoping we can maybe get a car together. Otherwise, we are going to be going into this thing criminally under-dressed."

"We're not actually competing in the thing, are we?" asked Wilkins. "I assumed this was just a delaying tactic so we can escape."

"It is," said Smithy. "The problem is that even in his messed-up brain, that thought's going to occur to Chaz, too."

"So, what do we do?" asked Diller.

"In the absence of any other ideas, we build a car. The three of us" – he indicated himself, Muroe and Wilkins – "can go scavenging for parts. Diller, you need to do what you do."

"By which you mean?"

"Go be a people person. Get out there in the camp and find out everything you can."

"Is that wise?" asked Wilkins. "The young lad might find it all a bit much."

Diller smiled at this. He had long ago decided that people underestimating him was something to be embraced and used to his advantage.

Smithy shook his head. "He'll be careful, but trust me – he's our best shot at getting the hell out of here." With that, Smithy raised his voice and turned to the guards at the end of the room. "OK, we need the two tow trucks that brought that Dragonzilla thing into the arena. We got to go find ourselves a car!"

"Yeah," said Diller, "and I need a pen and a clipboard."

CHAPTER THIRTY-TWO

At another time, this place would have been heaven to Smithy. It wasn't as if he were a real "car guy" – he could name most of the parts of an engine, maybe even replace a couple of them, but that was all. Still, the place was extraordinary. The junkyard stretched off into the distance. Whoever had owned it before it had become Nowhere had accumulated thousands of wrecked cars, for reasons unclear. Most of them were not much more than rusted shells, but there were plenty that looked as if they could be working vehicles again, with enough TLC. More than that, the place had a real sense of history to it. Cars from every decade were stacked on top of one another, like layers of rock concealing the treasures of bygone generations.

Now was not a time for a leisurely sightseeing stroll, though – they needed to find a way out of this madness. If that meant competing in this demolition derby then so be it. They had a day, little in the way of tools, and nothing in the way of a car.

Once they'd got their hands on the two tow trucks, complete with trailers, they'd headed to the arena. Unfortunately, by the time they got there, much of the remains of Dragonzilla had been stripped. So much for Zero's men protecting them. They really could've used those tank tracks, but all that remained was some of the steel armour that had been too heavy for the scavengers to carry away. Smithy took all they could, figuring he'd decide what to do with it later.

Once they'd finished up there, their little convoy rolled on to the junkyard proper. Smithy wasn't completely ignorant of cars, but at the same time, he didn't feel confident of really being able to build one from scratch, at least not in the time allowed. Luckily, as it turned out, he didn't have to. He, Wilkins and Muroe climbed down from the trucks and eyed the masses of metal stretching away in haphazard rows for as far as the eye could see.

"OK," said Muroe, retying her hair in a tight bun at the back of her head, "let's see what we're working with." She turned to Wilkins. "Jeeves, you got much experience with cars?"

"Well, I drove a Rolls-Royce for a few years."

"Super. If we need somebody picked up from the airport, you're our guy. Smithy?"

"I'm good with electronics and I've done some basic repairs but—"

"OK, you're my assistant."

Smithy raised an eyebrow.

"Yeah. Before I started making deals with the devil, I spent my awkward teenage years working in my uncle Bert's shop. I'm not saying I'm him, but neither of you two is either, so let's go with me. Now, what do we need?"

"A car?" ventured Wilkins.

"Good guess, but entirely wrong. We need an engine. That'll be the biggest get. Bigger the better, assuming it's working – or that we can get it to, in the crappy amount of time we've got. Then, we need a decent chassis to put it in. Something that can hold up that armour – assuming we're going with that, which I'm guessing we are. We don't have much in terms of offensive weapons, so I imagine hanging in there and hoping for the best is our tactic. There are lots of other things we need, but I'll explain as we go.

"Split up, start opening hoods. You find an engine that looks like it might work, come call me. Also, when you open a hood, stand well back. You're in the desert. Odds are the local wildlife might be using it for some shade and won't be too happy about you disturbing them. Everyone clear?"

Wilkins and Smithy nodded.

"Great." Muroe pointed at one of the three lackies with Zero – the beanpole with the broken nose and the forehead you could screen movies on. "You, tall guy, come with me. I'm going to need a hand carrying stuff."

"Not my job."

"Sure. Shall we go ask the mighty emperor if carrying stuff falls within your remit? He strikes me as the type of guy who loves to clarify small details."

The guy gave a disgruntled nod of assent.

"Super."

Smithy spoke in a low voice. "Are you sure that's a good idea?"

"Oh, yes," said Wilkins. "Ms Muroe wisely chose the homosexual amongst our captors."

"Really?"

Smithy craned his neck to look around her at the beanpole. "How can you possibly tell?"

"Takes one to know one."

"Oh. Right," said Smithy, looking up at Wilkins. "Well, this group is just full of surprises."

"It is confusing. People are often unsure if my manners, good deportment and high standard of personal hygiene are indicative of my sexuality, or merely a by-product of being English. It happens to be both."

Smithy nodded awkwardly. "Cool."

"I am so relieved to have your acceptance. Now, if you'll excuse me, I have to go and not get bitten by a rattlesnake."

CHAPTER THIRTY-THREE

Diller stood at the entrance to what had been the museum and was about to become their garage. The sun was already starting to dip as they headed towards evening, and time was of the essence.

His assigned chaperone was the guy sporting the toothbrush moustache, mohawk and scar that ran down the left side of his face. Diller had never heard the man speak – over the last couple of days the guy had spent their time together really focusing on his sneering game. Still, like Diller's mom had told him on his first day at school, people who seem unfriendly are often just scared or shy. You'll be amazed what kind of response you'll get if you're kind to them.

Those words had served Diller mostly well. He had been actively trying to keep thoughts of his mom out of his mind since they'd been here. Assuming what Muroe had said was true, her recovery back there – in what he was struggling not to think of as the sane world – would hopefully be going well. Nothing else mattered. OK, it did – but still, the thought of her getting well was a great comfort to him.

Diller remembered another piece of advice she had given him: 'Where possible, open with a compliment.'

He put on a smile and extended his hand to his chaperone. "Hi there. Cool moustache. You don't see that style much these days because of the, y'know, associations, but you really make it work."

The man looked at Diller's hand and then at his face, making no effort to accept the handshake. After Diller had left it there for a couple of lonely seconds, he threw his hand up in a jaunty salute. "Sorry, I'm Diller by the way."

The man opened his lips, revealing an unhappy collection of issues that could pay for a dentist's second divorce. "Adolf."

"Cool. Is that, like, a nickname you got because of the—"

"No. Mine since birth."

"Right. Sure, I mean, why not? It is crazy for a name to be off the table just because one guy had it. I mean, people still call their kids Ted and Charlie and, y'know ... whatever other serial killers are called. I like how you sort of leaned into it with the moustache too. Really owning it."

This earned Diller a confused look, before the man turned and showed him the tattoo on his right shoulder.

"Ah, cool. Nice tattoo. I'm seeing a theme here. 'White power'. I mean, 'power' doesn't normally have that many Os in it but, y'know, language is always evolving, isn't it?"

Not for the first time in his life, someone found Diller a disconcerting potential victim. The man was not used to a black guy complimenting him on his racist beliefs; he found it unsettling. Diller kept going, talking as if they were firm friends, to the point where Adolf was feeling as if one of them had missed something fundamental in their interaction, and he wasn't sure if it was him or not.

"OK, well, we'd better hop to it."

"What you doing?"

"That is an excellent question."

Diller spent the next fifteen minutes wandering about. Men were sitting around drinking in groups of three or four, sometimes more. As Diller walked by, people stopped to look, and often made remarks. He received quite a few compliments, or what he attempted to think of as such. However, it really was a stretch, seeing as they involved references to what could be politely referred to as "prison-style romance". Apparently, he'd be worth a whole carton of cigarettes, which, even as a non-smoker, Diller took to be quite a lot.

To casual observers, it would have looked like he was wandering about aimlessly, mainly because he was. He didn't have a plan, but he hoped that one would present itself to him. Smithy was counting on him and, more than anything, Diller didn't want to let him down. Well, that desire possibly came second to wanting the carton of cigarettes situation to remain hypothetical.

At one point, Adolf found a wrench lying about, and threw it at the back of Diller's head. Luckily, Diller followed the "walk softly and watch out for big sticks" approach, so he'd been half expecting it. He ducked and then, to Adolf's great annoyance, picked up the wrench and shoved it in his back pocket.

"Thanks, dude, we'll definitely need one of those."

Various shacks were constructed around other larger permanent buildings in the camp. Diller scanned them but did not attempt to enter. From the noises he heard, he figured some of them were being used to prep their competition for the demolition derby tomorrow. As for the others, well – he tried not to think about what was going on in those.

A friend of Adolf's came up and they had a chat which contained enough racial slurs to set race relations back a good decade all on its own. The overall tone suggested Adolf was a pussy for being Diller's babysitter. Diller had always known that there was a limited window of time before the guy ostensibly protecting him became the guy he needed protection from.

For a second time, they passed the boxing ring, where two relatively small guys were sparring in a reasonably civilised manner, while a few clusters of spectators sat around, half watching. Diller approached a group situated under a couple of large sun umbrellas, passing a bottle of whiskey and some funny-smelling cigarettes between them. There were half a dozen men in total.

It reminded Diller of the time he'd gone for a casting call for guys Jason Statham needed to beat up in a movie. He'd not got a callback. He'd not even made it into the room. The assistant had politely explained that Jason only beat up large guys in groups of three or more, or occasionally a duo of Asian guys who clearly knew martial arts. He did not slap skinny black kids around on film as it was bad for the brand. Still, Diller had got a free soda for his troubles.

None of these guys would've got the shove-off and free soda. There was enough muscle and latent belligerent violence in the group that the casting director would've got a bonus for this haul. Tattoos, scars, facial disfigurements – this group had it all. One of them even had a Pit Bull that was lounging around at his feet, receiving the occasional ear scratch. Diller figured to go for the group that was mean enough not just to have the only sun umbrellas available in the middle of a desert, but also feared enough that nobody else wanted to challenge them on the matter.

"Hey, guys. I'm Diller. I hope you're all having a lovely day here at Camp Nowhere."

His opening gambit was met with a mixture of raised eyebrows and laughs.

"We're having a super time," said the one with the hook for a hand, in a mocking falsetto. "Who the fuck are you – the Avon lady?"

This was met with more laughter, which Diller joined in with.

"Sort of. Hey," he said, glancing down at his clipboard, "is one of you a gentleman by the name of Zeus?" He'd spotted the tattoo and taken a chance.

The guy tilted his head to the side and squinted around the large blunt he was smoking. "Who wants to know?"

"Oh, I'm just checking. You see, I asked Adolf back there who the toughest guy here was, and he said you."

Zeus looked at Adolf, whose expression remained blank. He couldn't deny a compliment.

"Hey, Zeus," said the man with the dog, "looks like you got a fan."

This raised a laugh from the rest of the men, and a smile from Zeus.

"Yeah," said Diller. "He said Zeus must be the toughest son of a bitch here because nobody ever mentions his—" Diller stopped himself. "D'ya know what, never mind. Anyway, it's been—"

Zeus threw out his leg to stop Diller from turning around. "Never mentions my what?"

"Nothing," said Diller, before turning to Adolf. "Honestly, it's not that noticeable. I mean, I can't smell it at all."

Zeus stood up. "What the fuck?"

"Hey," said Adolf. "I didn't say nothing. I don't know what the hell he's talking about."

"He's right," agreed Diller. "I misremembered the whole conversation."

Zeus grabbed Diller by the shirt and pulled him close. "What exactly did he not say?"

"C'mon," said Adolf. "Who you gonna believe, me or some dumbass nig—"

The large black guy at the back of the group was on his feet and striding purposefully towards Adolf. "What you say, white boy?"

"No, I didn't say ..."

Zeus released his grip on Diller, as the offended man went nose to nose with Adolf.

"Seems to me you racist butt-munchers only ever get chatty behind closed doors and brave in large groups. How 'bout you and me have ourselves a little chat right now. *Mano a mano.*"

Zeus grinned. "You tell him, Darnell. The boy got way too big a mouth on him."

"Gentlemen, gentlemen," said Diller in a conciliatory tone, moving towards the two men. "There's no need for violence."

"The hell there isn't."

"I'm supposed to be following him," said Adolf weakly.

"Well, maybe I don't like seeing some racist shitbird following a brother around."

Darnell bumped his chest against Adolf. In most fights, Adolf would be the big dog, but Darnell was built like an NFL defensive lineman. He wasn't the size of Zero – nobody was – but he still had several inches on Adolf, who stood there, his mouth flapping open and closed as he tried to catch up with his rapidly deteriorating situation.

The altercation was gathering quite a bit of attention from around the camp.

"Perhaps," said Diller, "the best thing would be to settle this in the ring, like gentlemen?"

Several voices rang out echoing his sentiment. The fact that Adolf's wasn't one of them became irrelevant.

Diller stood at the back of the crowd as the two men were escorted to the ring, Adolf protesting all the way but being roughly guided by multiple hands.

As the bell rang, Diller slipped away. He hadn't even got around the corner of the large shipping crates before it was over. He'd glanced over his shoulder at just the right moment to see the crowd roaring on Darnell as he picked up his unconscious opponent, held him above his head and tossed him out of the ring.

Diller looked down at his clipboard.

"To do – lose chaperone. Check!"

CHAPTER THIRTY-FOUR

Smithy had ended up with Zero and the guy with the disconcerting twitch as his minders. He wasn't sure if he should take that to mean they saw him as the biggest threat of escape, or that they didn't want to be on the receiving end of any more of Wilkins's barbed remarks.

The two of them followed Smithy awkwardly as he clambered around the stacks of vehicles, opening the hoods of various wrecks to see if their engines looked useful. At one point, Smithy had found a lug wrench in the cab of a truck, which led to the twitchy dude mouthing off about him having a weapon. Smithy then reminded him that a lug wrench, despite being great for smashing some poor unfortunate over the head with, could also be used to remove the tyres from a vehicle, and they were going to need to do some of that. Twitchy had looked at Zero, who, after a moment, had given one of those nods he was so good at.

The wrench had come in handy when opening the hood on a Trans Am, which had brought Smithy face to face with two scorpions that didn't seem happy to see him. They'd possibly been interrupted mid-coitus, or else one of them had been in the middle of attacking the other. Either way, they'd both turned their attention to Smithy, who walloped one of them and got the hell out of there before the other could lodge any further objections. From then on, Smithy followed a policy of beating a quick rhythm on any cars he was investigating and then stepping away, giving any wildlife the chance to remove itself calmly from the area.

As the trio moved on to the third row of stacked cars, Smithy's enthusiasm was waning. So far, in the cars that still had engines, nothing had looked close to usable. In over an hour of looking he'd found only a wrench, a working jack and a crowbar. At each find Twitchy had expressed his reservations. For a man holding a submachine gun, he had a remarkably nervous disposition.

At the top of another pile, Smithy spotted a Volkswagen Beetle. He sighed and wiped the sweat from his brow. "Alright, I'm going to check that." He walloped the door of one of the lower cars loudly with the crowbar and then dropped all the tools. "Can one of you keep an eye on my stash of weapons? I'd hate it if they were stolen."

Twitchy sneered at Smithy as he began to climb. A couple of cars up, Smithy felt the pile lurch sickeningly towards him. He tried to jump down but his Hawaiian shirt was pinned between grinding pieces of metal.

"Fuck," screamed Twitchy, correctly assessing the situation as he scampered heroically to safety.

Smithy clenched his eyes shut and then, after a moment, registered that the anticipated pain had not come. Instead, when he opened his eyes again, Zero's immense arms were beside him, pushing the pile back into place. Smithy removed the tail of his shirt from where it was caught and looked across at Zero's bullet-like head.

"Thank you."

Zero gave him another of his trademark nods.

Smithy abandoned the Beetle as an unwise risk and moved on to the next pile, where he hit pay dirt in a Corvette. The engine looked great, and while he first needed to remove a rattlesnake using the crowbar and wrench as a pair of makeshift tongs, the fact that the reptile accidentally flew in Twitchy's general direction did wonders for morale.

Smithy ignored the man's expletive-laden diatribe as he inspected the engine.

"I mean, I'm no expert, but this looks like an engine to me."

He glanced at Zero standing above him, who regarded it impassively.

"OK," said Smithy. "Can someone go get Muroe, see what she thinks?"

Smithy looked at Twitchy.

"Screw you. That ain't my job."

Zero pointed in a way that made it obvious he felt otherwise. Muttering darkly to himself, Twitchy made his way down the aisle to go find the others. As he disappeared from view, Zero turned to Smithy.

"Thank God, you have got to help me!"

CHAPTER THIRTY-FIVE

Smithy sat quietly while the big man stood there, hands on his knees, having what – to Smithy's untrained eye – looked a lot like a panic attack. The whole thing felt incredibly awkward. What was he supposed to do? Climb up a couple of cars so he could reach across and pat the guy on the back?

"OK, just breathe," said Smithy. He had no medical knowledge but that seemed like safe advice for almost every situation.

Zero looked at him, his face flushed. "I'm sorry, it's just ... This whole thing has been an absolute nightmare!"

Until this point Smithy had heard little more than grunts from the guy. His voice was unexpectedly high with a hint of a lisp to it.

Zero sat down against a car, causing the whole stack to judder alarmingly. "OK, I'm sorry, just ..." He took a couple more deep breaths. "I have been trying to talk to you guys since you got here, but I could not find an opportunity."

"Right," said Smithy, still trying to get his head around this. "But you're Chaz's second-in-command?"

Zero looked as if he might faint. "He keeps calling me that! I got booked for this gig through my agent. I'm an actor."

"You're kidding me?"

"No. I mean, I also kinda do bodyguard work – sort of. Look, I follow rappers around to award ceremonies. People just like having a large guy to stand behind them. Y'know, for the look of the thing. I'm not actually protection. If you want that, you go get some discreet special-forces dude. I'm a bodybuilder. I don't even carry a gun – I hate the things. And my name isn't Zero – it's Keith! I turn up here, thinking it'll just be the usual. Y'know, follow someone about and look menacing, and then this Chaz guy starts calling me Zero and telling people he saw me twist a guy's head off. I didn't do that! I'm a Buddhist."

Zero, or Keith as he should apparently be known, put his head between his legs. "Oh God, oh God, oh God! I only took this gig because my mom is behind on her condo payments."

"But he's been giving you orders," said Smithy. "I've seen him."

"I know!" squealed the artist formerly known as Zero. "He keeps saying things like, 'Have the men been drilled?' I don't know! How would I do that? I'll be honest, I'd have got the hell out of here once I realised how insane it was, but have you seen the guys around here? These monsters find out I'm not who he says I am and they'll eat me alive. That's why I've just been nodding and grunting. I've been bluffing the whole thing!"

"I see," said Smithy. "Well, if it is any consolation, you are really good. I mean, I never suspected for a second."

The man placed one of his meaty paws on Smithy's shoulder. "Thank you so much. You don't know how much that means to me. I've been going to classes for a couple of years, but let's be honest, roles are incredibly limited for someone like me. I've been pencilled to get the crap beaten out of me by Jason Statham next year."

Smithy was taken aback to discover the man was a kindred spirit. Nobody knew better than him how frustrating it was to be pigeonholed as an actor because of your size. He patted the hand of the artist formerly known as Zero. "Hey, that's a tough gig to get. Don't put yourself down. My friend didn't even make it into the room at that audition."

Zero leaned back his head. "I just want this to be over. Chaz has asked me twice now to spank him for being a naughty boy. I keep grunting and walking off. Between you and me, that guy has some serious issues."

"Yeah," said Smithy. "I was getting that vibe alright."

The artist formerly known as Zero stood up as they heard the distinctive sound of Wilkins being withering coming from around the corner.

"Let's hope this row is the right one," the butler was saying. "I don't want to die of exhaustion while Pocahontas here leads us around in circles."

"Oh no," said Zero, flapping his hands in front of his face. "They're coming back. C'mon, Keith. Get it together." He leaned down and grabbed Smithy's shoulder again. "Please, I know you guys must be working on a way out of here. You've got to take me with you! I'll do all I can to help."

Keith straightened up just as Muroe, Wilkins and their minders came around the corner. Smithy looked up to see Zero once again, standing there impassively.

"See," said Twitchy. "I told you this was the place."

Zero nodded. Damn, he really was good.

CHAPTER THIRTY-SIX

"Where the hell is he?"

For the first hour they'd been back at the ex-museum, now garage, it had been Smithy who had been assuring all and sundry that Diller would be fine and not to worry about him. Now he cracked and admitted that he was terrified.

Smithy had held it together until the point at which Diller's chaperone had returned, sporting a badly bandaged head wound and a particularly surly disposition. All that Smithy had been able to get out of him was that Diller had disappeared, but only after getting him into a fight.

Zero was nowhere to be seen, having been called off to attend to whatever lunatic request Chaz had had now, which may or may not have involved spanking.

"Look," said Muroe, "you said it yourself – he's a resourceful guy. He'll be fine."

"Yeah, well, I'm an idiot. If I wasn't an idiot, not only would I not be here, but neither would he. I sent him out into this pack of feral low-lifes. What the hell was I thinking?"

Several of the feral low-lives who were sitting nearby, playing cards, reacted in such a way that made it clear they weren't wild about this description, but Smithy was past caring. As if they didn't have enough problems on their plate, Chaz had sent over half a dozen more guards to watch them around the clock. No reason was given. That was the thing with megalomaniacs literally high on their own supply – reasons are rarely given and dangerous to ask for.

Muroe had already spoken to the guards about getting tools, and despite her considerable efforts cajoling and threatening, they offered no help. If Smithy were able to care, he'd have noticed that the threat of Chaz's wrath no longer carried the weight it once had.

The mission to the junkyard had gone pretty well. They'd found a Chevrolet, a less precariously positioned Volkswagen Beetle and a station wagon, all of which had mostly working engines and out of which Muroe reckoned she could make something. They'd spent the last hour of daylight rushing around trying to find various parts. Muroe had said they might have what they needed, or else they'd have to go back to the junkyard at dawn to find it.

Of course, that was assuming they made it to dawn – Smithy was about to use some of the scant tools they had to fight his way out of the garage to see if he could locate Diller. He was trying and failing not to picture what might be happening to him when his thoughts were interrupted by a loud bang on the door.

Smithy ran over to answer it, which caused several of the card-playing guards – those who had a bad hand that they were delighted to drop, presumably – to get up and block his way.

"Well, somebody open the damn door, then."

Somebody did.

A wave of relief so strong washed over Smithy. He felt like collapsing to his knees.

"Where the hell have you been?"

Diller looked taken aback. "Sorry, Dad. I was out making friends in the neighbourhood, like you asked me to."

Adolf stood up from his seat. "I want a word with you, fuckface."

"Oh, hey, Adolf," said Diller cheerfully. "I was wondering where you had got to."

"Adolf?" said Smithy. "Seriously?"

"Since birth. Family tradition." Diller stepped to one side in the doorway and waved his clipboard. "Sorry, come on in."

Smithy watched in amazement as four men entered the garage, carrying equipment.

"I didn't know what we needed, but I asked some of the guys for suggestions." He pointed at the stuff as it came in. "We got a mechanic's full tool kit, a drill, a bandsaw that can cut metal – isn't that right, Fido?"

A guy wearing a dog collar – not of the clerical variety – nodded enthusiastically.

The last guy to walk in was Cobra – or the Cobra, to give him his full title, aka the guy who had fought the ninja assassin. "And last but not least, my man El Cobra is lending us his oxy-acetylene welding kit."

Diller's new acquaintances put the equipment down.

Adolf had almost reached Diller and was pulling a blade from his boot. "I'm gonna fuck you up."

Adolf didn't see the headbutt coming, so the first thing he knew he was on the floor, his head spinning, as three versions of the Cobra stood over him. They blended into one blurry one, which grabbed him around the throat.

"Anybody lays a finger on the Dill-dog, they answer to me. ¿Comprende?"

Adolf had the common sense to nod before falling unconscious.

The Cobra turned and embraced Diller.

"*Gracias, amigo*," said Diller. "I'm going to stick you down for an extra box of those cigars you like."

The Cobra extended his hands to indicate this was too much.

"No, I insist. You've been great. All of you. Thank you so much."

The quartet of killers waved their goodbyes as if they were leaving their grandma's birthday party, and made their exit.

Diller turned to the three stunned expressions looking back at him.

"Hey, guys, how'd it go at the junkyard?"

Smithy, Wilkins and Muroe looked at one another before Muroe cleared her throat. "Time for a team meeting, gentlemen?"

Their group huddled between the cars, away from the prying ears of their guards.

"OK," said Smithy. "First things first. I think I speak for everyone here, Diller, when I say how in the hell?"

Diller turned his clipboard around and showed it to the others.

"It's amazing how quickly you can make friends when you've been sent by the Emperor to find out what everybody wants for the big party tomorrow night."

"I see," said Muroe. "And what party would that be?"

"Oh, that would be the one I entirely made up."

Smithy read from the list. "Someone called Zeus wants three bottles of Paddy's Whiskey. A speedball. Ketamine." He started to skim read. "This list appears to contain what even Mötley Crüe might consider an excessive amount of drugs and booze."

Diller nodded. "That would be fair. Some of these drugs I had to double-check what they actually were. There are a lot of types, and some of the guys have exotic tastes. It was educational."

Smithy flipped through the next two pages. "I can see that."

"I tried to limit them," said Diller. "I told them – one bottle of booze per man and, like, thirty bucks worth of drugs."

"There's a lot more than that here," observed Muroe.

"Yeah. Then I did a lot of bartering, which is how I got all that gear."

Muroe shook her head in admiration. "I don't suppose you'd like a job after this?"

"No," said Smithy pointedly. "He would not."

"I hate to be the wet blanket in all this," said Wilkins, "but what will happen when these men realise that none of the tricks and treats listed here shall be forthcoming tomorrow evening?"

"Yeah," said Diller, with a nod. "I imagine they will be pretty angry. I strongly suggest we are not here for that." He looked around the group. "I mean, I assumed we were going to try to get away before then, right?"

Smithy nodded. "Well, we hadn't firmed that up, but a quick vote on that being the plan?"

Everyone raised their hands.

"Cool. And sincerely, well done, Diller. You are truly this group's Face."

"Face?" said Wilkins.

"I think they're referencing *The A-Team*," said Muroe.

"The what?"

"The TV show."

Wilkins shook his head dismissively. "Childish."

"You are such a B. A.," said Diller. "Also, I found out that Reed is with Emperor Chaz pretty much constantly, so that's going to be tricky."

"Why?" said Wilkins.

"To round him up for when we bust out of here."

Wilkins raised his eyebrows.

"I mean, I know he's not terribly nice, but we can't leave him."

"I most certainly could," said Wilkins.

Diller looked at the others.

Smithy went to speak but Muroe beat him to it. "Look, if we can get everybody out, then great. But believe me, I worked for him – the guy isn't going to be overly concerned about our wellbeing."

"Alright," said Smithy. "Let's just park that for a while. We don't even have a plan to worry about including him in." Smithy looked around to double-check no one was eavesdropping on them before continuing. "OK. In other news ..."

The others listened in silence as he explained about Zero, or Keith as he one day no doubt hoped to be known as again. When Smithy had finished, Diller shook his head appreciatively. "Wow. He is good."

"I know," said Smithy. "Talk about an understated performance."

"While I'm sure this episode of *Inside the Actors Studio* would be fascinating," said Muroe, "we still have the dual problem of getting out of here and this damned demolition derby."

"Right," said Diller. "On that score, some info. That plane that Mr

Wilkins mentioned – it's in a hangar about three miles west of the camp, and it's heavily guarded. I presume that's the one beside the airstrip where we arrived."

"OK," said Muroe.

"And I found out about our opposition tomorrow. Not good. Five other cars have entered. There's the Killertron – it's got spiked wheels and a ram that I know of. The Scorpion – which has some kind of ... Well, it's like a scorpion with pincers and a tail."

"You're kidding?" said Muroe.

"Nope. There's some really talented mechanics around here. It is a shame more of them didn't find a way onto the straight and narrow."

"A tragedy," said Wilkins. "You were saying?"

"Right," continued Diller. "The Black Dahlia has one of those big chain-fed machine guns. And the Rhino is, like, y'know, a rhino with a ram and stuff, but now they got that flame thing off Dragonzilla too. It doesn't fit the theme they're going for and the team are having discussions about a new name. Then there's the final car ..." Diller looked suddenly bashful.

"What?" said Smithy.

"Sorry," said Diller. "I know this is silly, but the name is so vulgar I'm not comfortable saying it in front of a lady."

Muroe rolled her eyes. "I think I'll cope."

"I just ... How about ..." Diller wrote something on his clipboard in the margin and circled it. He showed it to the others.

"Jeez," said Smithy. "That really is rude."

"I don't see how ..." started Wilkins.

"Say it out loud in your head," said Smithy.

"Alright, but ... Ahhh ... that is vile."

Muroe nodded. "Christ. I hope their design isn't as inventive as their wordplay."

"It might be," said Diller. "They've got a buzz saw, some kind of lifter thing, and stealth armour."

"Stealth armour?" said Wilkins. "That doesn't sound likely."

"I agree," said Diller. "I'm just telling you what I heard. The guy who told me that was really drunk, though. So take it with a grain of salt. Oh yeah," he said, standing up and shifting on his feet. "Then there's the bad news."

"Are you implying that everything else up until this point has been good news?" asked Wilkins.

"OK, the worse news. The prize for the demolition derby was twenty thousand dollars." He looked around the group. "Emperor Chaz has let it be known that anyone who kills our car? That's worth fifty grand. And I mean kill. As in ..."

"Yeah," said Smithy. "I think we all get it."

"What are we going to do?"

Smithy looked at the broken-down husks of the cars that they'd retrieved earlier. "I don't know, but whatever it is we'd better do it fast."

CHAPTER THIRTY-SEVEN

They had been working on the cars for what felt like not much more than an hour when Zero returned, accompanied by a half-dozen more men. Apparently, their presence was requested for dinner in the arena. Muroe had tried to make the case that they were already criminally short of time to be ready for the following day, but it was made clear that attendance was mandatory.

They were frogmarched to the arena where the nightly feast had already begun. The long table on the dais had been replaced with a throne. Apparently, Chaz felt the previous arrangement was too understated. Reed sat to one side, Junkyard Elvis to the other. Rake's cage was beside the stage. He looked dirty and emaciated, and was paying little heed to what was going on around him. The band was set up on top of his cage, because when it rains it pours.

In the corner of the arena the Taco King van was doing a roaring trade again. Despite the direness of the situation, Smithy had a real hankering for some quality Tex-Mex. They'd each been given another MRE a while ago, but freeze-dried military-issue food designed to keep you alive under enemy fire was no match for some spicy tacos.

Smithy, Diller, Muroe and Wilkins were placed before the throne, and their escort of a dozen guards fanned out in front of the stage in an approximation of military fashion. Smithy was taken aback – one of the few advantages they had in this situation had been that Nowhere seemed to exist in a perpetual state of chaos. This seemed no longer to be the case.

Junkyard Elvis nodded at one of the men.

HEAVEN SAVE THE WORLD FROM FAILED MUSICIANS.

Oh great, thought Smithy. *The annoying voice in my head is back.*

Junkyard Elvis approached the microphone that stood in a stand in front of the throne.

THAT MORON SINGS AGAIN AND YOU'LL BE BEGGING ME TO TALK.

Smithy couldn't argue with that.

"Citizens of Nowhere. Pray, silence, and listen to his greatness, our glorious leader, THE EMPEROR!"

The guards arrayed before the stage applauded enthusiastically. Smithy didn't look behind him, but it didn't sound as if the general populace was mirroring their wild enthusiasm.

Emperor Chaz, still wearing his gold crown and lamé cape, stepped down from his throne and stood before the mic. He raised his hands to silence the rapturous applause he could hear mostly in his head.

"My brothers, today is a good day. Arrangements are proceeding better than we could have hoped. Soon, we will be ready to put into action my audacious plan, and we will no longer live here in the desert. No – we will soon have our own country!"

He raised his hands again. The guards really went for it on the applause front as nothing was coming from the crowd behind Smithy bar the sounds of spoons scraping against bowls and general chit-chat.

"But, now more than ever, security is of paramount importance, which is why I have appointed a new head of our military command."

Junkyard Elvis took a bow.

A FAILED ARTIST. WHEN HAS THAT EVER GONE BADLY?

"Sadly, as we strive to achieve our goal, there will be those who do not share our vision."

Smithy shifted his feet nervously as Chaz stared down at them for the first time. His eyes were bloodshot, his pupils pinpricks in a sea of chaos. Smithy had been scanning their environment for escape routes, but assuming any of the dozen armed men in front of them could shoot straight, their chances of getting out of there if things went sideways were slim to none. Now that Smithy looked at the men again, they looked an awful lot like a firing squad.

I WISH YOU HAD NOT NOTICED THAT.

You and me both.

"There is a traitor in our midst! Someone who connives and schemes against us."

This seemed to get a bit more interest from the crowd, possibly because it sounded as if something might be about to happen.

Chaz removed the mic from its stand and stepped forward. He looked at Smithy, Diller, Muroe and Wilkins in turn.

"The traitor is ..."

The drummer broke off a drumroll that seemed excessive. Chaz looked Smithy in the eye, long and hard. Smithy refused to look away, not wanting to give the guy the satisfaction.

Eventually, the Emperor spun around and to the side of the stage where Junkyard Elvis was pushing forward a figure with its hands bound and a black bag over its head.

"Finley!"

Elvis ripped off the bag to reveal the shell-shocked face of Finley, who looked up at his old schoolmate pleadingly.

"Please, Chaz. No – I ... I ..."

"Silence!" hollered Junkyard Elvis, walloping Finley in the back of the head. "How dare you address the Emperor directly."

Chaz jumped from foot to foot and nodded excessively, like a shady preacher building up to asking for your bank details for Jesus. "This reprehensible piece of scum tried to use his money – his dirty money – to compromise the loyalty of my men. Little did he know, my brothers, that you cannot be bought."

Smithy reckoned that, for a wad of used notes, most of the

inhabitants of Nowhere would take out their emperor with a rusty spoon, no questions asked.

"This weasel's cowardly plan was foiled by a true friend, and my new second-in-command – Vice-emperor Reed."

Lousy Louis Reed stood up and gave a wave, moving down to stand beside Chaz.

Smithy watched as one of the guards opened Rake's cage and Junkyard Elvis shoved Finley inside roughly, causing him to fall on top of his new cage-mate, who wailed before being silenced by a guard walloping the bars.

Reed took the microphone and roared into it. "Fellow citizens of Nowhere, I am proud to be one of you." He pointed to Chaz. "And we are all blessed to have this great man as our leader. Such is his magnanimity that he has taken me in, after others led me astray with their evil deceptions. I now must tell you, I did not find the Lewinsky dress. This woman before you is a liar who deceived me!"

This revelation was met with total indifference by the audience, despite Reed's vehement delivery.

"Nonsense," said Wilkins.

One of the guards moved towards him.

Smithy placed a hand on the Englishman's arm. "Shush."

Reed handed back the mic to Chaz as if he were awarding him an Oscar. They shook hands.

"Hear me now, brothers," said Chaz. "If anyone else tries to derail our plans and leave Nowhere, it is your job to stop them."

Chaz looked directly down at Smithy and his companions again.

"And anyone who does so will get a reward of fifty thousand dollars per escapee!"

This announcement did receive an enthusiastic cheer. Chaz clasped Reed's hand and held it aloft. They stood there, basking in applause that wasn't really for them, looking like the presidential ticket from hell.

"OK," whispered Diller. "Screw that guy."

Smithy nodded. "Amen."

CHAPTER THIRTY-EIGHT

Smithy and Diller had come up onto the roof of the museum-cum-garage to watch the sunrise. Three of their guards followed them up there, looking hopeful. It seemed everybody was very keen for a shot at the fifty-grand prize for capturing someone attempting to flee. It had not escaped Smithy's notice that other inhabitants of Nowhere were keeping a close eye on them from atop the nearby buildings and walls of scrap. When they'd opened the door to the roof, Smithy had proclaimed in a loud voice that it wasn't an escape attempt and that anyone shooting them now would get nothing plus a whole lot of trouble. The response to this had been a couple of shouted swear words but, crucially, no gunfire.

And so, the two friends sat on the roof on a couple of deckchairs and watched the sun begin to rise over the wall of cars. Smithy looked at the three guards sitting behind them watching eagerly, and laughed.

"What?" asked Diller.

"Ah, nothing. It just occurred to me – we got into this whole mess because I tried to win fifty grand in that stupid leprechaun hunt, and now we've got an entire village full of lunatics trying to get us for the same prize."

MONEY IS THE ROOT OF ALL EVIL.

Not now.

"You need to stop blaming yourself," said Diller.

"Why? It's my fault."

"No. You agreed to go to Hawaii and be humiliated to make sure my mom was OK. All of this," he said, wafting his hand around, "is because there are some insane people in the world, and at least one of 'em had a lot of money and, well, let's just say some issues."

"That is a very kind way of putting it – for both him and me."

Diller handed Smithy a can of beer. "Here."

"Where'd you get this?"

"Wilkins has a cooler in that storeroom at the back."

"He doesn't strike me as the beer sort." Smithy opened his can and clinked it against Diller's can of soda in a toast. "Has he calmed down yet?"

"I don't think he's ever going to calm down."

They'd worked all night, doing what they could with the meagre resources they had. They did it all against the backdrop of Wilkins ranting that the Lewinsky dress was genuine and that he had gone to great lengths to verify its authenticity. He was more annoyed than Muroe, and it was she who had been accused of cheating.

After Wilkins had launched into his fifth monologue of the night on the subject, she'd slammed down the hammer she'd been holding. "Look, we all know it was genuine. Reed just sold us out to save his own flabby ass. Now, you can spend the night whining or stick it to him by winning this thing. You know – living is the best revenge and all that."

This had shut Wilkins up, at least about that. His umbrage at the authenticity of his collection being called in question was nothing compared to when Junkyard Elvis turned up a few hours later and demanded a couple of items from The Collection. For a minute, it looked a lot like Wilkins was going to go down fighting rather than allow them to be taken. Muroe had done some truly outstanding negotiations to prevent the whole thing from going to hell. If the woman used her powers for good there was no reason why she couldn't sort out the Middle East. Last they'd seen him, Wilkins had been muttering darkly in a corner. The man took his job seriously.

The car itself – well, Muroe was good, that much was obvious. Without her knowledge they'd have been screwed. Smithy knew electronics, but Muroe's uncle must've been one hell of a teacher because twenty-plus years later the woman could rig an engine using scavenged parts and an alarming amount of duct tape.

Smithy and Diller had left Muroe doing some final tweaks and testing, after she'd made it clear that not only was their presence not required, but actively discouraged. Everybody was exhausted, and tempers were frayed.

Diller looked at the burns, scrapes and cuts on his hands. "Man, that was a long night of work. I'm exhausted."

"Yeah. There's a reason that part would be a montage in a movie."

"Do you think it'll be enough?"

"What?"

"The car."

"Absolutely." Smithy had been going for confident, but he was too tired to clear that high bar. Sure, they'd done a good job in the circumstances and, fingers crossed, they'd managed to throw in a few surprises, but nobody was fooling themselves that they really had a chance.

Smithy was aware of Diller starting to say something a couple of times, and then stopping himself.

They watched the first rays of the sun peeking above the rusted wall of metal opposite. It was kind of beautiful. Smithy thought of Cheryl, and then wished he hadn't. Their last words had not been kind ones.

Diller coughed to clear his throat. "I still don't understand why it has to be you to drive the car. We should draw lots."

"Nope," said Smithy. "I appreciate it, but you don't drive – and Muroe and Wilkins barely drive – whereas I, my friend, have attended the greatest survival driving school known to man. I drive a New York taxi and I'm still alive to tell the tale. And besides, the car has already been modified for me. It's a done deal."

Smithy finished the rest of his beer. Maybe it was the moment, but it really did taste incredible.

Diller lowered his voice. "We could make a break for it."

"No, we couldn't. We're currently on an island surrounded by circling sharks. Somebody has us in the sights of a rifle right now."

Diller's head spun around, trying to look in all directions at once. "Where?"

"Over there. Eleven o'clock. On top of that pile of wrecks."

Diller squinted and then raised his voice. "Fido – is that you?"

After a moment, a hand was raised and waved at them. "Hey, Dill. No offence, man. I got child-support payments."

Diller shook his head. "And to think, I threw in an extra bottle of tequila on his order."

"Would that be the imaginary order for the imaginary party that you lied to him about?"

Diller shrugged. "Well, if he's got child-support payments he shouldn't be getting loaded. He should be out getting a job and being a responsible parent."

Smithy nodded. "While I agree with the sentiment, maybe don't tell him that right now."

Diller shifted in his seat. "I've been meaning to ask – Lousy Louis ratted out his friend Finley to Chaz, and pushed that bullshit narrative about Muroe having cheated and faked the dress. How come he didn't tell Emperor Chaz anything about us? I mean, he was there when we first discussed getting out with Wilkins."

"I don't know. Maybe he did tell him. Or maybe he realised that telling him over a day later about our little chat might have raised some awkward questions. Who knows? Seems like those two didn't exactly have the healthiest of relationships before all this happened. He clearly decided to say whatever he thought would save his lousy ass."

"Still," said Diller. "I can't believe he'd turn on his friend to save his own skin."

"Yeah. I was wrong about a lot of stuff, but I stand by my original assessment of that man's character."

They sat there quietly for a few moments, watching the sun rise.

"Look," said Smithy, when he eventually broke the silence. "We will be fine, but if anything goes wrong, y'know ... Could you ... talk to Cheryl?"

"Of course."

"And say ..." Smithy stopped to think. He squeezed the empty beer can in his hands, crushing the metal. "For the life of me, I can't think of a damn word to say. Wait ... Sorry. That's one word, I guess."

"It's a good start."

Smithy nodded. "In case I don't get the chance to expand on that, can you maybe throw in a little more? You're good with words."

"This time tomorrow you can tell her yourself."

Smithy smiled. "Sure."

The sun moved a little further skyward. As the light hit some shattered glass in a window of one of the wrecks, it refracted into a rainbow.

"Damn," said Diller. "Life is weird but beautiful."

They sat there a couple of minutes longer, watching nature's light show.

"I hate to break the moment," said Smithy. "But there appears to be a large monkey staring at us."

Diller looked across. "Oh, hey, fella. Hungry?"

Shitshow bared his teeth in what could've been a smile or a threat. "Ook."

Diller pulled a packet of the imitation-cheese spread that came with the MRE from his pocket and tossed it across to him. "There you go, big guy."

"Ook."

They watched as the orangutan ripped open the packet and squeezed it into his mouth.

"You made friends with Shitshow the monkey?"

"He's an ape and you know it. Did you also know orangutans are the only great apes – except humans – that can talk about the past."

"Is that so?" said Smithy. "I bet Shitshow here could tell some tales."

"Don't call him that."

"Alright," said Smithy. "How did you even get the time to ..."

"When I was out, y'know, getting us equipment and info. I saw him hanging out behind one of those shipping crates. Everyone around here is throwing beer cans or shooting at him. I gave him the cheese-spread stuff from my MRE. He loved it. Poor guy probably isn't eating well."

"No," said Smithy, "I can't imagine he is. Here ..."

Smithy had saved the apple turnover from his MRE. He handed it to Diller.

"Really?"

"Yeah. I'm not much of a dessert guy."

Diller held it up and the orangutan beat a hand against its chest excitedly.

Diller tossed it to him. "There you go, Bunny."

Smithy laughed. "Wait a sec, you call him Bunny?"

"Yeah."

"But he doesn't look anything like ..."

As they watched, the orangutan ripped open the second packet with his teeth. He shoved the contents into his mouth with one hand, while scratching his ass with the other.

"Oh, yeah. I see it now."

CHAPTER THIRTY-NINE

"OK," said Muroe for about the fourteenth time in five minutes. "Is there anything else we need to worry about?"

"Well," said Smithy, "I am missing having a phone. I'd really like to google if caffeine overdose is a real thing, because if it is, we might need to get you to a hospital."

"Hilarious."

"Relax, doc," said Smithy. "You've done all you can for the patient."

The car was unrecognisable from what they'd started with. Somewhere, under the armour they'd ripped off that idiotic Dragonzilla robot, was the skeleton of a Volkswagen Beetle the good people at Volkswagen would happily disown. The shell of the station wagon sat beside it, its bodywork having been stripped away. It had still fared better than the Chevrolet, which had been gutted for its engine and then used for scrap.

They'd used the armour on the Beetle to jury-rig something that resembled a metal military pillbox, complete with slots at the front and sides that offered a very limited field of vision. Mirrors were strategically positioned in the side-slots that offered Smithy some kind of view of what was going on behind him. The metal plates stretched down over the top half of the tyres and sat four inches above the ground. Ideally, Muroe would have liked to cover them a little more, but any lower and the thing would get stuck if it hit soft sand.

The top of the car was considerably less well armoured. The Beetle's hood and trunk had been removed and welded together to form a fairly soft shell. It clipped into place thanks to some clasps Wilkins had begrudgingly given them from the packing cases in which he transported his beloved collection. Any serious blows to the top and it'd crumple fast. It wasn't ideal, but there was only so much armour and so much weight that the chassis could take.

They'd also ripped out all the furniture and left Smithy with one pilot's seat bang in the middle. It wasn't as if he would be picking up hitch-hikers anytime soon.

Diller had christened their vehicle 'the Bug' and nobody had bothered to argue.

"OK," said Muroe again. "Remember, go easy on the engine. I've over-extended it to all hell, so it will not last that long."

"I know," said Smithy, strapping on the helmet he still had from his brief stint in the competitive lawnmower-driving business.

"And, just, y'know ..."

Smithy smiled at her as he clambered up over the side armour. "Ms Muroe, stop now, before you do any irreparable damage to your reputation for being a stone-cold bitch."

She laughed. "Screw you."

"Not right now, I'm busy."

Smithy jumped down into the cockpit and buckled up. Diller climbed up and looked in.

"You in?"

"I'm in."

Diller paused. "This is the bit in the film where one of us should say, 'Hey', before leaving an emotion-filled pause. And then the other looks up at him and goes, 'Yeah, I know. Me too.'"

"Yeah. Let's assume we did that."

"Cool."

Diller reached down, and they bumped fists.

"Break a leg."

"See you on the other side."

Smithy sat there as Diller pulled the makeshift roof into position and then reached up and flipped the levers to clamp it in place.

All alone inside the Bug, it struck Smithy how little light got in. In the gloom he double-checked the clamps and then made sure that the wooden box to his right was securely in place. It was very definitely something you did not want to have sliding about the car. They had precious few cards to play, but that was one of them.

He ran his hands around the steering wheel. One way or another, this was going to be the drive of his life.

He heard a fist pound against the garage's roller-shutters, and a voice roared, "It's time."

CHAPTER FORTY

As the roller-shutters opened, Diller, Muroe and Wilkins had to shield their eyes from the blinding midday sun. Junkyard Elvis was standing there with a quartet of his men.

"C'mon. Time to party." Elvis looked over Diller's shoulder and grinned. "Damn. Is that it? Ugly piece of crap, ain't she?"

"If you're going to start passing aesthetic judgements," said Muroe, "just bear in mind the fact that everyone here has heard you sing."

Elvis's head snapped around sharply as one of his men sniggered. "Shut up, dummy." He turned back to Muroe. "I want you to know, when we discussed the options for what to do with you, I was the one who suggested the raffle."

"Did I tell you," said Wilkins, as if speaking to nobody in particular, "I met Elvis Presley once?"

"Really?" asked Diller.

"Yes. He was the guest of honour at this big fancy function that was being held by the family I worked for. They had managed to get him there because of some link with his record company, or something like that. Money always finds a way. You could see them watching him as if he were an exhibit in a zoo. He clearly didn't feel like he had much in common with the guests.

"At one point, he excused himself by saying he was going to the bathroom, and then he nipped into the kitchens. Forty-five minutes he was in there – joking with the pot-washers, signing autographs. He even sang a song for one of the waitresses because it was her birthday. He was charming, polite – a true gentleman." He turned to Junkyard Elvis. "So you can call yourself whatever you like, and cut your hair however you like, but just know, you shall never be anything like him."

Junkyard's face formed into an angry sneer, but before he could say anything he was drowned out by the roar of a revving engine. The parade had started. He grabbed one of his men, shouted some instructions into his ear and marched off.

Diller, Muroe and Wilkins watched as the other competitors in the demolition derby trooped by, cheered on by the excited crowd.

"That must be Killertron," shouted Diller over the roar, as the first car passed by. It was long, painted bright red, with spiked wheels and a large ram that was pulsating in and out as the car moved slowly forward. Muroe shouted something, but Diller couldn't hear it over the engines.

Next came what he guessed was the Black Dahlia, noticeable for the manned gun turret in the back seat. Diller didn't know a lot about cars, but it looked as if there were a Corvette under all that sleek black armour.

The Scorpion was green and black, and had what looked like the arm of a miniature crane sticking out the back, and large clamps on the front. It also had its name helpfully spray-painted on its side armour. The crane arm had an enormous hammer-like bludgeon on the end of it. Diller tried not to think about their car's vulnerable soft top.

The Rhino looked, well, like a rhino, albeit one that had a flamethrower lifted off a certain robot welded onto its back. It was painted grey and had a large ramming horn at the front as well as extremely thick-looking armour. The flame assembly didn't fit the feel of the design, but given that it belched fire into the sky, none of the crowd seemed to mind.

Finally came the one Diller had taken to referring to as the Unmentionable, mainly because he absolutely refused to say out loud the horrendous name they'd given it. The thing's design was almost as horrible as its name. It looked boxy, but had the lifting apparatus from a forklift on the front and a buzz saw attached to the back. Diller still didn't know what they meant by "stealth armour", but there seemed to be odd-looking portholes in its side that were probably nothing good.

It struck Diller that most of these vehicles had a crew of two or more. He felt even worse for poor Smithy, sitting in there on his own.

Once the Unmentionable had passed, one of the guards waved the Bug forward.

Muroe shook her head. "We have to push it."

"What?" said the guard.

"We have to push it."

"You're shitting me?" said the guard.

"Can you guys help?"

"No."

"Fine," said Muroe. "I guess the three of us will do it."

"I'm not pushing anything," said Wilkins.

"What?" asked Muroe, not attempting to hide the outrage from her voice.

"It's been a long night and I am an old man who has had enough. I am going to bed. Good day to you."

"You can't do that," said Diller.

"Oh no? Watch me."

"I guess it's at times like this that you find out who your real friends are," shouted Muroe to Wilkins's departing back.

"Wait," said the guard. "I gotta bring all of you to the arena. Elvis said."

Wilkins didn't look back. "That man isn't Elvis and I am not going anywhere except to bed."

Diller and Muroe looked at each other.

"OK," said Diller. "I guess it's just you and me."

CHAPTER FORTY-ONE

As Diller and Muroe pushed, the sun beating down on their backs, they could hear Junkyard Elvis announcing each of their competitors in turn as they entered the arena. The Bug was lagging well behind. Given the weight of all the extra armour, it was more like trying to push a truck than a VW Beetle.

Diller ran his forearm over his brow to try to lessen the sweat pouring into his eyes. "Can't we ... turn on the engine ... for a little bit?"

"No," said Muroe. "It'll overheat. We have to wait."

"OK."

"C'mon, move it," hollered the lead guard.

"Either help or shut up," snapped Muroe.

He and his two cohorts were following behind them slowly. He'd seemed unsure what to do about Wilkins, before instructing two of the guards to stay behind to watch him, seeing as he refused to leave the garage. The head guard's order had been met with much bitching and moaning – nobody wanted to miss the action. He was looking nervous, as if he were having second thoughts about all his recent decisions. The pressures of being in command.

In front of them, all the other vehicles had entered the arena, and the Bug wasn't even halfway there. The last stragglers from the crowd were laughing.

"What's wrong? Doesn't your dumb car work?"

Somebody threw a beer can that bounced off the roof.

Smithy was still inside, and that was where he had to stay. Diller and Muroe would get the Bug there or die trying. The latter was beginning to feel like a real possibility. Diller turned around and set his back flat against the rear armour. He pushed with his legs, trying to gain any kind of momentum.

Muroe did the same.

On they went, feeling every inch, as the guards walked behind them, like unsympathetic mourners at a funeral. Then, the sun was blocked from view. The figure of Zero appeared above them. He turned and growled at the guards.

"What?" said the head guy. "I wasn't told to help them."

Zero placed his massive arms on the rear armour and started to push. Diller fell flat on his ass such was the change in speed. He picked himself up, and he and Muroe lent a hand, but Zero was the powerful engine, making what had felt like a mountain to them look like a shopping trolley. Once this was all over, Diller was going to see about investing in that set of dumbbells he'd been contemplating.

As they entered the arena a wave of noise washed over them. The walls were packed – almost everyone in the camp had turned out to watch the main event. The viewing platform was gone, which made sense. If it had wobbled yesterday when they had taken a pop at it with a ride-on lawnmower, it wouldn't cope with a direct hit from any of the competitors in the demolition derby.

Instead, Chaz and his new vice-emperor were positioned on a sturdy-looking wall down at the far end of the arena. Across from them, someone had taken the cage containing Rake and Finley, attached it to a crane and dangled it over the arena floor, so they had an incredible – if highly dangerous – view of proceedings.

Muroe, Diller and Zero pushed the Bug into position just in front of the gate. The other five cars were positioned around them in an approximate circle. Over the PA, Diller could hear Junkyard Elvis saying something, but he couldn't make out what it was – not over the sound of revving engines and "fans" screaming for blood. When they were finally in place, Zero stood up and arched his back.

Diller yelled "Thank you" and then ran around to the front slot. He clambered up to shout inside.

"Alright, Smithy, you're in position." He couldn't see anything in the darkness. Through the armour, he felt the engine rev ... and then die.

Diller looked over at Muroe, who blanched.

Oh no.

Diller hopped down and listened as Smithy tried the engine again.

It coughed, whined and died once more.

Diller could see people on the walls laughing and pointing. Maybe he could plead their case. Appeal to the Emperor for mercy –, for just a few minutes to get it working. Anything was better than leaving Smithy sitting there like that staked cow, waiting to be ripped apart. He saw Chaz and Lousy Louis Reed, clapping and jeering with the rest of the spectators, and knew with a sickening certainty that any appeal would fall on deaf ears.

Junkyard Elvis stood above the main gate, microphone in hand. Someone must have turned him up because Diller was able to pick out his words more clearly now.

"... starting in one minute."

Smithy gave it another try.

The Bug coughed, spluttered, whined, and then ... burst into glorious roaring life. Diller punched the air and looked across at Muroe. She looked relieved, and then collapsed to the ground.

Diller ran over.

She had passed out.

"Oh my God, wake up. Ms Muroe. Ms Muroe!" He shook her shoulder to no visible response. He looked around at the revving cars. "Please, we need to get out of here."

"Thirty seconds ..."

Diller stood up and tried to get Junkyard Elvis's attention. He pointed urgently at Muroe. All he got back was a wide smile.

"... twenty-five seconds."

Diller tried to pick up Muroe, but then Zero was there, snatching her out of his hands. Diller ran after him as he headed for the main gates, which had started to close. Diller ran ahead, trying to find a way to slow down the process. Big chains ran down into the earth from the stone pillars. The mechanism was buried underground.

"C'mon. Stop!"

He stood in the gap between the gates, watching Zero run towards him. The big man put his head down and charged. Diller stepped through the gate and out of the way. After a couple of moments, Zero squeezed through, Muroe still thrown over his shoulder. He collapsed to the ground, panting hard.

When Zero looked up he was shocked to see the seemingly unconscious Muroe now standing above him and looking fine.

"I'm not going to lie, big boy. As pick-ups go, that was one of the more impressive I've experienced." She looked at Diller. "How was my performance?"

"Next time, faint nearer the gate."

"Everybody's a critic. C'mon," she said, looking around, "let's get out of here. It worked. We need to go while they're distracted by all the loud noises. You boys and your toys." She looked down at Zero. "And if he needs to be carried, you're up."

CHAPTER FORTY-TWO

Smithy was already sweating profusely, his hands slick on the wheel. It could have been the fact that he was in a large metal coffin, under a sweltering midday sun, in the middle of the desert, with an engine three feet behind him.

However, you could also argue that it was partly because, through the slot in front of him, he could see five heavily armoured and armed vehicles, all of which had the clear intention of ripping him to shreds. His chances of winning this thing were zero. Luckily, he wasn't intending to win. All he needed to do was to drag it out as long as possible in the hope that he could give the others enough time to get away. Smithy had never been one of life's great winners, but he was a master at being awkward.

He'd watched through the slit as his opponents had driven by the garage earlier. It had been a sobering little parade. Hearing Diller describe the vehicles had been one thing, but seeing them in the metal-grinding armoured flesh was something else. They all looked infinitely capable of tearing him and the Bug to pieces, but the one that worried him the most was the Unmentionable, as Diller had taken to calling it. It had the lifting rig off a forklift amongst its array of tricks. If that thing got under the Bug's armoured skirt, he'd be flipped over and left as helpless as an upturned turtle. If he was going to die, he'd rather it be with his wheels on the ground.

It dawned on Smithy that he had no idea how this thing was supposed to start. If someone waved a flag or made an announcement, he was never going to see or hear it. In the absence of any better ideas, he sat there and waited.

ANY LAST WORDS?

"Ah, come on," said Smithy out loud. "Do we need to do this now?"

THERE MIGHT NOT BE A LATER.

"Thanks for the vote of confidence. By the way, if I hadn't saved Lousy Louis Reed back in that apartment, at *your* behest, none of this would have happened. So, you kind of owe me on this one."

WHAT DO YOU WANT? A MIRACLE?

"Honestly?" Smithy slammed the car into reverse as all of the other cars suddenly surged forward. As he threw it into a one-eighty he screamed, "YEAH!"

CHAPTER FORTY-THREE

Merv and Slappy sat outside the garage in the shade and listened to the distant roar of engines coming from the arena.

"Man," said Merv, "I bet it's really good."

"Shut up about it."

"Don't you tell me to shut up about it. It's thanks to your dumbass cousin ordering us to stay here and guard some stupid old man while he sleeps that I'm missing out."

Slappy slammed his hand against the metal shutter. "For the last damn time, he ain't my cousin. My uncle was banging his mom – that don't make us blood."

"Nah. It makes you some patsy he thinks he can order about."

Slappy stood up. "Do you want to go, homeboy?"

Merv mirrored him. "Maybe I do. Why don't—"

They were interrupted by the metal shutter starting to roll up.

"Cool," said Merv. "Maybe he changed his mind. We can catch the end."

Slappy bent down to look under the rising shutter. "Hey, old man, you ready to go see the show?"

The shutter completed its rise. Slappy and Merv stared into the darkness, their eyes slow to adjust from the bright daylight outside.

Somewhere in the darkness an engine roared to life.

"What is—" started Slappy, which is why Merv got out of the way in time and he didn't.

The skeleton of a station wagon surged out of the darkness, catching Slappy's knee as he tried to dive for safety. He hollered in pain as the car rocketed past and pulled a sharp left turn, sending up a cloud of dust as it tore off towards the arena.

CHAPTER FORTY-FOUR

Not that he had the time to think about such things, but if Smithy had been asked to sum up the first sixty seconds of his demolition-derby career, begrudgingly he would have to quote Mike Tyson: "Everyone has a plan until they get punched in the mouth."

It had been a chaos of collision and desperation. The one thing Smithy had in his favour was that everyone was so desperate to be the one to destroy him that they were falling over each other – or rather crashing into each other – to do so. Smithy had just been veering around wildly, trying not to give anyone the clean shot they were looking for.

The Black Dahlia bore down on him, its gun turret blazing away. Most of the bullets pinged harmlessly off the Bug's armour, but at least one found its way through a slot. Smithy flinched as he heard it ricochet inside the cab a couple of times before coming to rest in something. He didn't know what, but at least it hadn't been him. He angled the Bug, trying to keep the Dahlia behind him, so that the gunner wouldn't have a clear shot at his slots.

Ironically, of everyone in the arena, Smithy had the single worst view of the action. He was not doing much more than reacting to the glimpses of metal he caught through the various slots. He looked in the mirrors to check that the Black Dahlia was behind him, and saw a plume of flame and the Rhino ramming it out of his immediate field of vision.

Turning his attention to what was going on in front, Smithy noticed just in time that he was heading for the wall. He threw the Bug into a sharp left turn.

He quickly scanned the battlefield through the left side-slot. The Black Dahlia had been upturned and lay in the centre of the arena, so that was one opponent temporarily out of commission. Its two-man crew were out and trying desperately to tip it back over onto its wheels. So intent were they on their task that they didn't notice the Killertron approaching from behind. The Black Dahlia's driver didn't even get the chance to scream as he went under his opponent's wheels. The gunner jumped on the top of his ride and narrowly managed to avoid the same fate.

Smithy saw the Unmentionable coming at him from a 45-degree angle. He pulled the handbrake hard, spinning the car into a turn and then releasing it. It worked in that the Unmentionable flew past in front of him and collided with the wall. Unfortunately, it also left the Bug wide open – the Scorpion crashed into its left side and locked on with its pincers. Smithy floored the accelerator in an attempt to gain some purchase. Instead, the smell of burning came from somewhere and the first wafts of acrid smoke from the engine reached his nostrils. Smithy looked out the left-hand slot to see the Scorpion's driver beaming a golden grin at him as he pushed the helpless Bug across the arena.

The realisation of what was coming next hit Smithy just in time for him to duck his head. The Scorpion's "tail" crashed into the Bug's roof with a deafening clang. The metal warped inwards. It could take maybe one more blow. Smithy looked out the front slot and then back out the left one. The Scorpion's driver gave him a cheery wave, which Smithy returned. Smithy followed up the gesture by pointing out the front window.

As potential final moments go, seeing the grin wiped off the Scorpion-driver's face wasn't bad.

Smithy tried to brace himself as the Rhino tore into them, but his face still smashed against the steering wheel, sounding his horn and leaving him dazed amidst the cacophony of tortured metal ripping around him. He could taste blood in his mouth and his vision was fuzzy. Still, the cooling breeze helped. The reason for the breeze was that when the Scorpion had been forcibly removed, it had taken the Bug's whole armoured left side with it.

Smithy looked out of his car's new feature. The light dazzled his eyes. He watched as the Rhino, flame belching from its dragon's-breath addition, slammed the Scorpion into the wall with such ferocity that one of the spectators stumbled, and was grabbed by his fellow onlookers just in time to prevent him from becoming collateral carnage. The Scorpion was a flaming mess and Smithy watched as someone spilled out of the back of the vehicle and rolled along the ground in an effort to put out the flames that engulfed him.

Smithy's head was clearing now. At the far side of the arena he could see Killertron being shredded by the Unmentionable's whirring saw. The Rhino, meanwhile, had pulled itself free of the flaming mess that was the Scorpion's carcass and was lining itself up for an unobstructed run at him.

Smithy slammed the Bug into reverse. Nothing happened. At least, nothing he'd hoped for. Black smoke billowed from the engine behind him and the Bug's wheels made a sickening grinding noise, but the car did not move.

Smithy watched as the Rhino, now in position, belched flames and headed straight for him.

SO, ABOUT THOSE LAST WORDS?

CHAPTER FORTY-FIVE

"You were faking?" said Zero as he looked up at Muroe with big sorrowful eyes, as if hurt.

"Yes," said Muroe. "I temporarily put aside all feminist instincts and we agreed that me faking a faint was the best way to get us out of being forced to stand up there and watch proceedings, which is crucial to the plan. I should point out that it would've been the other way around, but we felt Mr Diller here would be marginally better at carrying me than I him.

"Also, I would like to point out that I built in a fricking night that war machine we were pushing, so I'm well stocked-up on feminist points." She looked up at Diller. "Am I rambling? I feel like I'm rambling. I had a lot of coffee. And then there was the exertion of trying to push the damn thing, plus the adrenalin rush from this part of the plan actually working."

She glanced up at Zero aka Keith. "Thanks, by the way. We really do appreciate your help. In fact, we're getting out of here so, y'know, if you want to come, your ticket to freedom is on us."

She said the last bit with a flourish of her arms, but then Diller noticed the smile fall from her face.

"Nobody is getting out of here." Junkyard Elvis was standing a dozen feet away, training a gun on them.

Behind him, the arena doors stood closed, but the roar of engines and screech of metal were still audible as the crowd screamed for blood.

"Ah, crap," said Muroe.

"Yeah. Bad for you. Great for me."

"Shouldn't you be commentating on the thing?" asked Diller.

As if on cue, everyone jumped as something exploded in the arena. "Can't hear me over the cars. Besides, three people trying to escape? I just got myself one hundred and fifty thousand bucks."

"Have you, though?" asked Muroe. "I mean, does your wise and noble leader strike you as the most stable of people?" She turned to Diller. "Did you see what he is wearing today?"

"I did and—"

"Shut up!" boomed Elvis. He pointed the gun at Zero, who was still on his knees. "And don't you dare move. I knew you would betray us. You couldn't take it that the Emperor promoted me over you."

"Oh no," said Zero, in the high-pitched, slightly lispy voice of a man who was really called Keith and was thoroughly sick of type-casting. "Honestly, I'm happy for you. I'm not cut out for this – any of this. You take it. I'll get out of your way."

"Silence!" roared Elvis. "Do not mock me. I will not be mocked."

"OK," said Diller, holding out a placatory hand. "Look, you got us. OK? We will come quietly. Before we do, though, how much do you know about Lou Reed?"

"The Vice-Emperor is a great man."

Diller looked into the man's eyes. In a town full of cutthroats who'd do anything for money, they'd managed to get caught by the one true believer.

"No, I mean the musical icon. Lou Reed, born Lewis Allan Reed, March 2, 1942 in New York. He was the singer, guitarist and main songwriter in the seminal rock band the Velvet Underground before leaving to pursue a solo career that spanned five decades. The album *Transformer*, featuring the single 'Walk on the Wild Side', was produced by David Bowie and is regarded as one of the great glam-rock albums. He followed it up with the album *Berlin*, after which his career entered a decline until the 1989 masterpiece, *New York*. He has been inducted into the Rock and Roll Hall of Fame twice – once as a member of the Velvet Underground and again as a solo artist. Why am I telling you any of this?"

Junkyard Elvis looked entirely mystified.

"Two reasons ..."

The arena seemed to shake as several things collided in quick succession.

"First, my best friend is in there risking everything for us and I never got the chance to tell him that I'd looked up Lou Reed and he was an awesome dude. Secondly, I was just trying to kill time."

"Why were you—"

The question was cut short by the fender of a 1968 Buick slamming into the back of his head. As Junkyard Elvis crumpled to the ground, the orangutan standing behind him grinned widely and slapped his chest.

CHAPTER FORTY-SIX

Smithy eyed the Rhino as it prepared to charge. The Bug couldn't move. Smithy killed the engine. He wasn't wild about the idea of dying engulfed in flames, but if it was going to happen he didn't want it to be from his own vehicle's engine exploding.

He could hear the crowd roar in anticipation of the kill. The other two remaining vehicles were too far away to have any effect on proceedings. From the corner of his eye, Smithy could see the gunner from the Black Dahlia scrambling up the back wall, trying to get out of the arena alive.

With his left hand, Smithy wiped his forehead. His eyes were burning from the smoke and the sweat pouring down from under his helmet. As he took his hand away, he saw that there was blood mixed in with the sweat – it was hard to know from where. Now that he'd stopped moving, everything was starting to ache. He dipped his right hand down to open the wooden box wedged by his side. He dug down amidst the bubble wrap and other improvised packaging to find what he was looking for.

The Rhino was spewing flames and had started to accelerate towards him. Thanks to all the armour, it wasn't moving that fast, relatively speaking, but it didn't have to.

Suddenly, Smithy felt the exhaustion tugging at his eyelids. The heat had been so intense. He was tired. So. Damn. Tired. He felt the large metal weight in his hands and took a deep breath, closing his eyes for a second, to try to stop the burning.

WAKE UP, IDIOT.

It was as if time had jumped forward. Suddenly, the Rhino was bearing down on him, eating up the ground between them.

Smithy's fingers scrabbled around and found the button underneath the discus-shaped object that would arm it. He heard the click as the pressure pad on the top activated.

His shoulder ached as he pulled back his arm. The thing was damn heavy. He heaved it with everything he had.

Wilkins had explained things in great detail. As anti-personnel mines went, the ones he had were responsibly manufactured. Meaning it wouldn't blow up from being jostled, or indeed thrown, as long as it landed the right way up. It wasn't that powerful, but it would severely curtail the ballroom-dancing ambitions of anyone unlucky enough to stand on it.

Smithy held his breath as the device landed ten or so yards from the Bug. As throws went, it had been a pretty good one. He watched as the Rhino passed over it.

For a second nothing happened. Then came an explosion under the rear of the vehicle. Dust flew up as the Rhino jumped in the air and came down again, minus the rear axle that the mine had removed. It gouged a trench in the ground as it came to a juddering halt just behind the Bug, belching flames uselessly into the sky.

Smithy leaned forward, ducking down to avoid the Bug's caved-in roof as he reached for the clasps that secured it in place. He needed to get the roof off, but the catches wouldn't budge. He unstrapped himself from the seat and pounded the surrounding metal with his fist, but the attack from the Scorpion had warped it too much.

The crowd cheered.

With a sickening thud, he felt the Unmentionable's forklift apparatus slide under the Bug's still-armoured right side and lift it up.

The car was utterly helpless now.

Smithy grabbed the hammer that was also in the wooden box and started to pound on the roof for all he was worth. His shoulders ached and his shirt was stuck to him with sweat. More of it poured into his eyes as he hammered desperately at the roof. Trying to get the metal to release.

He shifted his position and kicked upwards with all his might. As the Bug came to a halt, in a moment of blessed relief the roof fell away and sunlight poured into the cockpit.

Smithy looked up to see that the Unmentionable was holding him up below the point on the wall where Emperor Chaz and his vice-emperor sat. They were both applauding, their faces filled with glee.

Smithy sat back in his seat.

Emperor Chaz stood and shouted down to him. "It was a valiant effort, my midget friend."

Smithy sighed as he pulled the lever to remove the steering wheel. "Been meaning to mention. 'Midget' is the wrong word, you patronising asshat."

"Really?" Chaz said, laughing. "And pray tell, what should I call you?"

Smithy unhooked the steering wheel and tossed it to the ground. "Well, it doesn't really matter now. I doubt we'll be seeing each other again."

"Anything you'd like to say before our brave champions use that buzz saw of theirs to cut you into even tinier pieces?"

"Yes," said Smithy. "First off – are you wearing the Lewinsky dress?"

"It isn't the real one."

Smithy nodded as he casually strapped himself back into his seat.

"Regardless, a word to the wise – you don't have the hips for it. And more importantly, what do you and a former Miss Alabama have in common?"

Smithy watched as the look of confusion spread across the self-proclaimed emperor's face. Then the penny dropped.

"That's right," said Smithy. "You both got screwed by someone in this seat."

Smithy reached his left hand down and pulled the lever. If this didn't work, he was going to look briefly stupid followed by permanently dead.

He heard the mechanism fire as the ejector seat from the Space Shuttle *Enterprise* added to its already storied history, by doing exactly what it had been designed for.

Smithy might be dead in a matter of seconds, but the look on Chaz and Lousy Louis Reed's faces as the chair launched itself into the sky made it almost worthwhile.

CHAPTER FORTY-SEVEN

Although Smithy did not know it at the time, he would be forever grateful for the work of the Martin-Baker Aircraft Company. They were the people primarily credited with the invention of the zero-zero ejector seat, one capable of ejecting at zero altitude and zero airspeed. Any ejector seats designed prior to that would have left him as a smoking hole in the ground where he landed – or, more accurately, impacted. Given that the *Enterprise* was one of only two NASA space shuttles fitted with ejector seats, the fact that they happened to have zero-zero capabilities was extremely lucky.

It was just one of the fortunate happenstances that Smithy experienced in quick succession. The under-seat cannon whose role it was to clear the seat from the aircraft – or, in this case, the shattered husk of a demolition derby runner-up – detonated correctly. Then the under-seat rocket-pack fired on cue to propel the seat to an appropriate altitude before the small explosive charge deployed perfectly to open the parachute canopy quickly enough to allow for a successful descent.

All of the above were part of a series of miraculous technological achievements worthy of celebration. Doubly so, given the fact that the seat had been assembled around fifty years previously. In hindsight, it was therefore quite disappointing that Smithy spent his entire flight in the *Enterprise*'s magnificently preserved ejector seat screaming the most standard of swear words with his eyes clenched shut.

Miracles are often wasted on their beneficiaries.

As it was, Smithy only opened his eyes when the ejector seat was a few feet away from landing. Once it touched down, with a considerable bump but nothing more, Smithy repeated the swear words several more times while his trembling hands fumbled with the straps that secured him into the life-saving device.

In Smithy's defence, he was a nervous flyer. If nothing else, the experience clarified that it wasn't being in an airplane that he hated. It turned out that flying without one was way worse.

When he finally extricated himself, he stood there with his hands on his knees, trying to rediscover how breathing was supposed to work.

YOU ARE WELCOME.

"Shut up. That wasn't you."

OH, WASN'T IT?

Smithy watched as the skeleton of a station wagon tore across the sand towards him.

"Stop trying to take credit, unless you were responsible for a foreign diplomat banging some model in that seat."

YOU ARE WELCOME.

"And don't take credit for an escape that's barely half over."

Smithy shielded his eyes as the station wagon screeched to a halt beside him.

Wilkins sat in the driver's seat. "You were supposed to land over there!"

"Really?" said Smithy, waving a hand in front of his face to clear the cloud of dust. "I pull that off, and you're criticising the landing?"

"We have to go. We've already lost valuable time because your colleague was attempting to convince an orangutan to get into the car."

"He also saved us," said Diller from the back seat.

"Just shut up and get in," urged Muroe, who was also in the back seat.

Smithy did as he was told, and was barely in his seat before Wilkins floored it.

"You couldn't get the orangutan so you got Zero instead?"

"Please, call me Keith," said Keith, from the passenger seat. "And I'm glad you made it out alive."

"Thank you!" said Smithy, who was feeling as if the incredible feat he'd just pulled off wasn't getting the credit it deserved.

He looked behind them, and then spoke to Muroe. "Can I ask why there are several flight cases in the back of this station wagon?"

Muroe shook her head. "Oh, believe me, we've had that discussion."

Diller leaned forward and shouted to be heard over the engine. "How did we do?"

"What?"

"In the thing."

"Oh. We came second."

Diller looked genuinely disappointed. "That's not bad, I suppose."

Smithy felt himself grow slightly defensive. "Well, sixth place through to fourth place died so, y'know, personally I was pretty happy about it."

From the front, Wilkins shouted. "That's the trouble with your generation – far too comfortable with failure."

"Yeah," said Smithy. "By the way, Master Breddenback was wearing the Lewinsky dress."

The car swerved so alarmingly that Smithy nearly fell out.

Muroe grabbed him and held him in.

"What? What are you talking about?"

"He's joking," shouted Muroe.

Diller pointed out into the distance. "Look. There. There's some kind of building. Is that the airstrip?"

"Let's assume it is," said Muroe.

The car veered as Wilkins altered their course.

Muroe checked Wilkins wasn't looking and punched Smithy's leg.

"Ouch. What?"

"Only you could come through an automotive death match, escape using a half-century-old ejector seat and then get thrown out of the back seat of a car for annoying the driver."

SHE HAS A POINT.

"Shut up."

Muroe raised an eyebrow pointedly.

"Sorry. Wasn't talking to you."

CHAPTER FORTY-EIGHT

As moments went, the one when the station wagon's journey towards the building in the distance changed from being on a dirt road to concrete was quite something.

"This is a runway," said Keith excitedly. "This is a runway!"

Which meant they hadn't escaped to an empty tool shed in the desert.

Wilkins brought the skeletal station wagon to a screeching halt and they all piled out. The front of the hangar was closed with a large, sturdy metal door. Smithy raced around to the side and found the access door, which was padlocked.

"OK. I can pick this. I just need to find—"

He was interrupted by Keith shoulder-charging his way through it.

"Or, we could do that."

They all moved inside quickly and Diller found the light switch on the wall. The fluorescent lights buzzed into flickering life above them. The group stood in silence for a moment.

"It's small," observed Diller.

It was. They were looking at a single-engine Cessna airplane that could seat four uncomfortably.

"I ... I won't be able to fit all of the collection in that," said Wilkins.

"You won't be able to fit *any* of the damned collection in that," corrected Muroe.

"OK," said Smithy, "we need to move fast. Zero – I mean, Keith – I don't suppose you can fly a plane?"

"Ehm – no," said the big man.

"I thought you said *you* could?" Muroe asked Smithy.

"No," shouted Smithy over his shoulder. "I said I'd once looked into it when I'd auditioned for a part in a reboot of the sitcom *Wings*."

"Well," said Wilkins, pointing at Keith, "if he is of no further use ... I mean, the collection was part of this escape before he was."

Smithy left Muroe to deal with Wilkins and jumped up into the Cessna. He'd never been inside the cockpit of an aircraft before, but he'd reasoned that if they got this far, figuring out the basics of flying wouldn't be that hard – relative to the other parts of the plan. That had been the theory, at least. Besides, he'd have to figure out how to steal the thing first. Smithy knew about hotwiring cars and he was working on the assumption that planes more or less worked on the same principle.

He looked under the steering console to figure out how to get to the wiring. There, almost winking at him, were the keys taped against the worn plastic.

YOU ARE WELCOME.

"I'll give you that one."

Smithy put the key into the ignition just as Diller hit the button to raise the hangar doors. As they slowly started to rise, sunlight began to flood the space. Smithy turned the key and started to survey the array of dials and controls in front of him. In his head, this had seemed simpler. He started flipping switches and pulling or suppressing things, working on the admittedly weak logic that for the thing to fly, everything had to be in the opposite position to what it was in when it wasn't flying.

Diller was trying to ignore the argument occurring behind him.

"Absolutely not," Muroe was saying.

"But you said yourself, Zero isn't going to fit into the airplane."

"We're still taking him, and he is called Keith now."

"But we could leave him and perhaps draw lots so that the collection could take up one seat? It is of significant cultural importance."

"So am I. You're welcome to take the station wagon and you and your love can make a break for it."

"I'll never make it."

"Well, that's your choice," said Muroe.

"Guys," said Diller.

"You, madam, are a philistine."

"I've been called worse. We're getting out of here and we're going people first."

"Guys," repeated Diller.

"Ms Muroe,' said Keith, sounding terrified. "I found this cord. Will it do?"

"It'll have to."

"Guys!" hollered Diller, finally getting the trio's attention.

"What?" said Muroe.

He didn't say anything, just pointed out of the hangar doors and down the runway. A large cloud of dust was coming towards them – fast.

"Holy crap," said Muroe. "It looks like the whole of Nowhere is chasing us!"

CHAPTER FORTY-NINE

Smithy had found a manual under the seat and was trying to read it. His task was complicated by the fact at some point the book had got drenched in what he hoped was some kind of fruit juice.

"Suppress the ... what does that say?"

There were also pedals, but as far as he could tell they were brakes. He was unlikely to need brakes any time soon.

The entire plane lurched violently to the side. Smithy didn't look up. "What the hell is going on?"

"You don't want to know," came Diller's reply.

"Yes, I do."

"Alright. Keith isn't going to fit inside, so we're strapping him to the top of the aircraft."

"I take it back," said Smithy. "I definitely did not want to know that."

"How's it going?" asked Muroe, as the aircraft shook some more.

"It's getting there."

"Get there faster."

"Thanks. Helpful."

"Don't mind her," said Diller. "And whatever you do, don't look up."

"Why would I not ..." Smithy looked up and saw the line of vehicles hurtling across the desert towards them. "Damn it. I had to look."

Chaz was standing up in the front seat of the jeep, screaming instructions that nobody else could hear. Reed sat in the back seat watching him. A couple of motorbikes zoomed past. In the distance, through the open doors of the hangar, he could see the plane sitting there, facing them.

"Get them! Get them, get them!"

"Ehm, Chaz – I mean, Emperor?"

"What is it, LouLou?"

Chaz turned to look at his second-in-command and Reed saw that what little remained of the man's mind had gone. His eyes were wild, and he was all but foaming at the mouth.

"Never mind."

Now was not the time to tell him that he'd split the seam on his dress.

Muroe and Wilkins were crammed into the back seat of the Cessna – Wilkins held a metal flight case on his lap and Muroe had another one on hers. Neither of them looked happy about it, albeit for different reasons.

Diller sat in the co-pilot's seat, straining every sinew not to ask Smithy any questions, primarily about why they weren't moving. He looked around and reached down into the slot in the doorwell beside him.

"Smithy?"

"Not now, Dill."

"Yeah, but, Smithy."

"Not. Now!"

SHUT UP AND LISTEN TO HIM.

Smithy looked up. "Sorry. What?"

Diller held up a piece of paper. "There's something here that says it is a pre-flight checklist."

Smithy tossed the manual out the window. "Start reading."

"One – examine the exterior of the—"

"We've got a man strapped to the roof. Just go for the stuff about pressing buttons and pulling knobs."

Meanwhile, dangling over a now-deserted arena, Messrs Rake and Finley sat in their cage, the sun beating down on them. Forgotten men. They looked out numbly at a world that no longer made sense.

Without warning, their view lurched and the cage crashed to the ground. It tipped over and landed on its side, leaving Finley and Rake in a messy heap.

"This is it," said Finley in a soft voice. He wasn't expecting "it" to be a good thing – that wasn't the kind of day he was having.

After a minute, a truck pulled up in front of him. On the side it read "Taco King". Finley watched a pair of brown-leather cowboy boots as they stepped out of the driver's side door and walked towards them. He looked up, shielding his eyes from the sun, to see an old Mexican man in a cowboy hat looking down at them.

"Everybody's gone," he said.

Finley said nothing.

"You boys rich?"

It took Finley a second to realise that those last words had been a question.

"Yes. Yes, we are. We'll pay you whatever you want."

"I don't want paying."

"OK."

"But I got grandkids. My family, we make the best tacos and burritos you ever had."

Finley struggled to understand what the required response to this statement was.

The old man shifted. "I am looking for investors."

And he had found them. They could work out the finer points of the deal in the van.

CHAPTER FIFTY

Following one of the most tense readings of a checklist in the history of mankind, the plane was now moving and taxiing out of the hangar. Unfortunately by this time, the bikes – in what was hard not to think of as a hunting party from Nowhere – had already reached the end of the runway. Two quad bikes and a motorbike were tearing towards them.

"Guys," yelled Keith from the roof, "they're coming."

"Tell me something I don't know," hollered Smithy.

"I'm scared of heights," responded Keith, who hadn't mastered the rhetorical question.

Smithy pulled the throttle.

"Don't pull it too fast," warned Diller, "or it'll stall."

"Too slow and we'll die," said Muroe.

"Everybody shut up with the backseat flying."

"They're coming right at us," yelled Diller over the noise of the engine.

"I know."

Turning. Stopping. Doing anything that wasn't going full speed ahead meant they were dead. All Smithy could do was wait for the plane to reach the required velocity and take off, assuming it was willing to do that with all the extra weight on board.

He watched as one of the bikers pulled a handgun from the inside of his jacket.

"Get. Down."

One of the shots entered the windshield where Diller's head had been moments before, and exited via the roof above Muroe's head. The other shots went wild.

Smithy tried to ignore everything else. He was concentrating on keeping the plane headed straight down the runway and pulling back on the controls. At some point he'd presumably feel it was ready to take flight – assuming the large man strapped to the roof didn't mess with the wings somehow. As soon as the thought occurred to him, he wished it hadn't. Too late now.

"Come on, fly!" he shouted.

ASK NICELY.

"FLY!"

NOT UNTIL YOU SAY IT.

"Please. God. Fly!"

Smithy pulled back on the controls and felt the glorious sensation of the plane's wheels leaving the ground.

YOU ARE WELCOME.

"It's working! It's working! We're flying!"

Smithy looked down at the end of the runway and saw the man in a half-kneeling position with something large and metal resting on his shoulder.

"Ah, come on."

A plume of fire erupted from where the man was kneeling and headed straight for them.

Smithy screamed as he pulled the controls to the right as hard as he could. The ground appeared in the right-hand window as the whole plane banked sharply. The rest of the airplane's passengers screamed along with Smithy.

Something large and angry flew under the left wing.

Smithy jerked the controls again and, after some trial and error, managed to level out the wings while still climbing.

"Where did you learn to fly?" shouted Wilkins.

"I didn't."

The hunting party was now arrayed in front of them. Men poured out of vehicles, guns in hand.

"Hang on," hollered Smithy as he pulled the controls to the right again and the airplane banked sickeningly. Their one advantage was that Smithy's flying made them a tricky target. If he didn't know where he was going, then they couldn't possibly know either.

Smithy tried to level out the plane again. He felt it judder as bullets made contact with one of the wings.

He glanced behind him. "Is everyone OK back there?"

Muroe responded by pointing out the front window. "Look out!" she screamed.

Smithy had managed to turn the plane one-hundred-and-eighty degrees, which made sense in terms of an escape from the hunting party. The only downside was that they were now heading straight for the hangar they'd just left.

Smithy pulled back on the control, desperately willing the plane to climb.

Beside him, Diller covered his eyes with his hands and rattled out a prayer.

In moments such as this, your life is supposed to flash before your eyes. Smithy had never had that. Instead, he got ...

AFTER ALL THAT, THIS IS AN EMBARRASSING WAY TO DIE.

"SHUT! UP!"

The plane jerked nauseatingly as one of its wheels snagged against the corrugated-iron roof of the hangar, and then they were above it. Glorious blue sky stretched out before them.

"Holy crap," shouted Diller, grabbing Smithy. "You did it, Smithy! You're a genius."

"Genius?" shouted Wilkins. "We're in the middle of the desert and he almost managed to crash into the only building for miles."

The plane jerked again as Smithy turned around. "Do you want to take over?"

"Just fly the damn plane!" shouted Muroe.

Nobody spoke for a few moments, then Smithy turned to Diller. "What's that noise?"

Diller listened for a second and then nodded. "I think it's Keith screaming."

"Ohhh." Smithy nodded. "Well, at least that means he's still alive."

Diller banged on the roof. "Hang in there, big guy."

CHAPTER FIFTY-ONE

Down on the runway, Reed watched numbly as Chaz went into total meltdown. The man fell to his knees, his dress all akimbo, and pounded the concrete with his fists.

"No. No. No. No. No!"

His entourage stood around and watched impassively, never a group of individuals predisposed to empathy.

Chaz turned an accusatory finger on them. "You idiots! You let them go. Morons!"

Reed climbed out of the back seat as quickly as he could extricate himself.

"I asked you to do one simple thing, but you braindead—"

"Ignore him," said Reed, trying to force a smile as he rushed over. "Everything is fine. He's just a little upset."

"Don't you contradict me."

Reed bent down and lowered his voice to a hiss. "Shut up. Just shut up."

When Reed stood back up, the one known as the Cobra was standing in front of the others. "We want our money. And we want our party."

"Right," said Reed, who didn't fully understand but felt that agreeing was the best course of action.

On the ground beneath him, Chaz gave one of his demented laughs before screeching, "Party? Party? You morons don't deserve a fucking party!"

Reed tried to clamp his hand over Chaz's mouth but it was too late. When he looked up, the men were advancing towards them slowly, closing in.

"He didn't— Agh!" Chaz had bit Reed's hand.

"How dare you lay your hands on the Emperor. Seize this man! I am your Emperor. Listen to me. Why aren't you listening to me? LISTEN. TO. ME!"

CHAPTER FIFTY-TWO

Smithy's breathing was returning to normal. Sort of. He was still flying a plane, despite not knowing how to do so, but seeing as people weren't shooting at them any more and there weren't any buildings he was at risk of flying into, that was an improvement. Yes, he had to figure out how to land the thing somehow, but one way or another that was going to happen. The gauge said they still had a half-tank of fuel, and they were going to keep flying in one direction until they saw something resembling civilisation.

After some "spirited debate" they had turned the plane around again and flown north. Diller had a vague idea, garnered from something someone had said on his fact-finding trip, that there was a main road somewhere in that direction. Besides, judging by the climate, wherever they were had to be somewhere south of New York. It wasn't the most cast-iron logic he'd ever applied to a problem, but it had been a very long day.

The group all looked out of their windows in silence as Nowhere passed beneath them. For the first time they could see it in all its messed-up glory – a sprawling chaos of metal glinting in the midday sun.

Smithy whacked Diller's arm and pointed down to the right. Diller leaned over him to look out.

There, making its way across the desert, was a van with "Taco King" emblazoned on the side. On the roof sat an orangutan, waving the fender of a 1968 Buick.

CHAPTER FIFTY-THREE

Starchild's head bobbed back up as the music stopped and the tape popped out of the van's cassette player. That was the problem with driving through the desert on your own. Nobody to talk to. Nobody to share the driving. You could space out real easy. It had already happened this morning. He'd found himself veering off the road. Damn near hit a cactus. That would have been heavy. He had a strict rule about not killing any living thing.

He tossed the cassette onto the passenger seat, then reached down and rummaged through the tape collection. Janis. Crosby, Stills & Nash. Nah, man – he needed some Creedence. Something to lift his spirits and clear his head.

He'd come to the desert for the same reason he always did – to drop a shit ton of acid and get back in touch with the universe. Normally, it was him and Unicorn together, but she hadn't come this time. He'd hoped the trip would give him some answers on that front, but it hadn't. All he'd done was sit in the tepee and tripped balls while an elephant and Hitler had argued about ping-pong. He was starting to wonder if he was going to find the answers he needed that way any more.

Unicorn – or Carol, as she was also known – wanted to settle down. She was a registered nurse and he was a Certified Public Accountant, despite hating accountancy with a white-hot fury people normally reserved for disease and despots. They'd always railed against the conventional life, but somewhere along the line they'd changed. She'd changed. It was her sister having the baby. It had done something to her. Starchild didn't know what, but something, man. Something. Suddenly she wanted to be an old lady – his old lady – and settle down and do the Johnny Square thing.

It was heavy.

Starchild – or Darren, as he definitely did not like to be known – had never fit in. He was a man out of time. He should've been born to reach his peak in the Sixties, but no. He'd been born in 1980. Nothing good had happened since 1980. Not one damn thing. He'd been miserable as a child until he'd caught something on late-night TV talking about flower power. It had spoken to him. It was as if the universe had reached down into his mom's basement in Winston, Oregon, tapped him on the shoulder and said, *Hey – this is your purpose. Become a citizen of the world.* From that moment, that had been the plan.

Sure, to keep his parents happy he'd gone to community college and got his diploma, but then he'd embraced his dream. He'd met Unicorn over ten years ago and they'd clicked. Two people out of time, together, getting out of their minds.

The van veered as Starchild searched for a pen. He had to write that down. That was a lyric. *Two people out of time, together, getting out of their minds.* He'd broken his guitar and, truth be told, he couldn't really play it anyway, but he was going to learn. And then they were going to get the band back together.

The one thing about roads like this was that as long as you kept the wheels on the thing, you weren't going to crash. Finding someone to run into here was an achievement. It was a long and lonely road.

Then it hit him. Maybe the drive was the trip. The lesson. This was what the universe had been trying to show him. That no man was meant to travel these long roads alone. He needed a companion. Damn it. He would go see Carol – Unicorn – and sort their shit out.

She had said she didn't want to give up the life altogether, just, y'know, hang out on both sides of the fence. Suddenly, that seemed pretty alright to Starchild.

And there it was. He was no longer just driving. Now he was driving towards something and that felt right.

The road was long, but not flat. As he cleared the ridge, he was surprised to see people at the side of the road. Even more surprised to see the airplane that lay crumpled on its side behind them.

As they waved him down, Starchild pulled over the van. You had to help. We're all in this thing together. OK, he'd been jacked a few times, but c'mon, man – give peace a chance.

They were an unlikely looking bunch.

An old guy with two metal cases. A dwarf. A young guy. A woman. And a big, scary-looking dude. Must've been, like, ten feet tall.

Starchild rolled down the window. "You folks alright?"

The woman did the talking. "Hi. Yeah, we kinda broke down."

"In a plane?"

"It's a long story."

"What's up with him?" asked Starchild. The big guy was shaking slightly and mumbling to himself.

"He's a nervous flyer."

"Yes," said the old man in an English accent, "and none of us greatly enjoyed the crash."

"We got down, didn't we?" said the dwarf.

"Gentlemen," snapped the woman. "Now is not the time." She smiled at Starchild. "Could we get a lift to the next town?"

"It'll be a little cramped," said Starchild.

"When isn't it?" muttered the old man.

"It'll be fine," said the woman. "We'd really appreciate it."

"OK, then." Starchild got out of the van and went around to open the side-door. There was a real knack to it.

The woman and the young dude guided the big guy into the back.

Starchild picked up the old man's cases. "We can put these on the roof."

"You shall do no such thing."

"What's in there?" asked Starchild.

"The brain of JFK."

"Wow. OK. Heavy."

Eventually, they got everybody in. The dwarf and the smiling fella sat in the front with Starchild, and everyone else was in the back. The van started up on the third attempt and they were off.

Starchild took a joint out of the ashtray and lit it before turning to his two companions in the front seat.

"So, where are you guys coming from?"

"Nowhere," said the dwarf.

"Ohhh, OK."

"Actually," he said. "Could you tell me where we are?"

"Sure." Starchild grabbed the map on the dashboard, turned it over and pointed.

The two men looked at it for a few moments.

"Wow," said the dwarf. "Never would have guessed there."

THE END

FREE BOOK

Hi there,

I hope you enjoyed *Welcome to Nowhere*. If it's the first of my books you've read then there's loads more to get stuck into - just check out the following page. Smithy and Diller feature in the McGarry Stateside series, which can be read on its own or, if you're a completist, then there's the whole of the Dublin Trilogy too - which will give you the backstory of the infamous Bunny McGarry.

If you'd like to get my short fiction collection called **How To Send A Message**, which includes a Smithy and Diller story, then go to my website:

www.WhiteHairedIrishman.com

The paperback costs $10.99/£7.99/€8.99 in the shops but you can get the e-book for free just by signing up to my monthly newsletter.

Cheers muchly and thanks for reading,

Caimh

ALSO BY CAIMH MCDONNELL

THE DUBLIN TRILOGY

A Man With One of Those Faces (Book 1)

The Day That Never Comes (Book 2)

Angels in the Moonlight (Book 3/prequel)

Last Orders (Book 4)

MCGARRY STATESIDE (FEATURING BUNNY MCGARRY)

Disaster Inc (Book 1)

I Have Sinned (Book 2)

The Quiet Man (Book 3 – Coming Oct 2020)

The Final Game (MCM Investigations)

Welcome to Nowhere (Smithy and Diller)

And in January 2021 Caimh's alter-ego C.K. McDonnell releases *The Stranger Times* – details on the next page.

Go to www.WhiteHairedIrishman.com to find out more.

THE STRANGER TIMES – C.K. MCDONNELL

There are dark forces at work in our world so thank God *The Stranger Times* is on hand to report them. A weekly newspaper dedicated to the weird and the wonderful (but mostly the weird), it is the go-to publication for the unexplained and inexplicable . . .

At least that's their pitch. The reality is rather less auspicious. Their editor is a drunken, foul-tempered and foul-mouthed husk of a man who thinks little of the publication he edits. His staff are a ragtag group of misfits. And as for the assistant editor . . . well, that job is a revolving door – and it has just revolved to reveal Hannah Willis, who's got problems of her own.

When tragedy strikes in her first week on the job *The Stranger Times* is forced to do some serious investigating. What they discover leads to a shocking realisation: some of the stories they'd previously dismissed as nonsense are in fact terrifyingly real. Soon they come face-to-face with darker forces than they could ever have imagined.

The Stranger Times is the first book from C.K. McDonnell, the pen name of Caimh McDonnell. It combines his distinctive dark wit with his love of the weird and wonderful to deliver a joyous celebration of how truth really can be stranger than fiction. Available for pre-order in the UK and Ireland now.

Made in the USA
Coppell, TX
18 August 2020